T0114926

I AM KAGARA

I weave the sands of the Sahara

Mark Nwagwu

Published in Nigeria by
BookBuilders • Editions Africa
2 Awosika Avenue, Bodija, Ibadan
email: bookbuildersafrica@yahoo.com
mobile: 0805 662 9266; 0809 920 9106

Printed in Ibadan
Oluben Printers, Oke-Ado
mobile: 0805 522 0209

CONTENTS

PREFACE

This is the third work in the series on the life and times of Ms. Chioma Ijeoma, great-granddaughter of Akadike Okeosisi of Okeosisi. We first met Chioma in *Forever Chimes* (2007) (Stirling-Horden Publishers, Ibadan); we met her again, in *My Eyes Dance* (2011) (BookBuilders Publishers, Ibadan); and now in *I am Kagara* (2016) BookBuilders Publishers, Ibadan.

Chioma's life and times in each of these works are strikingly different. In the present work, *I am Kagara,* some characters from the earlier works are still present. Thus we find in all three works: Chioma's parents, Okeadinife and Onyebuchi Ijeoma; her grandparents, Maduka and Adiaha Okeosisi; and her great-grandmother, Ma Nneoma. Chioma's naming by her great-grandfather, Akadike, now late, is recalled in the present work to help explain the significance of her *Chi* that works in unison with her to fulfill her destiny. All the other family characters have their roles in the story. Thus, *I am Kagara* can be easily understood without a background in the earlier works, though they would help for a fuller understanding and appreciation of the character, Chioma.

GLOSSARY

Afang soup	a vegetable soup of the Efik
Akara	fried ground beans
Agidi	Steamed maize meal
Akamu	Ground sieved maize porridge
Edikaikong	Staple vegetable soup of the Efik
Egusi soup	Soup cooked with ground melon seeds
Ntong soup	A vegetable soup of the Efik
Ofe Owerre	Staple vegetable soup of Owerri
Onugbu soup	Staple bitter-leaf of Anambra State
Sukuma wiki	Vegetable meal typical of Nairobi, Kenya
Ugali	Corn flour meal typical of Kenya

PHRASES

Chukwu ji ike nine	Almighty God
Chineke muo o-o-o	Oh my God!
Nna'm	My father
Nwam	My son
Umum ndewo nu	Greetings, my children
Chukwu gozie unu	God bless you
Unu emeka	You have been good
Ndewo nu	Thank you

CHAPTER ONE

October 11, 2011

Kagara, Bokoro State, Nigeria

"Please, where is this? What's the name of this place?" Chioma asked four women she met on the street. She was still dressed in her Maryland pink suit with a bow-tie, her flowing hair draping her shoulders. They looked at one another in utter disbelief.

"You must be a stranger. Please come with us. Let us hurry, it is not safe here. We live in the police barracks. It is well-protected and the insurgents have not been able to attack it yet. Please we must run. Who are you? Oh, by the way, this place is Kagara in Bokoro State in Northeastern Nigeria."

This was real, Chioma was certain. She had been mysteriously transported from her bedroom in the serene and magnificent University of Maryland at College Park, Maryland, to this strange and dreary environment. She did not know what month it was, but it was hot and dusty. She guessed it would be some time in November because one of the women had mentioned they had entered the second of the "ember" months. Chioma thus concluded it would be November, counting from September to December. She had heard a lot in the United States about the insurgencies in Bokoro State and was frightened out of her wits that she was now in a terrorist territory. She must be fully on guard and did not say much about where she was from, not that she could have said much in her present predicament. She could only mutter that she was Chioma, from Imo State, and that the bus that was to take her to Maitama had a problem on the way and had to drop the passengers off. She said she had walked for over two miles before she fortunately met them and that she was very thankful for their kind assistance. Concerned for their safety, they did not bother Chioma anymore and rather sought to get home as quickly as possible.

The street seemed deserted with only men in white robes and white caps hurrying down the slope in the opposite direction to Chioma and her friends. The race uphill was slow but furious. On the left side of the road as they ran in the hot afternoon, there were electric poles with wires all lying on the ground except for a lonely one that stood firmly and refused to fall. Chioma loved this pole and saw herself in this singular 'hero'. The road was uncharacteristically smooth with few potholes. They did not have much further to run, but just about a hundred metres from their home, they took a shortcut through the fields and one of them, Aisha, accidentally walked into what must have been a land-mine that exploded—no sooner than she shouted "Oh my God!" blood sprouted from her lower torso as she was thrown backwards like a rag doll. They quickened their pace taking every precaution not to run into any foreign object. Fortunately, they were soon home weeping their hearts out. One of the ladies stayed behind to watch over Aisha and Chioma volunteered to keep her company.

"Dad, hurry, we think Aisha is badly injured. Her body is lying in the field not far from the barracks. We think she must have stepped on a land mine; her left foot was split into two. Blood was everywhere." Saisa waved her hand; she could not speak, as tears clouded her eyes and her voice was sobbing with fear and grief. Saisa's father, Mr. Kakadu Ibrahim and Aisha's uncle quickly ran out and called three police officers; they all rushed down to the site of the accident. The police had landmine detectors to guide them and keep them out of harm's way. Theirs was one of the better equipped police stations in Kagara, close to Bokom, capital of Bokoro State.

Mr. Ibrahim examined Aisha's body, felt a very low pulse, and could make out there was still some life left in her. He quickly rushed her to Bokom Specialist Hospital, run by the state government for senior civil servants, police officers and military personnel, a thirty-minute drive from Kagara. The vehicle drove to the rampart of the emergency ward and with alacrity and gentle care, two of the police men helped move Aisha to a bed. "God please save my child; God please save my child." Mr. Ibrahim prayed as the nurses promptly rushed to her aid. As fate would have it, two of the doctors were on duty, one of whom was a trauma surgeon. They quickly laid out Aisha on a stretcher and wheeled her to the surgery theatre. They operated on her for the better part of three hours, from two o'clock in the afternoon till after five in the evening, and after, one of the doctors, Dr. Shagaya, came out to talk to Mr. Ibrahim.

"How is she? Is she alive? Will she live? Is her leg cut off?" Mr. Ibrahim burst forth with all worst fears to the doctor.

"All is well, Mr. Ibrahim. Aisha is now sleeping with her left leg in plaster. Apparently, she did not put her whole weight on the mine so the explosion was not too severe, or the bomb was poorly made. Anyway, her left foot did not require amputation, only extensive sutures and we were able to remove some metal objects from her stomach. No organ was affected. She wore a metal cross under her blouse. We suspect this must have deflected the metal objects that erupted from the mine for we could see signs of abrasion at several sites on the cross. Only the skin of her stomach was pierced. The leg will take some time to heal but she will be able to walk normally in a few month's time. You have nothing to worry about, Mr. Ibrahim. We shall take good care of her."

"Thank you, Dr. Shagaya. Thank you very much."

"There is not much you can do for her tonight. Just let her sleep."

"Okay. But can I please see the patient?" Mr. Ibrahim inquired.

"Yes you can, but only you, and for a few minutes only. She hasn't come out of the anaesthesia and she won't be able to talk to you."

"That's okay, doc, I just want to watch her breathing, to see some signs of life in her."

"Fine, then I'll probably see you tomorrow morning, if you are here by 9 a.m."

"Oh yes, I will surely be here then, doc."

Aisha was fast asleep. Boma, Saisa and Mary sat by her

side and, bedraggled as they were, they could not contain their relief. Chioma sat on a chair by the bed.

"This whole thing is a miracle, my God. Aren't we lucky, where would we be without Aisha?" Boma queried in excitement. She continued: "Saisa, do you remember what she said yesterday, that this week beginning today Monday would be one of frightful events, that the terrorists were likely to strike at the barracks and that we should all move south until this terrible insurgency was over?"

Saisa nodded her agreement and added, "she even said one of us might be a victim of this unstoppable terrorist, BOND, Bring On Nigeria's Development. Can they be the ones who have mined the fields, and do they think they themselves would not somehow be victims of their dastardly machinations? What they are doing destroys all that makes us human, with dignity and freedom. Well, Aisha is a prophet. We should listen to her more often. We are all three of us from the South. How did we end up here in northern Nigeria, in Bokoro State. And now to add to our troubles we have this young woman with us. We know nothing about her. She is a total stranger. Chioma, can you please tell us something about youself?"

Chioma was at a loss as to what to say. She felt she could not tell her new found friends that she lived in the United States and just found herself in her new surroundings a while ago when they met her on the road! She knew this would be simply incredible and would only add to her worries. Instead she made up a story and told them she taught in a girls' secondary school in Okeosisi and was on her way to a meeting of school principals in Maitama. As for her luggage, she said they were attacked by armed robbers just after Lokoja and she had lost everything she had with her. She had hoped she would get a bus to Maitama, and as she walked along the road, she met the four of them.

"Well, you're in good hands. We will be able to help you. Just like you, we are all graduate teachers in the girls' school here, Kagara Girls' Secondary School. This town is Kagara, and ours is a good police station and we are not far from Bokom, the state capital from where you can get transport to Maitama. We shall be here all night, of course, till Aisha wakes up." Saisa concluded.

Saisa spoke first. "Boma, quick, quick, why do your parents live here, in this hopeless place? "

"Why pick on me, why don't you start with yourself?-- after all you came here before all of us? My father came here as a distributor for Falcon Breweries and he's doing quite well. At least he has been able to train three graduates including myself, how about that?"

"Ah, Boma, I'm sorry. Don't be annoyed. I know for now it's only Aisha's condition that matters. I simply want us to relax a little. I'm sorry, Boma, can we figure out how we can help Nigeria get rid of BOND?"

Mary, who had been quiet, completely absorbed in Aisha's plight, weighed in with her suggestion. "BOND will not cow us, never." She recapitulated the sordid events of the past few years that saw the emergence of horrendous, mercilessly murderous BOND: the bombings, the kidnappings, the outright plundering and vandalisation of police stations and utter disregard for any sense of law or order; now, they themselves were victims of this rabid insurgency: a mine had blown up Aisha's foot. Sensing Mary's agitated state of mind, Boma appealed to her to please just calm down for a while. After all, she said, they were all still alive, had a bed to sleep in and food to eat. They should be thankful to God while they prayed to him for Aisha's speedy recovery and, more generally, to save Nigeria from chaos, anarchy, and doom.

Chioma felt much aggrieved and wanted to learn more about BOND's atrocities. "Please, don't feel offended. Can you talk about the lives of some of the people who have suffered from terrorism? Many of my students ask me if I could please tell them stories of the suffering BOND inflicts on people. I try to shield them from these disasters but they insist they must know. And the newspapers don't tell us much except the numbers of people killed or injured without looking into the personal lives of the victims. So, please, tell me what you can."

Mary smiled, a long smile that spoke of sorrow and pain, but still a smile. She breathed in and out in self-control exercise: now she could void her mind of a sordid story that had plagued her for a long time. For her, one of BOND's most horrible crimes was the senseless killing of innocent men, women and children in Abuja, who were on their way home, after Mass on that fateful Sunday in March 2011, when death ran on rivers of blood. In rainbow details, Mary painted a picture of one family she knew about that was crushed in the bomb blast. She told the story of Obioma Ogbonna, a carpenter.

"Obioma was married with two children, aged five and

three. He had come to the Federal Capital of Nigeria, Abuja, in answer to that call of nationalism that directed the hearts of all able Nigerians to give of their best for their country. He did not have to come to Abuja to heed this call but felt that his heart must be one with this great city, chosen to be the capital because it lay at the centre of the country. Here he believed all Nigerians would be one, united in faith and duty to their motherland.

"Obioma was what could be described as a 'small-time" carpenter, maker of household chairs, tables and stools. He never ventured into anything grandiose like upholstered furniture made in the latest European style. Nor would he be cajoled into working for a major furniture company where he would work with fine equipment that produced magnificent work. No, he saw himself as his own master in his little world, and was satisfied with his little job in his little shop.

"His dear wife, Obiageli, sold family household provisions of oranges, bananas, and whatever fruit was in season, such as *udara*, mangoes, *soursop* and avocado pears. Her shop was a busy bazaar under an umbrella tree huddled with several other women in their own world. Although they all sold similar products, Obiageli made good sales and was able to augment the financial gains of her dear husband. When she got home at the end of the day, she would sit with Obioma, and tell him stories of her day's experiences. In between preparing the evening meal and carrying on a conversation, she would bring forth any profits of the day to him. She always started with, "I thank my God, Obioma, today was good. Every day we are alive is good.

Obioma *dim oma*, my dear husband, together we will always have peace and joy." She would return to the kitchen and in a while bring the dinner. After dinner, Obioma would return her profits to her with warm words of encouragement.

"Their children, Aham, the five-year old, and Ogoma, the little girl, both attended St. Cyprian's School, not far from their home; Aham in Primary 1, and Ogoma in her first year, kindergarten. Ogoma's class ended at 1 p.m. but the class teacher would keep her in safety until 2 p.m. when Obioma would come for her and her brother, Afam.

"Every day without fail, he would be there to take his children home at 2 p.m. on his rickety motorcycle. It was always a trying experience, for he had the two children squeezed closely to his chest so they would not slide and fall, with Afam holding firmly to his dear sister. He had a little bed in his workshop, removed from the dust and noise, where he kept his children to rest or sleep till he would take them home by 5 p.m. It was always five o'clock so the children would not be far too tired and restless. He regaled Aham with stories of life in their village in Umuaku giving her biscuits, sweets and soft drinks thrown in for loving pleasure. Soon they would sleep and he could return to work.

"Obiageli, on the other hand, usually got home by six in the evening. Some civil servants on their way from work would stop by a *buka* close to her shop for a meal and she would approach them smilingly to take something home to their loving wives and children. After some time, these same customers would stop by her stand and buy some fruit. Her reputation grew and soon long lines started forming in her stall. She would, thus, still be selling goods later than usual. On such occasions, Obioma gladly suffered her lateness and took care of Afam and Ogoma, who by then were exhausted and sleepy, as best as he could. As soon as their mum came back, they would rush at her with cries of 'Mama, I am hungry. Mama I am sleepy.' And Obiagelli would get their dinner without any delay.

"Their dinner would be of beans and stew with one or two small pieces of beef; or fufu with a variety of soups from okra to *ugu* to *onugbu*. When either Obinna or Obiageli had a great day in sales, it would be rice, stew, and some healthy lumps of beef. The children would have whatever they asked of their mother if they did not find the regular meal suitable. And their mother always gave them what they asked for if she had it. After dinner at seven, the children went to bed and their parents sat in each other's company telling all kinds of stories about their life in their villages, and what was happening in the country at the time, as much as they could follow the events.

"They did not have to pay any rent to a landlord: an elder, Chief Jerome Ulasi, from their home town, Umuaku, who was also the president of the town union, Umuaku Development Union, Abuja Branch, gave his boys' quarters of three rooms free to Obioma. This was most unusual in Abuja where rents were at cut-throat prices and no one would be seen to give another any rooms for free. It was comfortable and to add to their ease they had free running water from the borehole provided by Chief Ulasi.

"On the fateful day, when they were blown into pieces by BOND's bombs, I found out that Obiageli woke up early, at five in the morning to get the children ready for Mass. Ogoma woke up readily but not Afam, her brother. He would roll and roll in his bed, wake up, lie down again, sleep off until his mother had hollered herself hoarse. She had put the water to boil and gave Ogoma a bath urging Afam to take the rest of the boiled water and have his own bath. This day, however, he complained the left-over water was not enough and that he would start to boil some fresh water. This angered his mother who would have none of his dilly-dallying and lounging around without end. Afam had to use whatever water was left over after his mother warned he would not eat of their usual sumptuous Sunday meal. Afam loved his food and quickly dashed into the bathroom and complied with his mother's directives.

"Obiageli offered the children a special breakfast of corn flakes and a hot drink of Ovaltine. An omelette completed this special fare which she whipped out on special occasions of celebration and merry-making. Obioma and she were ruled out because they would be receiving Holy Communion. The ride to St. Cyprian's Church took about thirty minutes with Afam sitting in front of the *okada* and Obiageli behind cradling Ogoma in her lap. Obioma felt a proud father.

"After Mass, Obioma picked up his dear wife, Obiageli, and the children, Afam and Ogoma. They sat on the *okada* and were as relaxed as the narrow space would allow. Just as the vehicle moved forward, no more than twenty metres, they were all blown to pieces by bombs planted on the road."

Everyone was speechless, weeping and coughing and drying

their tears. It seemed they had had enough, but Saisa had her own tale.

"The victim I'll talk about was James Ofanta, a secondary school student at a boarding school for boys in Jos, St. Augustine's Secondary School, then in his final year, in SS3. He had come to spend the long holiday with his parents in Abuja. He was their only child and you would say his parents had spoiled him with lots of goodies—he would get practically anything he had asked for. His father was a civil servant and his mother, a nurse at the National Medical Centre, Abuja.

"By eight in the morning of that Sunday, while his mother was getting breakfast ready, James told her he would be attending Mass in the morning rather than in the evening as was their usual custom."

"But why?" the mother queried, "What is so special this morning?"

"Yes, Ma, you're right; but you're not from St. Augustine. Some of us Augustinians on holiday here in Abuja had agreed we would attend the 9 a.m. Mass in our college blazer, looking bright and cheerful, and show the community that our school would be a worthy place for their sons to gain a first class education. Please, Ma, Brian will soon be here and I'll join him in their family's SUV."

"Surely, son, you can go," his mother replied.

"And James went, and met his unfortunate death on that same road that received the blood of so many parishioners after Mass."

CHAPTER TWO

October 11, 2011

College Park, Maryland, U.S.A

Chioma was in her office with a friend, Vivian, when Palm Frond Fern came to see her. She had had a dream some days earlier that she would encounter evil spirits whom she would see in their human form. When they appeared, only Chioma would see them and would be able to hear and understand them. Chioma could not make sense of the dream and gave it no further thought, until the strange looking green spirit showed up in her office: "You know, Ms. Chioma, great professor of African Mysticism, I was there during your lecture but not as I am now. Yes, I was one of the students. My full name is Palm Frond Fern but you can just call me, Fern, and just as ferns grow on plants, so I will grow on you. You cannot shake me off."

Fern threatened he would do her harm should she accept to lead the organization, GAP, Girls Are Precious. His words flowed like running water into Chioma's eyes and came out of her ears but no one could see the water. As the sound gurgled in her ears, she could clearly make out what Fern was saying.

Chioma offered some coffee and cake from a party she had attended over the weekend to Vivian, an African-Canadian friend of hers, who was a lecturer in sociology at College Park and with whom she frequently played squash.

She took a bite, then another, joyfully exclaiming, "Wow, Chioma, this is great chocolate cake, which party was this I missed, you did not invite me?

"I'm sorry, it was a last minute affair, the Nigerian Minister of Cultural Affairs was visiting and at the last minute, the embassy sent a car to bring me to a party in his honour. I had told them the notice was too short and that I was otherwise busy. But when they threw in the bit about the car, I was moved to be charitable and attended. And it was well I did for apart from all the lovely discussion about African spirits and the survival of African culture amongst Nigerian children in the States, I came back loaded with lots of goodies neatly packaged and brought home in the same limo. All in all, I was quite happy. You must come again and get the whole story."

"Come on, Chioma, you know how I feel about culture and time in the face of ever continuing change in an ever-troubled Africa. As we know Africa may be fast disappearing, especially as the best brains on the continent come to the US, settle here, and never return home. If they do, it's only for a time," Vivian replied.

"Well, you're right, that is, African culture may be receding into oblivion. But we are here to give it a new lease of life."

"Chioma, let's get this right: the cake you gave your friend that she liked so much was not from the batch from the embassy."

"So, where else could it have come from? I myself put it there in the fridge and I have eaten out of it too." Chioma replied. "Tell me then where it's from."

Fern obliged her. "Ok, let us start then. Do you remember that when the driver dropped you, you had left one of your bags in the car and you had to call the embassy to say so. It was brought back without delay and you were very relieved. Is this correct? Well, I put the chocolates there in your bag. Yes, I, Palm Frond Fern, put them there. I shall bring you some more."

Chioma found that her words did not come out in English and made no sound whatsoever, so Vivian could not have figured out there was a third party with them with whom her dear friend Chioma was deeply engaged in disquieting conversation. She was tongue-tied and thought, 'How could this evil creature have done this? Was Fern now ever to follow me wherever I went? Will I now be accountable to this supernatural being? Whether an evil spirit or a wraith, why must this nuisance meddle in my life?' These thoughts tormented Chioma. She broke out in a sweat to Vivian's notice.

"Chioma, what's the matter? A while ago we were having a great time and now your look worries me. You must be sick or something."

"I'm sorry, Vivian, there's no cause for concern. It's just that this whole story of the life of our children in the States leaves me in a state of hopelessness and I find myself lost in a world I cannot understand. Then you see what you're seeing in me now—quite flustered."

Chioma continued for a while describing her own life in the States, how she came here in her teens, her years at

Georgetown University, and her ever changing decision not to reside in the United States. She had regained sufficient balance and peace while she poured out her soul, as it were.

"Chioma, I did not know all this you're telling me now. I could have sworn I knew you closely but could never have imagined that this cultural question was one you strongly took to heart. Anyway, now things are more relaxed, could I have another piece of that nice cake?"

Chioma complied and they chatted on and on for a long while. Vivian talked about her childhood in Kaduna and the difficulties of growing up as a Christian in Northern Nigeria where her father was a reverend. She sensed she had perhaps just as much pain as her dear friend Chioma, but she simply told her story from the standpoint of history.

When Vivian got up to leave, Chioma walked her to the door. Fern accompanied them; in fact, this unholy spirit was the one who opened the door though it would appear to anyone watching that Chioma had done so.

"Now it's you and I alone, no one else here to interrupt." Fern asserted with all the power of his spirit-world authority. "You and I have a long way to go and we're just beginning. I know you very well and we have picked you out for special attention, for this enterprise of keeping our girls at home, and not in schools. Your curriculum vitae throws you up as one we can sacrifice, our first martyr, as it were, to get rid of all your learning and to show that girls do not need your kind of learning with degrees and awards and prizes. No, all the learning they need they will get from their homes, from their

mothers. Take a look around you now, what do you see?"
Fern disappeared.

Chioma tried to collect herself and take control of her
actions for she could not now understand what was
happening. She tried to remember her immediate past and
take it from there. She had finished her class on
anthropology where she sought to teach her students the
Aro of Arochukwu in South-Eastern Nigeria. She had laughed
a lot during this class for her students tried to make fun of
learning, and she had just been with her friend, Vivian, and
somehow their conversation had drifted to culture and the
past glorious days of African culture. She could recall all this.
This was as far as she went. She remembered nothing of
Fern nor that he had talked to her. She looked around and
realized she was in a tropical forest in a place that seemed
to belong to the skies. She saw trees but no land. They all
seemed like spirits; they were not rooted to anything and
seemed to be floating in space.

It dawned on Chioma that this was to be a new learning
experience. She tried to say her prayers but the words would
not come; tried to kneel down but her limbs would not
bend, they stood straight. She could not find her hands, she
felt helpless. She felt the temperature was as hot as an oven,
quite unlike the Maryland autumnal coolness she had just
left. A kite flew by and got caught in the thick vegetation.
She thought, "But kites don't fly low, and certainly don't fly
around in forests unless these forests did not have any skies
above." And indeed Chioma looked up and saw nothing she
could call sky. The sky, if any, was not visible.

The forest trees totally blocked her view, but there was

light, so she reasoned there must be a sun. She swiftly climbed a tree and just as swiftly, climbed down. Hot as it was, she was not perspiring and she basked in her newly-found climbing prowess. A hand held out a ham sandwich to her, straight into her mouth and she gobbled it up, drank the fluid offered her. She fell asleep on the grass, tired as she was. When she woke up, she was on a road in Northern Nigeria. And then she met Aisha, Boma, Mary and Saisa.

Chioma now remembered her encounter with Fern in her office and concluded that Fern must have transported her to Nigeria, to kill her, just as he was likely to be the power behind BOND's horrendous terrorism. She spent the night with her friends, Boma, Mary and Saisa. They were all wide awake when, in the early hours of the morning, Aisha turned and asked, "Where is this, where am I?"

October 12, 2011

Kagara

The nurses on night duty visited Aisha regularly, every half hour and checked her vital signs. Satisfied with her status, they would leave her in peace. No one gave her an answer but Boma quickly ran out and called the chief nursing sister: Aisha repeated her question, "What is this white stuff on my leg? What am I doing here?" The sister simply quieted her down and she soon fell back to sleep. But not for long; she now woke up in great pain and started hollering. The nurses came to her assistance, administered an injection, and she then slept off more deeply after some moments of wailing.

Chioma must find some way to get to Maitama. She

reasoned that if she waited till 9 a.m. when Mr. Ibrahim would be visiting, he might ask one of the police officers to take her there. She thought it might be better if she said she would be returning to Okeosisi and so gave the reason that she did not feel very safe on BOND's mined roads. It was then about 8 a.m. and she saw that taxis were coming and going from the hospital. Her friends were taken aback when she told them she would be leaving that morning back to Okeosisi. They had hoped she would spend a couple of days with them before continuing to her destination. But Chioma could not take this risk, fearing whatever spirits brought her to Kagara might just suddenly return her to Maryland right before Saisa, Mary and Boma.

"No, Chioma, you are now one of us; please come and stay in our home with my mum and dad. Dad you've already met but not my mum."

"And me too", Boma and Mary each quickly added. "You just can't go. You are one of us. Come and stay with us. We can give you our clothes to wear. You can see you are our size and our clothes would fit you well."

"Many many thanks, Saisa, Mary, Boma," Chioma answered, feeling disturbed and unhappy. "It's not that I want to leave you, to run away from you. No, it's not that. I must return to my school in Okeosisi quickly to tell them about my mishaps and how you saved me. We shall exchange addresses and phone numbers and keep in touch. Surely I'll be back soon to see Aisha walking."

After exchanging their personal details, they

accompanied Chioma to the taxi park from where she took a cab to the car park. She took a bus bound for Lokoja and would, from there, continue to Onitsha. As the bus was not yet full and was not yet ready to leave, Chioma went to a *buka* for breakfast. She finished the meal of *dodo,* fried yam, and omelet and was walking back to the bus. The next thing she knew she was back in her room in Bethesda, Maryland! It was three o'clock in the morning of October 12, 2011, and she was astonished she had been gone for only one hour!

CHAPTER THREE

October18, 2011

College Park

Chioma went to her office at College Park and spent much of the day reading up on the history of Arochukwu, in eastern Nigeria; in particular, the qualities and distinguishing features that made them a dominant group in Igboland before the advent of colonialism. She was captivated by their high level of social formations and loyalty and service to the community. She felt proud to be Igbo and to be associated with such an illustrious and highly organized clan. She had lunch in the school cafeteria, nothing much, just a cheese sandwich, salad and a glass of white wine and left for home around five in the evening.

When she got home, she picked up Isidore Okpewho's *Call Me By My Rightful Name* and buried herself in its narrative and characterization, recalling haunting memories of an ancestry. She was about turning down the lights when she noticed that one of the flowers in the vase by her bedside had withered and was drooping, its head resting on the table. She was sad she had neglected her flowers for the past two or three days, a bouquet of red carnations, yellow daisies and strips of green fern. She promptly took the vase to the kitchen, changed the water, added some salts and returned the thirsty flowers to the vase. She smiled, said her prayers, turned off the light, got into bed and neatly tucked herself into her quilt from her grandmother, Adiaha. She slept till her alarm roused her at five in the morning when she noticed she had woken from the left side of her bed!

October 19, 2011

College Park

What sort of day would this be? She had spent some time in prayer and had gone to Mass as was her wont. It was Wednesday; her favourite day of the week, when she felt her abilities peaked seizing her in a frenzy of delight and joy. She was determined this Wednesday would be no different. She would insert fresh acts into this day; in fact she decided everything she did that day would be something she had not done for a long time. Whatever was well and good and proper she would attempt. Rather than drive to work today, she would walk from her home in Bethesda, Maryland, USA, to the University of Maryland at College Park, a three hour walk at best. She was fit and athletic and though it was a warm, September morning, she could easily contain the dripping sweat of a brisk exercise.

Everything moved on perfectly till she got to the junction

of Brenner and James Avenue, when a woman, well tanned, slim, large-boned, her muscles tightly bound, probably in her thirties, with dusty long hair walked up to her. Chioma was taken aback, for this was most unusual in these parts of Maryland; for someone to rush up to you in a surprise and start talking to you.

"Good morning, Miss Chioma."

Taken aback, she wondered, "how could this stranger know my name?" Still, she accommodated this uncalled for experience in the need to make this getting-out-the-bed-on-the-left-side something interesting.

"Good morning, Miss..."

"Awarah Mengei, Awarah for short."

'so, Awarah, how are you? How do you know my name? How do you know me?"

"I got to know you are the only African female professor at College Park; that you have a huge name in the university; that you are a fiery supporter of the girl-child. We have kidnapped knowledge."

Chioma did not know how to proceed with this affront. She must summon the courage to reply, for this woman might just be a kidnapper of some sort, not just of knowledge, but of humans as well. She could well be carrying a gun!

"Thank you for the compliments, Awarah. So how did you trace my whereabouts?"

"Ah, that's quite easy. Once, I gate-crashed into one of your lectures, I simply waited for you to finish your day at school, watched you get into your car and then followed you home, or rather to your new address; for they tell me you change your address frequently, that you don't live in just one place."

This was only an illusion well constructed by Chioma for security reasons: in fact, she had one home and one home only; but she would sometimes spend long evenings with her friends, returning to her Nesbit home before late in another car, well disguised. She would often adorn her identity in different ethnic outfits when she went to work in consonance with her appointment in African cultural and spiritual philosophy. When however, she went into class, she would always wear a dress, cut in traditional western style, usually a suit, a skirt-suit, or a dress. From time to time, especially when the weather grew warmer, she would dress in good Yoruba attire, such as adire, *aso oke*; or *akwete* of Afikpo renown, or Ghanaian *kente*, to drum the beat of her African descent and spirit.

"Well, now that you've found me, Awarah, what can I do for you?"

"There is a group of young women who want to lead the fight for the education of women in disadvantaged circumstances, irrespective of their cultures, in different countries of the world. We have our headquarters in England, at the University of Cambridge. We want to start a branch here at the University of Maryland and I have been asked to make sure I recruit you as our head; and then we'll move our headquarters to College Park. They tell me there's too much learning in your head and that we must keep you to ourselves. No one else will have access to you."

"No one else would have access to me, did you say?" Chioma repeated, with a look of consternation.

"Well, don't take it that way, Chioma, I'm sorry. Of course, you are a university professor and the world is your school. I'm sorry, I exaggerated just to drive home the point that we sorely need you and want you to devote yourself to our cause, a noble cause, I dare say." Awarah answered apologetically and proceeded to tell her story of how GAP, came to be.

The group consisted of sixteen women in various disciplines—engineering, law, medicine, biological sciences, literature, theology, economics and psychology from different nationalities—Iran, South Africa, Sri Lanka, Australia, Canada, England, Sweden, Nigeria and Pakistan—who believed that girls should be given every opportunity to go to school and there should be no barriers whatsoever to girl s' education. Generally the association believed that the human person, whether male or female, was the means and the end of knowledge.

They chose the University of Cambridge for its fame as one of the world's most renowned universities and any output from there would be widely acceptable, and they themselves were top academics in their various fields. They lacked a leader and had not yet fully developed their ideas. They sought one from anywhere in the globe, but preferably a woman, black and African, a world leader with a close attachment to the family, love for children, an engagement with history and an acute grasp of the essential rudiments of everyday living.

"What strange day could this be? Chioma wondered. "I have heard of insurgents killing pupils in schools, especially girls, saying women were mere chattel in the hands of men, to do no more than cook and have babies; that the educated woman was an affront to any decent society. We could have a world organization for the education of women but how would we ensure their safety in schools? How would we deal with the selfsame terrorists who do not want to see women in schools, for it seems that's what GAP was really out to overcome?"

Chioma felt faint, and realized she must be careful as her life might be in danger. Not knowing what to say but aware that Awarah, who came from nowhere, might be up to some disguised evil, she kept her silence waiting for this unwelcome guest to speak her last word. Soon, Awarah did just that: "Chioma, please do not worry about your safety. Nothing will happen to you, nothing, and there is nothing for you to do at this stage. And if there's anything for you to do, you would be the one to tell us and lead us, as you please. I have been sent, and I have delivered the message. But I have done more than that: I assure you nothing will happen to you. I will watch over you. I will protect you in this new battle of the girls. The bastards who think women don't matter will burn. Yes, women matter!"

Awarah disappeared just like that! Chioma could not find her anywhere. Was she in a dream? Was she in another world? Did she not just talk to someone? Were words now meaningless? Was this to be the Wednesday when all manner of pains would visit her? She could not make sense of what could be going on especially after her meeting with the Spirit Fern, being transported to northern Nigeria, and back to Maryland. Nothing made sense to her anymore.

All manner of thoughts flooded Chioma's head but she decided to continue with the day as though nothing had happened. She had come to the United States when she was fifteen after her childhood years in Yaba, Lagos. Her mother, Onyebuchi, was the granddaughter of Akadike, her great grandfather, of Okeosisi legend. Her father, Okeadinife, and her mother were both barristers, practising in Washington, D.C. She had studied at Georgetown University and Obafemi Awolowo University and now taught at the University of Maryland at College Park.

Steeled in mysteries, in African mythologies and their gods, Chioma had received from her great-grandfather, Akadike, when she turned seventeen, the walking stick that had been in the family since time immemorial. Each first son of the legendary Akadike dynasty simply passed it on to his own first son until the walking stick finally was transferred to a female child, who had been ordained as the last recipient of this mysterious heirloom. Chioma, who turned out to be this chosen female child, called the Walking Stick, *Uzo,* and gave it a female identity, since she, the final possessor, was a woman.

She recalled that one day, after she had brought *Uzo* with her to the United States, *Uzo* disappeared. Chioma knew she would not see her anymore but felt that she would be able to make out *Uzo's* voice whenever she spoke, if she still wanted to participate in the physical world in which Chioma lived. When she considered what was happening to her, she felt that *Uzo* could not have been reincarnated in

Awarah for, if so, *Uzo* would have made known her presence. Nevertheless, Chioma was perplexed and did not know what these occurrences meant, in particular their foreboding for the future. She walked more slowly as she thought things through.

It was now past nine o'clock in the morning with cars riding on top of other cars as the traffic coiled into a fastening rope. Chioma thanked her stars that she did not drive on this day in this hideous traffic. One of her students in a Toyota sedan saw her and offered her a ride. She graciously declined and no further than two street lights ahead, the car was in a horrendous accident. A truck had run through the red light and slammed into three cars heading toward College Park, all of them with college professors or students. Only the first car suffered immense damage, the one with two of Chioma's students, Frank and Olive, his girlfriend. She stood by the scene of the accident as an ambulance quickly sped to the spot, soon followed by police vehicles. She could not get close to her students and quickly followed the ambulance to the hospital.

When she got close enough to recognize them, the female passenger she thought was Olive, her student, turned out to be the selfsame Awarah Mengei! The other passenger, the driver of the vehicle, was her student Frank quite alright.

"You are shuddering with fright, Ms. Chioma because you find me in this inexplicable situation, inexplicable to ordinary human minds used to reading books and learning from books. Human knowledge comes mainly from the written word. But you are different. You are an Akadike and you are able to piece together matters, celestial and earthly alike. We will use you in the best way for our ideals. You must work for us; somehow we'll get you to work for us. As you can see, this whole business of knowledge, women, and society is way beyond ordinary human reasoning or I would not be here in this hospital bed all in the effort to see you."

This was Awarah speaking to Chioma from her hospital bed after the doctors and nurses had completed their medical tests and examinations. They allowed Chioma a few minutes with her believing she was their patient's teacher, for Awarah had told them she was; that her parents and close relatives lived in Iran and her teacher was her only next-of-kin in the United States. Chioma quickly took a taxi and was driven to school distraught and bewildered.

Chioma thought to herself: "how could all this be happening in one day, this day she got out of her big bed on the left side? For that matter she wondered why she never slept on the left side of the bed. Why would she need a big bed if all she did was simply crawl to one side and lie there dormant?

She could not make any sense of the day's happenings so far. She showered when she arrived at College Park and got into fresh clothes. She examined herself closely in the mirror, taking particular care of her hair which she had combed scrupulously. This was a morning for one of her Akwete dresses, in traditional checkered white and blue squares adorned with strands woven in gold and purple colours. It was a simple shirt-dress draping Chioma all the way down to her heels. Her nails would do with some colour and she took time to put on a fresh coat of purple nail polish to match her Akwete dress. She closely examined herself in the mirror and was happy with her look.

Around 4 p.m. or so, two security officials came from Bethesda General Hospital to tell Chioma that Awarah had left the hospital and asked if she was with her by any chance, or, if she knew where she might be. Chioma replied Awarah was not with her and she had no idea whatsoever where she might be. She was by now far too nonplussed to do any work and took a cab home.

CHAPTER FOUR

October 20, 2011

College Park

Chioma tried to take the events of the past day in her stride but could not: they were too far intense and complex for reasoned human resolution. She locked herself in her office to think things through and see whether she could make sense of her mysterious experiences. As strange as things were, she felt that Awarah, who ardently solicited her leadership of a women's association for women's education, might be a good soul.

She began from her birth and recalled what her great-grandfather, Akadike, had said at her naming ceremony: "I name this sweet little thing here, this charming princess, fragile as the eagle's egg, this my great-granddaughter – I name her CHIOMA. She is our good fortune, sent by the gods. She will fly high like the eagle. She will be phenomenal. She will set the world aflame with her genius. She will be the first among her peers. Yes, Chioma, my child, will hold the world spellbound." She turned her mind to the Igbo word, Chi, and its various meanings, in the effort to relate her recent experiences to any apparent link with what her name portends. She realized this was no more than mysticism and might have no bearing on reality; but then her experiences were both mystical and real.

She understood that the name, Chioma, as Pa Akadike had used it himself, meant "good fortune". But then Pa went on to include, 'sent by the god s'. For Chioma, the gods would of course, in traditional Igbo parlance represent God himself. Thus, she had no difficulty of seeing herself as a child of God. But Pa had described her in the most glowing terms. Why should this be? She wondered. Then she remembered that Pa's other words about the circumstances of her birth. He had said: 'my people, this is a great day. Who could have thought, six months ago, that we would be here today, a baby in our arms?" She recalled the stories of her birth and her childhood and why Pa had said all that he said on the day he had named her Chioma.

The story went that while she was pregnant with Chioma, her mother had been shot in the hip by armed robbers. One of the bullets had hit her and miraculously missed a large blood vessel in her thigh and was lodged in the bone while another bullet pierced through the stomach and passed out of the body. From Pa Akadike, her great-grandfather, down to her grandfather, her parents, and the entire Akadike dynasty, Chioma was to all who knew her a gift from the gods who gave her life and made sure she lived, the bullets notwithstanding.

From her studies on African culture and from her own life experiences, she knew that if you wanted to find out how life had treated an Igbo man, a good place to look was the names he gave his children. Thus, his hopes, his fears, his joys and sorrows; his grievances against his fellows, or complaints about the way he has been used by fortune; even straight historical records, would all be revealed in their names.

Chioma knew that *Chi* was regarded as a pervading principle that is a part of one's life; a dominant force that has a special hold over a person such as no other powers can muster. Understood thus, *Chi* can, for example, dispense with the physical endowments and terrors of spirits. She recalled a famous Igbo proverb: "No matter how many divinities sit together to plot a man's ruin, it will come to nothing unless his *Chi* is there among them."

Chioma often dwelt on thoughts of her birth and this time sought to relate them to the appearance of the spirit-human, Awarah, whose transition from human to spirit, as it were, was puzzling; but she could conclude Awarah meant well. Slowly, she was regaining her composure and then directed her mind to how she would proceed with her life from then on. She knew *Chi* also meant destiny, or fate and had long believed, through her faith, that destiny was nothing more than the sum total of the decisions and choices one made in life, in full collaboration with God's grace, in full personal freedom. Thus, she knew it was not what she met in life that determined the outcome of events, but what she herself did with what was presented to her. In full conscience, she would accept full responsibility for her actions.

She returned to her name and what Pa Akadike had said about her, and would confidently assert: "Yes, I am Chioma: whatever I may meet, be it a spirit, like Fern, be it Awarah— or by whatever name she may be called — whatever may happen to me, with the grace of God, I shall do all I can to turn evil to good, and bury evil with a lot of good."

She would rejoice: "Yes, I am Chioma, I am Chi Oma, Good Fortune; no evil will overcome my spirit. I am Chioma; no evil can ruin my destiny. I am Chioma; I must get on with my life in the manner to which I am accustomed, according to my training, according to my faith. Yes, I am CHIOMA."

October 21, 2 011

College Park

Fully invigorated, the following day, Chioma went to her class on human settlements, taught about the emergence of societies and communities and touched on the plight of refugees in various parts of the world. Her students just could not grapple with the massive suffering of many people all over the world. They sought for the source of these miseries and could readily place it at the doorstep of the world leaders who seemed to care more about themselves than their own people. They saw this every day without end on their TV sets and found that the human person was slowly and steadily degenerating into a selfish wolf devouring all others in a world brought into increasing closeness by the tools of communication and knowledge. Knowledge, it seemed, was at one and the same time its own life, and its own death!

Chioma steered her talk away from the United States but her students kept pulling her back to the pitiful life of African-Americans, giving many examples of how they were denied justice and, in some cases, being hanged for crimes they did not commit. She would return to innumerable instances throughout history of genuine social formations for human well being but her class would quickly give her other intolerable human-made conditions that adversely afflicted people, that left large populations homeless and hopeless, without food or water to drink—when water became a luxury to people who had lived a simple, ordinary existence. Of course, war effectively turns everyone into a refugee, rich or poor, without any inkling of dignity.

Though not a part of their lecture, the ways and means to ameliorate the suffering of so many, especially children and women, gained the interest of the students, and they asked: Could we invite some of them to our homes, in the United States? How would we go about this? It would be impossible. Should we rather distribute whatever donations we were able to raise to refugees all over the world, or should we maximize our meagre efforts and channel them to refugees in one country alone, such as Syria, Somalia, Ethiopia, or Mali?

Before the end of the class, the students had formed an organization 'students United For Refugees', SURF; and, right there, put their hands in their pockets and were able to raise one thousand dollars. This was to be the beginning of a large humanitarian refugee effort.

'let us consider what to me was the worst form of refugee-ism", Chioma stood up firmly gesticulating with her five fingers as if to count off the worst forms one after another. No, it was simply to show her utter disaffection with the world of self, self, and self alone. She continued, "Please tell me, whoever can, what to you would constitute the most miserable condition of life?"

"You ask us, Ma'am, a very difficult question, for what I regard as a miserable life may be quite bearable to another, and vice versa."

"Yes, I know that, Bob, still, we would like to know what you consider intolerable misery."

A hand shot up at the back of the class. Chioma's class was always full, and attracted the largest enrollment in the faculty of the social sciences. She did not see the hand in time so the young man stood up.

"Ah, Greg, I'm sorry I didn't see your hand in time. So what do you say?"

'ma'am, perhaps we can begin by defining misery, what really is misery?"

The rest of the class was stunned for it seemed so obvious to all that misery would be something that anyone was well aware of, and may have lived with at some time in their lives, or may have met in someone else's life. Perhaps, Greg had not listened to the lecture and had not contributed to SURF.

"ma'am, perhaps you would tell us something about misery and we'll see if we both share the same sort of feelings."

"Well, how do I begin to take you through what misery might be all about. Let's take the light ones first."

Jim interrupted the lecture saying. "Ma'am, I'm sorry to say that what you consider light might be heavy for me."

The class laughed off his remark for they felt Greg and Jim were now stretching the point, and, if they proceeded at that rate, they might never come to the end of the matter - what really was misery, what made one miserable, what made one event more miserable than another?

Chioma did not know how she could quickly and charitably address this preposterous response from her students. She kept silent for some time, better to regain her composure. Before she said a word, however, Jim apologized for his obtrusiveness and implored the class that they should further explore all aspects of the refugee and grief problem. Chioma was still silent and Jim took this to mean he could continue. He agreed they all knew what grief was and went on to give an example of the suffering in his family when his dad was laid off from work, from there to receive unemployment benefits and soon the family lost their comfortable house in Bethesda. They then had to move into an apartment in an ugly part of the District of Washington, with rats running in and out of their rooms. For three years his dad was unemployed and his mum had to do all sorts of odd jobs to keep the family housed and fed. When he was done speaking, again he apologized for his earlier brazen interruption.

In the light of Jim's apology and the story of his family's misery, Chioma now felt that all this was thoroughly engaging. She had struck the right chord and she would fully explore the problem to good effect. She did not forget her main interest was the miserable life of refugees, but she wanted her students to go deep into their own experiences and describe what they felt touched their minds and hearts so terribly it deeply affected their lives.

"Okay, dear friends, we are friends, aren't we?" Chioma asked rhetorically.

"Yea, yea, very much so, Ma'am," they all shouted out in a quaint voice, distant yet endearingly close. They had grown fond of their professor who was ever challenging their minds, taking them far out into the outer fringes of knowledge and human experience.

"Jim, as you rightly said, we need to fully explore refugees, misery and suffering from all angles," Chioma assured her class. "Ok, I know you are all out to pursue happiness; happiness is all that counts. Forgive me for taking you into the suffering territory where rats feed on garbage, on left-over food, and snakes feed on the rats. And the beat goes on; each finds what to live on, animal instinct feeding on self- interest."

When they heard their teacher speak this way, they all stood up in rousing thunder, stomping and c"ping, their voices at their peaks. This was unusual, what could have caused this, Chioma wondered. She was thrown off guard and just did not know how to move forward with her lecture. And so she repeated what she had said earlier, 'let's do this again; selfishness is all about vain pleasure."

"Yea, that's it, Ma'am, the capitalist state is a selfish

state." The class responded in loud acclamation.

Greg weighed in with a new opinion to explain his earlier obtuse statements: "ma'am, kindly look at things this way. You are the playwright producing the script, the plot, and the whole array of different scenes. We, your students, on the other hand, are the ones to produce and direct your play and put it on the stage for all to see. What the audience sees, what the world knows is what we show them. We can even change the script to suit our purpose. So, you see, Ma'am, we shall put to practice what you teach us that the world may know who you are, who we are, where we stand, where we come from."

CHAPTER FIVE

March 9, 2010

College Park

Swinging her head left to right, up and down, the air flying, her eyes wide open, Chioma happily went to her class, Anthropology 417, The Aro of South Eastern Nigeria. It was now four o'clock in the afternoon, her last class for the day. This was one of her favourite courses where she distinguished herself as a true child of autochthonous African transcendence.

"What was the black person, the African, doing before the imperialists, who descended on his kingdom, plundered his wisdom, his industry, his culture, and left in its wake a subterfuge of insipid progress?"

Chioma was not expecting an answer to this question

and treated her proposal at length, convincingly demonstrating that Africans had a life of invincible worth and meaning all through their existence as humans in the warmth of the sun. The more she proceeded in this discourse, the more it struck her that though Africans did not record their thoughts, ideas, events, and their variegated cultures in the written word, they were able to preserve themselves in the tightly-woven niche of knowledge, understanding and social organization. Nothing was committed to writing and the preservation of books. Chioma went on, "Was anything lost in this mode of life? No, there was thrilling history going on and a life lived to the full with all the trappings of the permanence of truth."

A student in the middle of the class raised her hand, eager to ask a question which she said had engaged her mind for a long while about Africans, namely, why spirits and *juju* and their priests held such pride of place in African culture, even till the present day, in parts of the continent. She recalled the saga of *Ogwugwu*, one of the feared jujus in Igboland, that engulfed Anambra politics in the early days of the return to democratically elected governments. Finally she asked the dominant question, "Why do spirits and their like dominate African political, social, and religious life even in the predominant presence of Christianity?"

Chioma gave a simple answer that it was a matter of the power of deities; that in the absence of any knowledge of monotheism, humans had created all sorts of gods, from biblical times to the days of early Grecian social organization, to our own day now. There was nothing to worry about on the dependence of Africans on their deities.

She referred to *Orunmila,* revered as almighty god in Yoruba ancestry, and how *Orunmila* gave *Ifa divination* to his children, by which means they could predict the future and decipher whatever was happening in one's life. Thus, the powers of *Orunmila* gave birth to the *Ifa* oracle, an exceedingly intricate means of divination.

Chioma also talked about the feared *Ibinukpabi,* the Long Juju god of Arochukwu, as a manifestation of cultural superiority owed to the gods.

"Surely," she said, "the mythical gods of ancient Greece and Rome, for example, Zeus, Hermes, Aphrodite, and Venus held much sway in the identities of their people, until the spread of Judaism and Christianity, and have no place in Western culture today. Myths may be tenuous; however, their apparent impact on cultures and their belief-systems, would make us ponder the realms of human understanding of reality."

She felt that the great deities, *Ibinukpabi, Ogwugwu,* and *Ifa,* may still exert an influence in the culture of the people, but this was no longer as commanding as it once was, except in some pagan societies, or in those individuals who sought their presumed powers, for good, or for ill.

Chioma considered the matter further and gave an example from her own paintings. She admitted that she often could not explain the movements of her hands when she painted, and she found that the different colours in their different rivalries and agreements sometimes took over her plans and imposed theirs on whatever she had wanted to paint. She also found that even the different spaces in the canvass, each had a life of its own and would not permit any encroachment from another space. Each wanted to be the master of its environment. In fact, each space saw the whole painting as its own, expressing its peculiar thoughts and desires, turning the art work into something thrilling, something profound, and something mystical.

She would, thus, move out of the limitations of her material experience and work in a medium suffused in surrealism. This, she said, might help explain some interest in other non-physical media we would refer to as spirits.

A hand shut up from the back of the class. "Ma'am, this is way too much for me: it seems we are ever moving between the real world and the world of spiritualism."

"My dear students, my friends, some of you have been with me for four years now and are about to graduate from this impressive institution. So, let us say that if you got nothing from College Park, College Park got something from you. The walls of the rooms you've slept in, laughed, studied, and danced in, all have memories of you, some of them delightful, others painful. But whichever it is, the rooms will remember you."

There were whispers of: "How could this be? Since when did rooms recall past or present events? We might soon be told that the rooms can even reveal what their next set of students would be doing."

When the whispering had subsided, Chioma continued: "Do not be surprised my friends if these same rooms met you on the street and told you about their tomorrows. Nothing is ever lost; it is captured somehow on this vast universe by elements of history, in one form or another. That is how culture is formed; how your mum and dad tell you stories about their rooms at Georgetown or Connecticut, or in a high-rise apartment. The stories your parents tell you have lived a life somewhere before."

Andy's hand quickly shot up, "Ma'am, what you are telling us is that we are the world and that the world is us and that the two can never part. We heard this on that 1985 magnificent collage of songs from Michael Jackson, Bruce Springsteen, Ray Charles, and many other stars arranged by the incomparable Quincy Jones for the famished people of Ethiopia. I believe, Ma'am, we can all identify with the cause of this music, and to that extent we can identify first with suffering and with death, and with the spirits that wander around us in one form or another."

'Where did this come from'? Chioma was astounded. She shared her thoughts with the class that she could not believe her ears and wondered whether all the theoretical lecturing that went on in universities and schools could be compared with an awareness of human experiences as they occurred. She said she knew that the blood of an eye wrote far more masterly than a mere pen that could be bought and sold; and that what we 'see' goes beyond what we 'read'. She considered the sad plight of Andy, who had earlier told the class that his father had been without a job for over two years and whose mother had resorted to all sorts of trades to keep the family fed and housed. This horrible life must have affected Andy adversely. But she raised the question, "must it all be adverse; did something of value not accrue from this unique experience; for, surely, if Andy believed that he was in this world to help others; that we were the world, and the world was us, can there be any learning experience greater than this?"

Chioma quickly returned to the topic of her lecture. "You will all recall that this lecture was supposed to be on the Aro of Arochukwu of south-eastern Nigeria and their predominant Influence in Igboland. I had said nothing yet about them when you came in with your edifying contributions, though they seemed funny at the time. Now that we are coming to the end of our class, please tell us, what would you say you have gained from this exposure, bearing in mind that I did not do much teaching, that you did all the work?"

Lisa stood up, smiled, and came forward toward the front of the class, as though she were going to take over from Ms. Chioma and give a lecture. But she came only to apologize; that what she had said earlier about learning was just to provoke a lively discussion; that she was sorry she had not given her professor time to take them through what must be a thrilling topic. She finally said learning was everything, and though the university was the prime place for this purpose, that life was more than what was learnt in a university and that human experiences made that education practical. And she repeated, "We are the world," and added, "with all its spirits and jujus. We are even in Ms. Chioma's paintings, in their colours, in their spaces, and in everything else in-between."

Everybody cheered and the class ended here.

CHAPTER SIX

November 15, 2011

College Park

One Tuesday afternoon, when Chioma had no class for three consecutive hours, Awarah came in to tell her more about the sixteen women who formed the Cambridge Group with the name *Girls Are Precious* - GAP. Chioma had kept this time free usually to do some research on African deities and their spirits. After all that was happening in her life with spirits and humans appearing and disappearing, and she herself being transported out of Maryland, and then returned, she was all the eager to dig deeper into the study of spirits. When Awarah came to see her, she saw this as one more mystery she could explore.

Awarah commenced: "This must be a good time to tell my own story so that you can get to know us better and come to our aid. Do you think your presence in your new College Park surroundings is for nothing? Some of our enemies want to sacrifice you as their first martyr, as the person they call PF Fern told you. We, on the other hand, want you to champion our cause for knowledge, for girls. You will therefore find that any time our adversaries make what they consider as a useful move to destroy you, and thus destroy us, we too shall be there in the same place at the same time to save you with all the tools we have."

"They had brought you to Nigeria and you were quite near the home of BOND. The spirits are behind BOND: and, I pray, you will be behind GAP. You have seen me and you know I am human as you are, and also live in another world that is not known to you. This other world does not mean much. But I am fully with GAP and I teach chemistry at Cambridge, as you also know. We need your full support for, with all our powers, we cannot force you to do anything you don't want to do. There is nothing in this world comparable to human freedom. We would like to work with your full support, freely given."

Chioma could follow Awarah alright but her mind kept returning to the BOND Sunday massacre. Awarah pressed on with her story and narrated just how Baraah, Cheryl and Funeka met purely accidentally for the first time and spontaneously began to pour out their minds on the intriguing question of men and women equally obtaining and using knowledge.

Baraah Hasni, born in Pakistan, was a lecturer in physics at the University of Cambridge. Legend has it that her ancestors had lived in the Western Himalayas, in the region of Nanga Parbat, a very dangerous peak, and over the course of about three thousand years had migrated first to several towns and cities before coming to Hyderabad and then settling in Jhang, in present day Pakistan. Working amongst some of the brightest brains on earth, Baraah found herself ever weaving thin threads of knowledge into a more fervid and resilient climbing twine, the threads wound around each other in a humane helix. While studying at London Imperial College, she met the great Nobel Laureate, the Pakistani physicist, Abdus Salam, who told her to serve Almighty God fiercely in her work. Herself a Muslim, like the Laureate, she poured herself into her work and, from then on, grew to become a leading figure in her chosen field of optics.

While at Cambridge, she had listened to many a scholar delve deeply into their particular fields, and had heard those who wanted to take the world by storm and move knowledge at the fast pace of one thousand ideas a second, awaiting verification, leading to a world of peace and joy. Over and over again, knowledge as a service to humanity was drilled into her with the ontogenic nails of virtue and honour.

Knowledge should not exist on its own and should always wear the garment of charity and selflessness, she learned. Slowly and steadfastly Baraah began to believe that women are repositories of both knowledge and human culture all over the world. She felt books could serve any purpose one had in mind, good or ill; and if ill, it would take someone else to point this out. Of course, she realized that was the whole purpose of the university—to take issue with whatever was untoward or untrue; that is, to discover the truth and make it known to all and to engage in all possible arguments and research until the truth was known.

Baraah had asked herself: 'should women not be at the forefront of selfless service to humans; in fact, should women not concentrate on humans and their culture'? She thought, 'we have pregnancies; the soul comes to the embryo right after sperm and egg meet and human life begins right then. The mother provides all the functions needed for the foetus to grow and actually become a human person'.

"Nine months later, without the mother doing no more

than keeping healthy and alert, she would give birth to a whole new and different human being, who also did no more than depend on the mother for everything. Why do women have this unsurpassable urge to bear children and put all of themselves at work for the child, nurse the child, feed the child, see to the total comfort and well being of the child? Does all this not tell us unshakeable truths and uniqueness of women?

'Can all the books on physics surpass the incalculable wonder of the foetus'? Baraah was more and more convinced she should devote her life, all of it, to serving the human person in society. She pondered after Abdul Salam's death in 1996: 'Look at it, this great man is gone and will be remembered for his contributions to theoretical physics, but is that all? Was this great man not greater than all his immense works, including his infamous contribution to the development of the atomic bomb'?

'What of the lives he touched upon with the light of an exemplary life, is this not of far more significance than all the papers he published and his Nobel Prize put together'? She concluded, 'surely I would like to live as he lived, even if I do not accomplish one millionth of what he accomplished. And if I accomplished nothing at all, still I would be satisfied just to be true to my being. GAP it is, GAP it will be; keep our girls in school that their knowledge may help humans to grow. Knowledge, your name is woman. Yes, we shall weave the sands of the Sahara into humane ropes of knowledge, culture, and service'.

She thus formed in her mind an organization that would marry knowledge and human growth in societies together, to produce the distinct social species that human are.

* * *

Cheryl Conrad loved life, she loved taking photographs of the outdoors and she loved painting landscapes. She immersed herself in the outdoors and was ever reluctant to make new friends or go out and meet people. One could say her whole life was lived in her mind and her personal view of the world she lived in. She defined the world clearly in her own terms and was not easily persuaded to see any other point of view different from her own. She took photos of her parents, her brothers and sisters and their children and in the process built a huge album of memories of her parents who had passed on when she was in her twenties. Out of her striking fascination with photography, she took a keen interest in light, in particular, how all of nature depended on light.

She grew up in Calgary and had an unusual keenness to detect the first rays of the sun in the breathtaking bright summer months, and took photograph after photograph of the sun as it peeped out of slumber at sunrise. The red piercing glow warmed her soul and drew her more and more into a supreme world of silence and meditation. She would make sure she woke up before the sun was out in the summer and would be there to catch the glittering giant before six in the morning. And she would be there too at dusk, after ten at night, in the long glorious daylight to catch the slumbering sun before she went to bed. After the sun, she was her own best companion and saw the family mainly as an extension of her own person. In every sibling, she saw a Cheryl inseparable from herself.

Cheryl came to the University of Cambridge to study photosynthesis. Her Ph.D. thesis was of such landmark contribution to the knowledge of how plants utilized darkness for some vital life processes that she was immediately offered a lectureship after her thesis defence.

Gradually she grew out of herself and turned her whole life to taking the light of love to someone else, someone she did not need to know. She saw the need for writing but would, instead, give deliveries, off the cuff, of whatever she was required to teach, or do. She believed she could pass on all she knew to another person, in much the same way light entered into our life and makes it possible for us to know the world we see. She would be heard saying:

'A man gives you his sperm, just a single cell, and you, the woman, nine months after, give him a baby, if he is still there. The man can leave, and you, the mother, now have the responsibility to bring up the child, giving her the social skills that would transform her into a distinct human person. Let all our girls go to school, that knowledge to keep societies humane may be well developed in our women. Knowledge would then live in persons, grow in persons, and be transferred to persons by humans themselves'.

At this point in her life, she knew nothing of Baraah nor of anyone else who might share her views. South Africa gave Cambridge University one of her outstanding poets in Funeka Luxolo, from Stellenbosch in the Eastern Coastal Region of South Africa. Her parents worked in grand vineyards, some of whose Cabernet Sauvignon were among the best in South Africa. As a child, in apartheid South Africa, Funeka worked with her father as he went on the daily rounds—pruning the vines, artfully guiding new shoots to embrace the long ropes on which they would climb and grow, or cutting the grapes and dropping them into waiting baskets, whichever was dictated by the season of the year. Apartheid did not grant her parents the luxury to fully live the life of the breathtaking grandeur of the landscape.

But not Funeka: she poured her early energies into writing, unknown to her parents. She kept her writings to herself and no one else saw them. She did not want her parents victimized in her struggle for justice, equity and fairness for her Xhosa race and other blacks in South Africa. She turned to poetry and laid her heart on the table of truth and beauty, translating the magnificence of the Cape Ford Mountain into elegant masterpieces of verse at a tender age. Funeka chose poetry to express her deep, fierce, and interminable hatred for apartheid; and could thus vault into the heights of her dreams for freedom and equity.

Stellenbosch University recognized her genius and granted her a personal scholarship in her own right. She cleverly sidetracked the anti-apartheid movement and its activities to gain freedom for her black people, for so-called *coloureds*, and for all people who desired justice for everyone. Born in 1974, she would learn of Nelson Mandela in her early childhood and as much as her poetry flowed in the waters of landscape and beauty, she gradually developed a style of defiance that would find appealing application in the songs and lyrics of young South African musicians.

She had a passion for their staple meal of maize and sugar beans, *Umngqusho*, and she ate it with the gusto of a gladiator out for his final fight. Though a vegetarian, she could not resist the local 'bush meat', *Umleqwa*, made from wild fowl. Her father, Mr. Luxolo, loathed the rich white man's wines though he meticulously manicured the vines that twirled on extended twines of horizontal equality and justice. That was the way they saw it: the life of the vines in their vast and guided extensions came to represent what the black man clamoured for—equality, freedom, the right to be as one chose to be. He ate the grapes, red or white, but preferred the red to the white, that bore the image of the reprehensible white settlers. Instead of wines, which his employers graciously provided, he relished the local beer, *Umqombothi* and, on weekends, indulged his taste at the neighborhood bar.

Funeka came to Cambridge bitter and forlorn. She examined herself closely and took ample time to know who she was. She could then look at South Africa with the eyes of love and humour. In this mood, her mind dwelt on her country's richest source of capital wealth, gold and diamonds, all buried in the mines for millions of years, in the hands of the all-white settlers, rogues she called them. She remembered the classic lines from Grey's elegiac poem:

> *Full many a gem of purest ray serene*
> *The dark unfathom'd caves of oceans bear;*

This placed in clear focus what she would devote her life to — the full development of the human person, not as a mine of knowledge that is buried in unfathomed bottoms of souls, but of humans as the total expression of knowledge as service, directly transferred from person to person in all simplicity and truth. The womb of knowledge would be the human person.

In Funeka's world, books would be written on the human mind; the human mind would be the home of books. The word would live in humans who would go on to live a life of selfless service. Funeka endlessly went on and on and her poems were never written again. She told them to persons and to persons only, much like what the elders did in her home town, Stellenbosch, telling each other story after story. She believed the only way to achieve her dream would be for women to be the light of societies through learning and through bringing up children in the light of learning.

In the summer of 2009, there was an International Conference in Hamilton, Ontario, Canada, on Climate Change and Development, which attracted contributors from all over the world. This was attended by some of the women at University of Cambridge, who cared deeply for the ecology of the world they lived in and who were fiercely dedicated to the social development of the human person in total self giving. Up till this time, they had had no meeting, did not know one another, nor did they know their separate societal interests. They had a passing knowledge of one another's work just as they knew that of any other lecturer at Cambridge, and since they were in different colleges, they did not get much chance to socialize in the Senior Common Room, a bastion of Cambridge culture.

During one of the morning coffee breaks, as luck would have it, Baraah, Funeka, Cheryl and two other Cambridge staff shared a table and got to talking about the endangered availability of wood pulp, the raw material for books, as the forests of wood pulp were diminishing. Funeka then blurted out, "Who needs books anyway? . . . they are fast obsolete." With raised eyebrows, Cheryl asked, "And what do you plan to do about this?"

"Come on my friends, why don't we take this up fully at dinner or so?"

"Hey, what of tonight?" Cheryl quipped, 'let us go to Niagara-on-the-Lake this evening for dinner. And we don't have to hurry back, if we don't want to. My parents have a holiday bungalow there and we can take in some sights and spend the night there. What do you say? Oh, I forgot I'm Canadian, from Alberta; it would give me great joy to show you something of my country."

"It's okay with me," said Baraah.

"It's fine with me too, but we have to get back tonight, I am sorry to say. I need to go over my papers for presentation tomorrow."

"Okay then, I'll get a car and we leave at 2 p.m. As we're all in the same hotel, let us meet in the lobby, "

Funeka and Baraah agreed and the conversation shifted to other matters. The other two ladies begged off and declined the offer, but they kept returning to the question of humans, knowledge and books, albeit in a tone filled with humour and love of the girl-child.

"You know, this whole business of the human person

leaves me stunned." Funeka led her new-found friends into a relaxed conversation as they sped on the St. Lawrence highway past St. Catharine's to Niagara- on-the-Lake. "As a black woman growing up in South Africa, I was ever made to feel that I should bow in reverence to the white man who was far more developed than I was, and who had brought the free market enterprise to us blacks. Without the whites, they said, South Africa would be just like the rest of black Africa, undeveloped, unskilled and ignorant, though our parents drilled into us that one day we would be free and developed, our destiny in our own hands. Then the gold, the diamonds, the wines would be at our service for our own development as we saw fit."

Funeka sat in front of the Toyota sedan and tried not to be a source of irritation to Cheryl who, she noticed, was having some difficulty navigating the highway. She said no further as she was then negotiating a dangerous curve. Now on the straight road, Cheryl asked Funeka why she suddenly stopped; to which she replied, ruefully, that she was lost in her thoughts. Now agitated, Cheryl herself expressed her disdain for apartheid and not just apartheid but for any form of oppression that led one human being to oppress, or to think he or she was superior to another. She recalled the crisis her country suffered through the insidious perception that English-speaking Canadians were 'superior" to backward Québécois French Canadians that fueled the call for Quebec as a separate nation from the rest of Canada.

With the details still clear in her mind as though the events happened only some days ago, Cheryl delved into Canadian terrorism of the sixties with the formation of FLQ,

Le Front de Liberation du Quebec, whose nefarious activities reached its dastard ugliness with the abduction of British diplomat, James Richard Cross and Pierre Laporte, in October 1970. Pierre Laporte, a minister in the Quebec Government, was assassinated later that same October by the FLQ. James Cross was released the following December ending the crisis.

Wherever we went in the world, Cheryl would observe, humans were under one form of slavery or another. All this burned holes in her aching heart and Baraah had to ask her to just drive so they could take in the sights and enjoy the landscape. Neither Baraah nor Funeka knew just how charged Cheryl could be and left off any further reference to the terrorist experiences of the past. They were already close to their destination and now drove past some notable historic restaurants of the city, such as where Winston Churchill had come for dinner.

Village restaurant, which Cheryl had chosen, was not in the main city centre of Niagara-on-the-Lake and she had to ask for directions. This lugubrious group of three professors of Cambridge University out to hinge the mind of the world to the humour, idiosyncrasies and vigour of individual persons, soon cast their worldly concerns to the sky as they were greeted by the warmth and commanding energy of *Village* restaurant. Before they were taken to their table, they were allowed to walk through art works, and workshops for carpentry, black smithing and handcrafts with the artisans actually at work.

Baraah observed as they walked from one workshop to another: "Here we have them working, the learning experience is immediately transferred person to person; they understand and work at their own pace and each work becomes a product of the human mind and human adroitness. Can we do this at Cambridge, all of our attention directed to the students and the students alone, without concerning ourselves obtusely with the written word? Can the word live in our hearts, in our minds, nay in our works, whatever work we did?"

They came upon a lady knitting what looked like a table cover and Funeka complimented her on a fine piece of work. She thanked her for the compliment and pointed out that, in fact, she was knitting a quilt for a bed being made in the carpentry workshop. She said a customer had come in and ordered the bed to be made to his specifications. She then walked over to him and invited him to her handicrafts workshop close by, and told him she could make a suitable cover for his choice bed. He had examined what she had on hand at the time and told her to craft something of her own making; something she thought would go well with the bed. And so what they were looking at was the intricate but simple embroidery that would be a fitting cover for his adorable bed. She had asked the customer what were his wife's favourite colours, thinking these would be the traditional pink but he surprised her when he said it was gold and olive. That had put her to some trouble for she did not quite like those colours and now had to produce what must be a masterpiece that the customer would love much to *Village's* pride. She got her visitors to appreciate the axiom on the entrance to the restaurant: **You Are Our Joy**.

They now walked over to the smithing workshop where

Funeka was reminded of the mines in South Africa and the smelting of gold nuggets to yield pure gold from fierce, purifying coals. She would mutter: "How much good comes from suffering; nothing good in humans can come without smelting out evil."

They found they had spent all the time on just two of the engaging workshops but it was already getting late for their dinner and not to disappoint his guests with a cold insipid meal, the steward ran over and pleasantly pleaded with them to come upstairs for dinner. There before their famished eyes was the large, copious kitchen open to diners to watch meals being prepared. The waiter apologized that their meals were already prepared for they did not know that they, their valued guests, would spend a long time going through the workshops, given the elegant ambience of *Village*. He told them, however, that if they chose to watch their meals being prepared from scratch, he would gladly accommodate their interest and give them fresh plates of their orders, for it was indeed important to *Village* that guests had their heart's desire in whatever way they wanted this satisfied. But Cheryl quickly and graciously thanked him and said they would gladly have their dinner and just watch as the chefs went on to prepare other dishes. They had placed their orders when they came in so their meals were ready for a hearty consumption.

"Thank God we came here today. It seems our job has received an apt solid description. Knowledge is precious when it finds a home in the woman, transcending mere human accomplishments," Cheryl openly spoke her mind.

"How did you come to this conclusion? What do you

mean?" Baraah queried.

"Well, look at it, those workmen at their workshops are doing nothing more than what we ourselves are out to do and which humans have been doing since time immemorial, namely, honest good work using their brains and skills as they know best. They transfer what they know directly to other workers they train, who continue the trade. Isn't this good old honesty and sincerity at work? Is this not what we want to champion: that knowledge may be selflessly transferred from person to person, from womb to womb, that humans may live and learn and have their being? There's nothing new here, if societies would only give women every opportunity to light the world with their precious minds. Yes, girls are precious," Cheryl concluded.

"Well, there may be nothing new here. But tell me, how many places do we have where people successfully and profitably work as they do here at Village?" Where in the different industries and companies of this evil-ridden, capitalist, self-driven world do you find selflessness, peace and joy? Please tell me," Baraah retorted.

Funeka had been engrossed, listening to Cheryl and Baraah and found the conversation exhilarating as it was moving in a direction for which her native South Africa had rigorously trained her: self-effacingly, to depend entirely on herself, to train herself to the highest degree, and be able to bring forth a new generation of South Africans who would never depend on the white settlers for the future development and growth of their country. She was strong in her belief that the human person transcended all knowledge, whose true value is expressed in love and service.

They were by now far into their dinners: Funeka, had oysters with quiche and shrimp salad. She had *Angel's Gate,* a Chardonnay; for the first time in her life, she found herself drinking wine which she had obtusely associated with white-supremacy apartheid. Now she was the one who was supreme. She laughed and laughed and even brokered the idea that they should just go ahead and call their movement *The Village.* Cheryl laughed her head off wondering how the name *Village* would sound in sophisticated Cambridge. She had ordered a Canadian burgundy, *Blue Spirit,* to go with her beef steak and baked potatoes; and Baraah bean curd, bean sprouts, Spanish omelet, and a drink of grape juice. Baraah confessed that their company had freed her from a number of disdains and exposed her to a genuine friendship she had not experienced ever in her life. For dessert they had strawberry and whipped cream, cheesecake, and carrot cake and whipped cream. More laughter all round, Cheryl invited Funeka to a silky liqueur.

Awarah ended her story, and as much as Chioma did not really want to join GAP, (Girls Are Precious), especially as she did not quite understand their objectives, she was irresistibly drawn to the group and found herself giving Awarah her support. She was particularly enthralled by the tale of Baraah, for whom knowledge meant service and for whom life had no meaning unless it was lived on the towers and gardens and rivers and oceans of charity and service, flowing through her eyes, her ears, her nostrils, even out of her toe nails. And she could accept from Baraah, Cheryl and Funeka that knowledge was all indeed enshrined in the human person developing in the womb of the mother. Chioma could completely internalize the spoken word as the person. In fact, for her, now, the word was inseparable from the person.

CHAPTER SEVEN

July 26, 2013

Okeosisi, Imo State, Nigeria

Chioma's grandfather, Maduka, lately professor of chemistry at Obafemi Awolowo University, was beside himself with grief. Ordinarily, he would take the events of the day as they came and nothing whatsoever would disturb his peace as he quietly and resolutely attended to any matter before him. But these were not ordinary times: Nigeria was in dire straits and there were no solutions in sight for the teeming problems made all the more intractable by the rising pace of insurgencies in different parts of the country. The recent kidnappings of SureGas employees by BRAND, Brothers for the Advancement of the Niger Delta, with a ransom of two million dollars on their heads to be used for the rehabilitation of the Faculty of Engineering of University of Kokoma, widely called Unikoko, riled Maduka's conscience without end. How could this be happening in his dear country, which at a time—before the ignoble oil boom—treated education with the abiding interest of a mother out to train her children to the highest level of their abilities.

Suddenly, while it seemed all were asleep, Nigeria's education was in the doldrums. What could he do, he worried. Retired and spending his waking hours writing books, Maduka did not know how else to contribute to raising the standards of education in his beloved country. Something must be done, he was certain; especially now that criminals masquerading as an armed insurgency, had come in to nail the coffin of higher education. Blood money was the saving grace for the rot! If this continued, if the insurgents demanded ransom for their captives and turned around to transfer such monies to schools, what would stop students themselves from engaging in such dastardly acts to fund their training? Maduka grieved beyond consolation.

He received a phone call from an unknown number, and true to his habit of not answering calls from numbers he did not recognize, he continued with his writing. The call was repeated again and again and Maduka was now roused to answer. It was his dear old friend, Prof. Willie Briggs, from his student days at University College, Ibadan, calling from Kokoma. At first he could not recall the name for he had not heard from Billy for over fourteen years.

"Billy, are you still alive?" Maduka asked.

"You Fool! You mean if I had died you of all people would not know? What's wrong with you?"

"Well, Billy, suppose it were the other way round, and I was the one that died, would you know?"

"Of course I would know, from a number of sources,

especially from the UI Alumni Association, Enugu branch. and I presume your obituary would be in the papers."

"Sorry for this bric-à-brac. It's just that I am very, very angry with you for your protracted and unprovoked silence. For over thirteen years now, you've stayed in your Kokoma enclave, without regard for the rest of us. We retired about the same time, some twelve years ago or so; and before this, the last time we met was in Kaduna, I think, at the Nigeria Economic Congress Conference in 2000; I remember because you were the president at the time. So what happened?"

"You, keeper of dates, you're the one who should be apologizing for I have phoned you, times without number, and no answer. Then I learnt you had gone on sabbatical in the US, then on leave of absence for a year or two. So, I stopped calling hoping you would make contact with me once you returned to Ife. But you didn't. So, who's to blame?

"Ok, ok. . . . I get it. I'm sorry I'm not good at making phone calls."

"So how do you expect your so called dear friends to keep in touch with you?"

"Never mind, why are you calling now?"

"You first have to apologize for your long and unprovoked silence."

"Yes, as you say, I'm a fool who doesn't know he's a fool. I just carry on with my business and get it done. I'm very very sorry. I, not you, have been silent for a long long time.

It will no longer be so, from now on."

"It must change because you and I and others like us will stand up to the crass insurgency in this country and rout it out."

"You call me a fool, Billy, but who's the fool now?"

"It's the one who chickens out of a brave confrontation with death."

"Are you in any way suggesting you are trying to bring about my death before its due time, and if I should chicken out of such a bad deal, then I am a fool?"

"Maduka, Maduka, listen, can you remember the last time I called you by your name, can you?"

"No I truly can't. To you, I'm always 'You Fool'. Say what you want to say, or is what you're saying now something I should take seriously?"

"Good, you're getting the hang of it. This is serious business. It's not one of your foolish escapades."

"Please, Billy, get on with it. This call must be costing you a fortune. You know I don't like to waste time, fool though I may be."

"Ok, here it is. The retired professors of some of Nigeria's universities want to get together at your home in Okeosisi to plan how best to combat the new horns of insurgency that now butt the University of Kokoma with severe effects on our educational ethos. If this were to spread, we might be fast approaching an age when funds from insurgents would be the source of succour for our mendicant universities. Okeosisi is the right place: your great father made it one for discourse, for heads to meet in an environment of friendliness and oneness.

"Ah! This is very serious business. I'm at my wits end how best to tackle the ugly demon of insurgency in our country. I'm happy you've come up with something. I spend much of my time these days in Okeosisi; so I'll be available any time you sound the battle horn."

"You Fool, you think I'm the one who's going to sound the battle horn, as you put it. The onus is on you. You're the one we are counting on. I already have fifty names from both north and south of Nigeria. I believe at least twenty of these would be able to attend any time you call us, even at short notice."

"Well, come over to Okeosisi today, tomorrow, or the day after, and I'll be waiting for you. Surely, we both need to meet to rehash things before the whole gang assembles here."

"You Fool, you're using all sorts of expressions to say simple things. I'll come to Okeosisi on Saturday. I'll be arriving around 4 p.m. and will spend the night with you. How's your dear old woman? Does she still cook, and Adiaha, is she in the country; the last time I asked I was told she's with your granddaughter in the States. We have a lot of catching up to do."

"Yes, my dear mother still cooks, but not often. Don't worry she will have your favourite fresh fish pepper soup ready. Adiaha is in Enugu but will come down tomorrow. She was in the States last year and there met a group of women academics who formed an organization to assist the girl child. They are well funded and have done a lot already. I'm sure Adiaha would be only too happy to tell us all about this group, of which her granddaughter, Chioma, is the leader."

"Chioma is at it again; she's ever restless, involved in many activities all devoted to women and their welfare. You Fool, isn't she your granddaughter too? I can't wait to see Adiaha and hear what Chioma is up to this time."

"Billy, old boy, till Saturday then, God be with you."

* * *

Maduka's grief grew worse, enlarging to encompass everything he wanted to do. His usual gaiety and laughter were slowly vanishing with each passing thought and he found himself embroiled in a myriad of problems for which he had no answers. He remembered the favourite name by which Billy called him, "You Fool" because he always brought laughter to impossible situations with his tomfoolery and rib- cracking humour. He would not take anything too seriously not to laugh; he found life thrilling and wonderful. He therefore thought, "Am I still the same man who found the world a happy place?" Yes he was, he told himself, and he would now face life squarely, do all he can, laugh at it all and pray for the rest. The whole issue of insurgency would not bear him down, would not defeat his steeled mettle, and would only urge him on to do better, and better, at whatever confronted him.

Ma Nneoma sent to see her son, Maduka. It was about seven o'clock in the evening when Ma would be having her dinner. And true to her usual habit, she was eating some boiled corn and pear. She offered some to Maduka who graciously received the cob and then took a slice of pear from the saucer on the stool.

"Mama, is this your dinner for the night; is this all you will eat? Today, Friday, is the day you usually have your favourite rice and chicken, what happened?"

"My son, my teeth are getting too weak. I don't chew things well any more. I don't use them; they just are becoming useless to me. This is boiled corn, not roasted, so it is quite soft and I can eat it without too much trouble. Chicken is sometimes hard to chew, so I don't eat it too much now. Anyway I am fine.

"Yes, my son, I called you just to tell you something that is troubling my mind. Do you remember that time when you were at Ife when termites ate your books?"

"Mama, I remember it like yesterday. It was a horrible experience; termites ate all of my valuable journals. What was most painful, Mama, was they were gifts from the University of Uppsala, covering a period of over fifty years. Mama, why do you remember this?"

"My son, you know I am an old woman, so things are not too clear to me anymore; so I have to ask: do you think these people on the Niger Delta, these people who take others and ask for money so they can free them, don't you think they are like the termites who ate your books?"

"Mama, you mean the insurgents who call themselves BRAND, who kidnap people and demand money for their ransom? Perhaps, they are like those destructive termites. But termites are not people, they are not human beings, they do not reason. They just follow their instincts, that is, whatever their body tells them. They will eat anything when they are hungry."

"My son, all I see in my dreams are termites and termites and it is termites everywhere. And they eat people, not books or trees. They climb over a person in thousands and slowly and slowly eat him. I am sure these Niger Delta people who want to kill other innocent human beings if they don't get their money are simply termites. I ask you my son, when you were growing up, was there any of this money-taking in our country; were people not hungry?"

"Mama, since when did you become what we call a socialist, someone who wants the goods of a country to be shared equally amongst the people according to need?"

"Call me what you like my son, I will soon die and I want to see my country the same happy place where your father and I brought you up to serve and train others."

"Mama, things are not what they used to be, and may never again be what they once were. I don't want to say we are now in the age of the termites. It is up to the young people now to watch over their books so that termites don't eat them. You are right: human beings have lost their senses and do anything they please for whatever reason pleases them."

"My son, are termites not better; they ate your books because they were hungry for food. That's all. They were termites and lived the life of termites. But we are different as human beings. We can think we can reason. My son, that's all. These dreams are killing me."

"Mama, these dreams may have their meaning. Thank you, Mama, thank you."

* * *

Maduka's world was now turning round and round and it seemed the centre was yielding. He had to make sense of what Mama had been telling him, that the terrorists were no better than termites; in fact they were termites themselves. Did the terrorists really believe that the tree of higher education was best served with the blood of martyrdom, for that was what would happen if their demands were not met? In the past, their terrible activities had given Maduka much pain, but the recent emphasis on tying better standards in education to blood money was so reprehensible to his reasoning that he felt he was fast losing himself, and whatever made him human; for he believed on the totality of life, that he shared his life with every other human person whom he saw as his own brother or sister. How could this be, he worried, when those he considered his own were no better than termites?

CHAPTER EIGHT

July 27, 2013

Okeosisi

The following day, Saturday, Professor William Briggs came to see his old-friend, Maduka, as he had said he would. He drove in a black, well-used BMW, no more than seven years old, arriving Okeosisi by two in the afternoon.

"Welcome, Billy, welcome. How was the trip?"

Billy was about the same age as Maduka, that is, in his late seventies, but, unlike his friend, he still drove himself.

"Well, all went well from Kokoma to Aba where I had a puncture in the right front tyre. I had to swerve quickly to the kerb for the car meant to sway left onto oncoming traffic. I had to steer full right into stones on the kerb. Dear me, I nearly had it."

"Well, what did you do?"

"You Fool, like your true self you ask foolish questions. I just told you my tyre was punctured and needed a change, so what do you suppose I would do in such a situation, stand there and let the car fix itself, or, perhaps, hop into another car and come to Okeosisi?"

"I'm sorry. I just don't fancy you stooping down to change to your spare tyre."

"You Fool, you think everyone is like you whose father takes care of even after his death. He takes care of you from his grave out there and your life just goes on smoothly. For some of us, life is backbreaking and tough and we have to fend for ourselves or we'll be swamped by all sorts of problems."

"So what are you saying, is that you changed the tyre yourself. You're not good at anything technical."

"You Fool, there you go again. Yes, I'm not good at anything technical. Since when is changing a flat tyre a technical feat?"

"Just tell me what you did. Yes, the last time we were together must have been about fourteen years ago, or so. I never saw you drive yourself, I must confess and I'm indeed at my wits end to figure out why you would be driving yourself when you don't see too well."

"You Fool, don't you know of ophthalmologists, or do you think it's only an optician's world? Do you have any ophthalmologist in this remote God-forsaken town? It's only your father who gave it a name, and he was not an ophthalmologist, or was he?"

"Ok Billy, you have not changed, still irascible, ever obstreperous."

"Look at the pot calling the kettle black. You Fool. Don't make any pretence about your prowess in English. You studied Chemistry, mixing all sorts of liquids and solutions to get another sort of liquid or solution. And you call that university education. Don't forget, I studied economics, with particular interest in monetary policy. Do you know what money is, all you care about is simply to have some money to buy fuel for your generator. Your dear wife, Adiaha, is the one who does all the rest."

Adiaha walked into the living room as though she had

been waiting to hear her name.

"Madu, Billy is here and you didn't call me. I've been hearing voices wondering where they came from till I heard my name. Welcome Billy. It seems you two are at it again. Look, I've been hearing your voices for the past thirty minutes or so and, if I did not come out, you may have continued into the night without any drinks, even without dinner. What can I get for a drink, dearest, dearest Billy?"

"The usual, please, that will be fine."

As soon as Adiaha left, Billy continued:

"You Fool, you don't know how best to take care of your friends. We've been talking talking, that's all."

"Well, what's wrong with talking and talking; when did I see you last, and when have I had the chance to open up my mind to any one?"

"You just sit there in your palace, quiet and all alone. Who is foolish enough to come around to talk to you? All you ever did was mix up things, and sometimes tried to separate things in the attempt to purify them. That's all. This does not train you for conversation and sociability. You are darn good in what you do, in chemistry, what else do you know, only to say "irascible", "obstreperous". What other big words do you know, You Fool."

"This is my house, don't forget. And here I am king."

"That's if Adiaha says so, otherwise you are king of caricature."

Just then Adiaha came in with a plate of roast chicken and some salad. Maduka had Guilder and served Billy his regular Guinness stout.

"What of your legendary kola, You Fool, even here in your classic Akadike Igbo roots? All this time you forgot about kola, or don't you have kola in this house?"

"Billy, please, don't mind Madu, these days it seems he has too much on his mind. The terrorist killings in Nigeria are killing him too, and I mean this literally."

"Come on my friend, you mean anything mortal can kill you? I thought only the gods would dictate the day you would join your ancestors."

"Come on, Billy, are you alright? Here is some kola. I offer it to you in love and friendship."

"Well, *Ojinwayo*, the one who takes it at slow pace, who takes it easy, who is not in a rush, who will not be killed by terrorists, thank you. Here, take the kola, I return it to you. Say the prayers to the gods."

"Oh God of our ancestors, almighty and invincible, full of love, full of mercy, we salute you. Bless my good friend here, Billy, whom you gave me many years ago. He is here for a big meeting. May it all go well. Bless all who eat this kola from the Akadike compound, from your own soil, from your own precious earth. Let us live to give you glory."

"Amen."

"You Fool, you forgot to pray for the terrorists, so that they may drop the weapons of war and hate and, instead, love their neighbours. That's why I'm here, for us to find a way to negotiate for joy and peace for all."

"Yes, Billy, we shall search for a way. Here's your share

of the kola, and here is a whole one you must take with you back to Kokoma, to your good friends. I have taken mine. You might save a piece for the terrorists.

"Let's go over and see Mama. I told her you were coming; otherwise she won't let me rest till she has seen you."

"You Fool, how then will I get my favourite fresh fish pepper soup? You don't have any waters near you here, so how will you get fresh fish, not that frozen stuff from Japan?"

"Don't forget we are Akadike, Billy, and all good things come to us."

"Well, we'll see just how fresh fish will crawl from the rivers of Kokoma to Okeosisi."

"Do you remember that line from Macbeth: "Fear not till Birnam wood come to Dunsinane? It's the scene where the witches, soothsayers, proclaimed the invincibility of Macbeth. Today, my good friend, you will see Birnam wood come to Dunsinane."

"Hmm? Is that all the Shakespeare you know? Don't forget Okeosisi is not Dunsinane and Birnam wood has nowhere to go. The fish of Kokoma belong to Kokoma, not to Okeosisi."

Maduka and Billy walked across to see Mama Nneoma. She was asleep and Nkeiru, her maid, had to wake her up.

"Mama, Papa Maduka is here to see you with another man."

"Have you seen this man before?"

"No, I have not seen him since I came here."

"Ok, tell my son I'm coming."

"Good afternoon, Mama."

"Oh my God! Oh my dear husband Akadike, all you angels come and see what I am seeing. Come and see Billy. Wonders are happening! I will soon die, I think. People I have not seen for many many years are here to see me. Oh, my God, what more will I see? Oh God thank you for bringing Billy here."

"Mama, you still remember me though I have not seen you for over ten years now."

"How can we forget you, Billy? You and my son were one those days when you were in far away Ibadan; and you have always been one, so you are like my own son to me, and my son you will always be."

"Thank you Mama, this is my home indeed. And you will always be my very own mother, my Mama."

"Alleluia! I will be able to make you that pepper soup you like. Yes, the gods love us. Yesterday was Friday and many Catholics don't eat meat, only fish, on Fridays. So, we were able to buy fresh fish from Ijeobi. They are still swimming in the pond outside. Nkeiru, please help me. Get the biggest one, clean it, and make it ready for cooking. Then go to the farm behind the house, pick some vegetables and spices. Then call me. My son, Billy, please tell me some happy stories."

"Mama, the only happy story I have is that I am here. I have seen you, Mama, and I have seen my dearest friend,

Madu. As for the rest, you may have heard what is happening in my place, in Kokoma."

"Yes, my son, nothing good these days: it is all killing, killing and more killing. Yes, my days are here."

"No, Mama, not yet, not yet, Mama, you will still be here with us. Chioma your one and only great-granddaughter wants your company for many more years. Perhaps you will bring her back from the United States."

"Yes, my son, she will want me to stay with her for many more years, and I would like that too. But is that what God wants? Yes, yes, he wants me to see Chioma again. Beyond that, I don't know."

Nkeiru came in and said all was ready for the pepper soup and Mama then took her leave and shuffled to the kitchen. She turned and said,

"Please don't go anywhere, food will be ready soon."

"Let me show you the compound, Billy. So much has changed since you were last here. You know seven years ago, that is, 2006, Chioma brought her students here to spend their summer holiday with us. We did not quite know what to do but we reasoned that every able-bodied American would love swimming and basketball. So we had these built, with the help of my dear brother, Onyekwere. A tennis court we already had.

"Yes, You Fool, the last time I was here I beat you 6-3, 6-4, in two straight sets, yet you pride yourself as a tennis champion."

"That was in those days in Ibadan, not now. You know I

lost the use of my right eye after our Ibadan days and I couldn't see the ball clearly. So you beat me; big deal."

"Can you shoot some baskets? Do you need your right eye too for this?"

"All you know is economics, the meaning of money and policies that affect the money in your pocket. You seem ignorant of anything else in the practical world."

"You Fool, one eye is enough for basketball. So, if I beat you, don't say it's because you're one-eyed. Let's try it out. You start. Here's the ball."

Maduka and Billy played their hearts out checking each other and making good jump shots. Try as he could, Maduka was no match for "dribbling Billy", who had perfect ball control. The final score was 20-12 in favour of Billy.

"Let's not try swimming; there I will beat you hands down."

"Oh yes, you will beat me hands down in swimming. In fact I can't swim," Maduka admitted.

"Well, humility has its place. Good. So I can beat you in any game you would like to play on this formidable Akadike estate."

"Isn't that wonderful; I now know we shall win any battle in which you lead us."

"You Fool, swimming and tennis and basketball are mere games. They do not measure up to battles, where weapons are used. Are you alright in the head, great professor of chemistry? I have come here to ask you to lead us in war and now you're telling me because I can beat you in basketball, that I should lead you in battle."

"What did you say you are here for? I thought you came just for Mama's pepper soup."

"I told you there was something I wanted to talk over with you, or don't you remember; is your brain now sawdust?"

"Billy, I know you too well. I don't listen to your reason for doing anything. You are far too brilliant not to find a good and satisfactory reason for any of your actions."

"You Fool, what you are saying is that you can read my mind and construe what it is I am going to do. Well, well, I did not know your great father, Akadike Okeosisi endowed you with prophetic powers."

"Come on, I know you well-well, as we Nigerians say. You are truthful. You are sincere. You are absolutely trustworthy. Why else are we such good friends, or, as Nigerians would say, "tight friends"?"

"Don't give me this goody-goody line. I know you too. Why else am I the only one who ceaselessly calls you, 'You Fool'. It has been so from the fifties, from Ibadan. That is why you will lead us. You know where to go, what to do, when to run, and when to dance. We need you to lead us in this fight against terrorists."

Mama called them through the window that dinner was served. When, after some time they had not returned to the house, Adiaha came out and asked them not to keep Mama waiting.

"Sorry Mama, this other son of yours just won't let me

rest. He keeps talking and asking questions and he forgets we are in his house and he should take good care of me."

"Billy my son, it is too late now for us to change Madu. He is just like his father, looking here and there for things which are there and here. And he does not stop. Please, eat as much as you can and don't mind him."

Adiaha had helped to prepare a hearty meal, including her incomparable edikaikong, which meant they would eat some yam fufu along with everything else.

"Mama, I thought this was supposed to be just fresh fish pepper soup and nothing more. Now we have a whole feast."

"Call it a feast, call it what you like my son, it is all for you. My dear Adiaha is the one you should blame. You know for her food is not just food. She says it is a way of life; that what people eat tells us who they are. You know she goes on and on about food. For me, please just eat till your stomach is full."

Billy took a hero's helping of the fresh fish pepper soup, and disposed of it in a twinkling of an eye. It was exquisite but he had to do justice to Adiaha's edikaikong and pounded yam, to boot. Even if it killed him, he would eat of Adiaha's culinary panache. He dove into his meal with his typical bravado and in a while he was done. Maduka could not believe his eyes.

"Billy, wonderful; you've really dealt with the dishes with the gusto of a famished prisoner."

"You Fool, may a thousand thunders rumble in your

bursting stomach, spilling all its fervid contents."

Adiaha returned with some fruit desert but Billy had had his fill. It only remained for him to thank Mama, so he started:

"Mama thank you plenty, plenty; more than this world can thank you. Live for us, Mama, live and go on living that we too may live and know what life is all about. Mama, thank you. I am a very lucky man to have this family as my own. Mama, thank you."

"My son, this is your own home. Come and live here any day you like. It is your own place. It belongs to you. I know you and Maduka have some business. Don't worry, my granddaughter, Chioma, will make all things well. Akadike told me in my dream you will come, that the katakata in Nigeria will come, but Chioma will make the sun shine again. I don't know what you and Maduka will talk about. But Chioma is my sun. We shall shine again. She is the last Akadike with the sunshine of all her forefathers."

"Thank you Mama, my stomach is too full to talk any more. And Adiaha, well, you are the expert who looks after us all, in all sorts of situations and ever makes us comfortable, thank you, thank you immeasurably. God bless you."

"Billy it's late now; I think we should call it a day."

"You Fool, call it day, we've not yet discussed the thorny issue I came here for. Do you think I came here to sleep? Even if I came here to sleep, I must first disgorge my mind of all the troubling matters living in there, while they are still germinating before they come out and grow to tall trees of tribulation and agony, all in a short while. No, let's get on with the job at hand. You know too well the workings of BRAND in the past few months. Your own son, Emeka, was a prize in their boot. And they have now shot their way into funding higher education. Are we now to fund our universities with blood money? We have thought this through, a group of us, that only the Akadike mystique can save us; that you have all it takes to find an answer to this apparently intractable problem and that, in the end, we shall win with you"

"Billy, what you are saying frightens me. Never in my life have I been thrust with so huge a responsibility and I'm not sure I can bear it. I don't even know what it is I'm supposed to do."

Billy told his dear friend he had the habit of not sleeping until the matter he was dealing with was well resolved. Maduka insisted he needed a clear head to know what to say and how to say it. But Billy would have none of this impasse; all had to be well defined, well articulated and well executed.

"You can't be serious, Billy. You come here this evening and in a space of less than six hours you want my soul past, present and future. You want me to commit myself to a cause you and I don't know much about. How do you expect me to do this?"

"You Fool; there is only one reason, because I am here."

"Billy, you know I'll do anything for you except commit murder. Please let us talk about this in the morning when my head is clearer."

"No. It's not that you want your head clearer, no; you are afraid. Don't worry. I too, am afraid. But fear gets you only to the point where you decide once and for all that live or die you will fight and fight to the end. I know you, You Fool. You fight and you fight hard. We can count on you. Whatever you say we should do, we shall do. We are with you all the way. There is no going back. We must defeat terrorism, even with its own weapons."

"Billy, this is not just between you and me. Many others, as you tell me, are involved."

"What more can I tell you? Will you lead me in battle or won't you? Will you take me by the hand through thick and thin or won't you? When the battle gets hot, will you abandon me or won't you? Should you see me dying, will you come to my aid or won't you? And if, for some inconceivable reason I am dead, won't you take my body back to Kokoma?

"Come on, Billy don't get so emotional. Of course, I will do all you say and more."

"So, what else are we talking about? See this whole thing as our own enterprise, between you and me. The rest is mere details."

Maduka was in a new world: how would he fight terrorism? He was an ordinary retired professor, living mainly on his pension with some support every now and then from book sales and from his children. Adiaha also makes her contribution; but these are mere trifles if he was to confront BOND, or BRAND, let alone both. Perhaps, Billy had something more to say.

"You must have heard of the group GAP, Girls Are Precious, founded in 2009 or so and which has devoted a lot of resources to the girl child. In fact, they were responsible for the rehabilitation of Buthyiana after she and other students in her school were shot by terrorists in Pakistan."

Maduka gave further details: "You might know that Chioma in her inimitable style has agreed to be the Leader of GAP. She would give her life that girls may be in school and learn all they are able to. She believes that the blood of all the victims of insurgency, especially the blood of mothers, and their children, is not shed in vain; and that ultimately it will weld all the peoples of the world together. It is for this reason that she accepted to head GAP, an association owed to an incomparable group of women all at Cambridge University, England. She keeps in touch with me on this. So far, I have not offered any suggestions as to what they could do in Nigeria with BOND. Any discussion will wait till I can see her in person and speak with her one on one. You never know, the walls may have ears and our plans may be spilled to our adversaries ever before they get off the ground."

"Well, we are getting somewhere. This is exactly why we chose you to lead us, Madu. Perhaps, ultimately, Chioma will lead the whole fight against BOND and BRAND. We believe there is no family like yours to get things done and done well. You know, I have been thinking; why not get BRAND to fight BOND, one group of terrorists to fight another?

Though, I must admit, BRAND is not really out to kill dastardly and needlessly"

"Billy, you might be right here. You have been close to the underground ever since our student days. You were an active unionist and you were ever a bone in the throat of the colonialists. And you are a big rascal, who has the passionate zeal, armed with trust and forbearance, to easily gain the listening ear of any underground resistance organization. And when you put on one of those your war garbs, you can pass for a freedom fighter."

"You Fool, don't forget that, like you, I'm in my seventies; and my days of resistance and irascibility are long gone. What you call my war garb won't fit me now. I don't even know where they are. Look at my waist size, look at yours. Were they as broad fifty years ago as they are now?"

"I hope you don't go on and chicken out of this enterprise."

"You Fool, am I not the one who came here to enlist your support and leadership? If we could find another leader, or, if I considered myself worthy of this role, why would I be here? Yes, we are old *babas*, but a number of young Turks will join the fight. All they want from us is the long reach of wisdom that would take us to distant places all over the world, what with your connections and mine. As you said, I can fish out the operators of BRAND and you have the overarching Akadike dynasty that can stand up to any malaise or danger. So let's get going."

"Billy, look at the time; you know I am not a night person. You could stay up all night and I don't think that has changed. As for me, by 9 p.m. I'm fagged out, ready to hit the hay."

"Don't you think this is an interview; that I must know that you can last through a whole night without sleep, without food and still be alert in the morning, and this could go on for days?" Don't forget you are over seventy years old now, closer to eighty than seventy. And suppose you were kidnapped by the terrorists and held captive for weeks, or months, how would you cope?"

"Come on Billy, when that bridge comes we shall cross it. Right now we are on firm ground for miles and miles."

"I'm sorry, this is not an interview. Forgive me, but we have to finish this whole business in one go."

"Ok, then when you get back to Kokoma, set to work without delay. Get to the underground using your young friends to search out BRAND's hideouts, to reach out to them. I have my own people there too. You know Emeka who was kidnapped already had some ideas of his own. He has said a few things to me. So, how much time do you need before we meet again. Of course, the identities of BRAND won't ever be divulged. Only you and I will negotiate with them under conditions acceptable to both sides."

"I think we shall have enough to discuss in a month or so and we can then have a meeting of the group. I anticipate no more than fifteen core people. This hard core would, of course, have their necessary support personnel. Oh, we've not said anything about funding. Leave that to me. Someone —actually it is a company—will bear all the costs we incur and have already pledged a million dollars to our cause.

Once I return to them and confirm you have agreed to lead our effort, you and I will meet and complete all our plans."

CHAPTER NINE

July 10, 2013

Kokoma, Rivers State, Nigeria

Maduka's nephew, Emeka, returned to Kokoma as he had planned, not to work, but to the home of one of his colleagues, Bjorn, a Swede who worked with him at SureGas. Bjorn had packed his bags and was ready to go home, back to his teaching job in chemical engineering at the University of Lund. He had been on a two-year leave of absence and was due back to Sweden in September. It was now July and he felt he and Emeka could holiday in his aunt's home in Bordeaux, not far from Margaux, where they could keep company with some of the finest wines in the world.

Emeka rang the bell twice, even a third time, but no one came out to answer the door. He had phoned Bjorn to say he would be in his apartment by 2 p.m. on that day, a Wednesday.

"Sorry, old boy, I went out on an errand for our Dean."

Bjorn lived on the campus of University of Kokoma, where he had a contract to teach a Master's course on molecular engineering. Nobody in the university knew he worked at SureGas and only a few at SureGas knew he worked in the university. The company kept it this way to protect his exact whereabouts. He developed a warm rapport with the students and they were often together at the Student Union junior common room, cafeteria, or gym. All in all he was a likable and genial fellow.

"Please come in, let me take your bag, for how long have you been here?"

"Oh, I got here about thirty minutes ago, then went for a walk and came back when I saw you drive in," Emeka replied.

"I'm really sorry, never thought the traffic downtown would be that awful. Well, here we are, you must be thirsty, hungry, tired. How's Mama, can she still get about, the last time I saw her, eh...like a year ago she could walk round the whole compound. How is she?"

"She's still her old restless and workaholic self. Yes she gets about in the compound and she still makes her own cassava herself. That's still your favourite Nigerian dish, *lafu* and Mama's Okeosisi soup, and she would always make sure you had your fill each time she saw you."

"Just add to that some fresh fish and lafu with Okeosisi soup will get me any day."

"Wonderful. Yes, Mama still cuts the cassava tubers into about six-inch pieces, then peels off the skin, making sure the tuber itself is now pure white without any of that green layer that binds closely to the skin. Then she soaks the tubers in water for five days, not three, not four, but five days, till they are soft and can be masterly sieved in a fine-mesh sieve to conserve only the wholesome globules of starch. She leaves the cooking to Nkeiru, her helper, for not much can go wrong with the consistency of the lafu after her thorough treatment of the tubers. I can only get lafu this good from my Mama."

"Well, I am sorry I cannot offer you anything so irresistible but we can have yam flour and *egusi* soup. Angela, the young girl helping me, is off duty today so you and I will have to rumble in the kitchen and whip up something to eat. I'll put on water to boil for the yam flour.

"And I will stir it up into a malleable paste ready to swallow", Emeka completed the sentence.

They had only eaten a bolus or two when four people, three of whom had the stature of heavyweight boxers, hooded and armed with pistols, one with what must be the notorious AK47, ran out of the bedroom and immediately tied the hands of Bjorn and Emeka and gagged them. Pandemonium galore, they tried to free themselves. The more they tried the tighter the ropes became.

The one with the automatic gun held it up pointing toward the ceiling saying,

"We're not going to hurt you in any way. We are BRAND and hope you will cooperate with us for you will be held hostage for some time and the conditions will be more and more atrocious the longer your intransigence holds on. We want to help UniKoko to obtain funds for its erstwhile world-renowned research in chemical engineering. SureGas will be informed you have been kidnapped, that they will fund the departments in the Faculty of Engineering with a paid ransom of two million US dollars to the University of Kokoma."

The second man took over. He spoke with ease and quiet determination: "Already all the departments have submitted the list of equipment and consumables they require ready to be acted upon by the dean. Now SureGas will receive the lists from the various departments and provide all the requirements before you are released. Scandinavian countries are tops in offshore oil and gas and will be quite conversant with the equipment, etc. We expect all the equipment and materials needed will be delivered immediately, certainly within one week for we don't intend to hold you hostages for a long time. But make no mistake about this, you will be held until our demands are met. You might even be martyred for the cause of knowledge."

The third person, a woman, for her voice was soft and her long hair peeped out of her hood, spoke softly and gently. She waved her pistol before their faces over and over again as she continued the seminar: "Once your disappearance is reported in the news, BRAND will claim responsibility for your disappearance and will give the conditions we have here described before you are released. Dr. Erlander, Mr. Akadike, you are both wonderful people and no harm will come to you as long as SureGas meets our terms."

Finally, not to be left out, the fourth person, the hugest of the lot, laughed out loudly. "Don't you wonder how we came into the house? Dr. Erlander, you might recall you told your class about a month ago that you were looking for your keys, that very likely you left them in the lecture room after the class. Well, one of your students had picked them up and within ten minutes or so had made copies before you returned to the class to ask if anyone had seen your keys. You were surprised to find them right where you usually left them, on the far right of side of the table. Yes, this operation was well planned and we don't expect any hiccups."

The first speaker then blindfolded them as they walked out of the house. Bjorn's house was on a lonely part of campus; his nearest neighbours were no less than fifty metres from his house, on either side. No one would notice what went on there and they easily departed without any qualms except that both Bjorn and Emeka were locked in the boot of the car. They had been warned to be absolutely quiet and still; and that if for any unforeseen reason the boot was opened, the opening act would release swords which would pierce them in at least twenty points on their chests. At a safe predetermined distance from the campus, having successfully navigated the entrance gates, their leader stepped out, disengaged the knives, brought Bjorn out of the boot and transferred him to a waiting car, and left Emeka still in the vehicle they came with, driving behind Bjorn's. One armed man sat on either side of Emeka, their pistols firmly nudging his sides. The woman and one man sat on either side of Bjorn. Their leader had earlier removed their mouth gags leaving them still blindfolded and their hands tied together. Though they could each now talk or scream neither did for fear of their life.

The radio, TV stations, of Friday, July 12, 2013, all carried the report of the kidnap of Emeka and Bjorn.

"We are the people out to rescue Nigeria from the mess

into which we have all been plunged. We are the Brothers for the Advancement of the Niger Delta, which you all know as BRAND."

That was from their leader, Comrade Dagogo Fubara's written statement to SureGas. It continued, "Yes we shall brand matters to suit our purpose, and right now we want to brand the universities to assume a more rightful stature in teaching and research. We have kidnapped Dr. Bjorn Erlander and Mr. Emeka Akadike, both of whom work for SureGas. We have asked SureGas to place the two million dollars in a special account of the University of Kokoma for the sole purpose of purchasing teaching and research equipment for the Faculty of Engineering. The transfer must be made within ten days or their workers will be beheaded in front of TV cameras."

SureGas went to work to meet BRAND's demands and secured the safety of their staff. Two million dollars was a lot of money and seemed high, but they would, of course, do whatever was necessary to get their staff back. They would negotiate. Mr. Clyde Douglas, their public relations officer, had already reported the incident to the Police Commissioner for Rivers State, Mr. Cantena Vantu, and they were to meet once BRAND sent its demands. Mr. Vantu strongly advised him not to negotiate with the terrorists under any conditions, that they should not pay the ransom and that they, the police, would through their network free the hostages in the following three days at the most.

The hostages were taken on a Wednesday, and the statement from BRAND was released on Friday, after two days of searching, and excruciating suffering for SureGas and for the Akadike family. The police, as they had promised, were poised to secure their release through armed onslaught. They were certain they would find the seclusion where the hostages were kept and would be able to rout the militants in any armed confrontation. But SureGas would have none of it: they could not accept any iota of danger to the life of the staff for a mere two million dollars that can be spent in a twinkle of an eye. No, it would be strictly as BRAND had demanded. They utterly and completely refused any attempt to free the men by military force.

In the end, the police yielded but would not forgo their traditional role to follow the track of the militants and fish out their hiding venues.

It was now the fifth day of the kidnap and SureGas had not transferred the required ransom. Tempers were rising to breaking point, but SureGas wanted more time to negotiate and to see if the police in fact would surreptitiously secure their freedom. Emeka had been driven to a residence in Asaba, a well furnished bungalow with high narrow windows no wider than a man's head. Two iron doors were the only routes of communication with the outside world. The ceiling was burglary proofed and there was no way to escape through the roof. The building had been recently completed, was secure, and could not be easily penetrated. Emeka was still blindfolded when he was brought to his new home by the two armed men who had accompanied him from Kokoma.

"Old boy, you can have anything you want, just yell and

we'll provide it", one of the guards gladly told Emeka. They had removed his blindfold and he could see his surroundings. He did not say one word, however, not even to ask for water. One of the kidnappers, still hooded, asked Emeka to have his lunch: "Old boy, we want to take good care of you, you know, we are not out to hurt you, just to get some money out of these bastard capitalists bleeding our country of our flowing gold. Please eat something. We know you love your pounded yam and pepper-hot *egusi* soup washed down with well chilled *Gulder*. Well, here you are, you have both." Still Emeka was unmoved.

"Well, we'll help ourselves to this marvellous dish and whenever you want yours, just holler, as I said earlier."

Six days after the kidnapping, SureGas was not yet persuaded to pay the ransom. They were convinced they could hold out somewhat longer since BRAND's stance that the ransom money was to be used for teaching and research at UniKoko gave them a more hostage-friendly outlook. They were serious, yes, and might kill their hostages but they were not likely to do so hurriedly, SureGas believed.

Bjorn, on the other hand, was taken in a boat to Opobo, blindfolded. BRAND did not want him and Emeka to be together for a minute. Being academics, they would soon use their fervid minds to hatch their escape, even in the absence of weapons. Besides, Bjorn was the big fish in the waters of SureGas: they would surely be prepared to pay a high price for this freedom. On the seventh day, BRAND struck. They showed a video of Bjorn blindfolded, standing on a high table, with a rope for hanging round his neck. He read from a piece of paper in his hands pleading with SureGas to transfer the ransom without any further delay or he would be killed by hanging.

SureGas working with the police tried to make out the environment of the video and where Bjorn might be but everything was faceless. About an hour after the release of the video showing Bjorn, another of Emeka was broadcast except that in his case his head was laid on a slab ready to be chopped off. The police had not seen such dastardly monstrous demonstrations before: they were more used to hostages being gunned down with one automatic rifle or another, never with a guillotine or by hanging. It was now the ninth day. Reason mired in palpable fear pervaded the corridors of SureGas. The employees demonstrated outside the main building housing the office of the managing director and that of the chairman of the Board, Mr. Stefan Englund. He had flown into Kokoma on the morning of the tenth day.

Straight from the airport, without a bath or breakfast, he hurried to his office to meet with the Board and to receive advice on how best to or resolve the quagmire without any harm to his personnel. The demonstrators/agitations that the payment must be made helped solve the impasse for the Board. At one o'clock in the afternoon of Saturday, July 20, 2013, on the eighth day after the kidnap was announced, Mr. Englund went on national television and most sincerely appealed to the terrorists to release the hostages since all the equipment had been paid for and receipt acknowledged thirty minutes earlier. The Vice Chancellor, University of

Kokoma, spoke immediately after Mr. Englund confirming his statement that the equipment and materials were on their way to Kokoma.

"This is a most unfortunate situation for this university. A member of our staff was kidnapped and the ransom the kidnappers sought was for the provision of equipment to improve the atrocious conditions in teaching and research in the faculty of engineering. I say unfortunate because evil need not be done that good may result from it. Kidnapping is evil and, surely, education is a good. We will never accept evil even if we do benefit, as in this case, from its outcome. We would have gladly rejected the offer from BRAND, the militant kidnappers, but they had warned they would kill the hostages. Freeing them was paramount on our mind and all we wanted was to help secure their release. And this we have done. Thank you very much."

It now remained for the university to confirm to BRAND that the equipment had been received before they released the hostages. Without any further delay, SureGas delivered all the required equipment to the university.

Thirteen days after their abduction, on Tuesday, July 23, after hope of their release had thinned into mournful prayers, Emeka and Bjorn were brought separately in boats to swampy Bankoko, a village in Bayelsa State, fifty kilometers from Yenagoa blindfolded without any notion of where they were. Emeka took off his blindfold and screamed for help. Bjorn heard him on the tenth scream or so and started his own rounds of relentless screaming, one calling the other as their separate voices soon coalesced into one loud glorious "Thanks be to God. Alleluia", repeated times without number.

Emeka could not believe his eyes; he had feared that he would never see Bjorn alive again. This was a new heaven, ecstatic and imponderable, where the impossible was possible and joys and hosannas resounded on the Everest heights of indolent Bankoko. Emeka embraced Bjorn and held him, rather squeezed him like lemon till he could drink of the juice of his joy. Bjorn on his part wept uncontrollably as they stood in the early morning dew.

It had all been well arranged: SureGas had sent a helicopter to sweep through the skies of Bankoko and bring their staff home safely having been intimated by BRAND of their point of release. Bankoko was not bushy, and its skies bright and uncluttered on this wondrous day. Bjorn and Emeka waved furiously as the pilot maneuvered his way overhead and was not able to make out the golden persons of his subjects both of them in a navy blue caftan. On close inspection Emeka noticed that the embroidery on the neck and sleeves of his clothes were fresh and even had some threads hanging loose suggestive of a hurried sewing. The neck was tight and the waist meant for a man of meagre stature. The legs were long and Emeka had to roll them up in several folds without their sweeping the floor. He had washed his underwear a number of times during the days of hostile captivity. In fact, he had just finished washing it when he was given the new clothes and told to be ready to be taken away. He was wet on his waist and it showed in the pants and even through the caftan.

Bjorn's was blue alright and being taller than Emeka his pants did not require rolling up to fit though the caftan swept the floor in the manner of the rich lords of Northern Nigeria. Fortunately, he and Emeka had not been dropped in the deep swamps; instead they were decently taken to dry land. No native of Bankoko had been seen to dress in flowing adorable, kingly caftans, to the consternation of the niggardly swamps. No sooner had Emeka and Bjorn taken off their blindfolds than they found themselves in front of a crowd of villagers who had gathered in stern consternation as to what this Nigerian and his white companion might be up to. They even thought they might kidnap them for a handsome ransom.

A man in a long-tail brown shirt, long sleeved and collarless, in typical River's style, raised his voice and spoke in English.

"Why don't we first show them some hospitality with our traditional drink of *apeteshi* and then discover what they are about. From nowhere a bottle of local gin appeared, then three glasses and some crabs. The apparent leader poured a drink into the glasses, took one for himself, picked up a sliver of crab, and offered a drink to their strange visitors. All hailed, "Cheers!"

"My brothers and sisters today is the type of day we have not seen before. We have here two total strangers, such as we have never seen before. We have seen white men, yes, but we have not seen one here dressed in Nigerian costume like he was going for a party and with him one of us. Please tell us your names. What has brought you to this no-man's-land, you would say?"

Emeka spoke for both of them. "I am Emeka and my friend here is Bjorn. We were kidnapped . . . ." Before he could finish, the spokesman for the group interjected his remarks, completing what Emeka was going to say. "By BRAND. We heard this on our TV, in the radio and read it in the papers. Everywhere the local conversation was on you, on the kidnapping. Well, we shall undo all the evil they had done and treat you right."

Just as he finished his sentence, the helicopter came around a second time and all attention turned toward the surprising sight from the sky. Emeka and Bjorn waved with all their might joined by the now ecstatic crowd waving their hearts out. The helicopter came down and they all ran to their new guests. Satisfied that they were surely from SureGas, for Emeka recognized the emblem on the plane, the crowd happily led their kidnapped guests to their final departure.

"Please come back to us again soon as our good friends in a much happier mood." Goodbye", the leader said as he shook hands with Emeka, and with Bjorn.

CHAPTER TEN

August 1, 2013

Kokoma

Billy went to work once he stepped on Kokoma soil. He was firmly in his social milieu: he had published a number of papers on poverty and militancy; why people turn to militancy to fight poverty. He had maintained close ties with a number of radical groups and was ever keen to smell out students who were likely to be drug addicts or cultists. In this regard, he was quite friendly with those who would be regarded as deviants. He was ever keen to bring them back to the fold of normal humans. He went to this group first with the assistance of his young activists.

Thus, the word went out that Billy wanted to meet with militants of BRAND. He hoped they would have heard of him and what he had done for a number of down-and-out students. To give things a fillip, he started pub-crawling, going from one hotel to another on the outskirts of the main city where he reasoned the militants might hang out.

This time, he did not drive himself for his visits were often after 9 p.m. One of his assistants took him round in his car. And he did not visit the same hotel two days in a row nor was he driven by the same person two days in a row. He would arrive, order a Guinness for himself, and whatever his assistant needed, beer or soft drink. They fully avoided eating in any of the bars. Billy did not spend more than two hours anywhere he went. Certainly by 11 p.m., whoever wanted to be anywhere would have arrived there. He went from bar to bar, from hotel to hotel without any luck. Then one day, while he was leaving, a man walked up to him and observed he had seen him in about five different hotels in the past week. He wondered if there was anything he was looking for.

"Who are you, if I may ask?"

"Sir, you may not know me, though I know you very well

for you taught me economics for two years when I did my Master's degree at UniKoko just before you retired. But, sir, what you are feeling by your side is the nozzle of a gun. Just come with me."

Professor Briggs was disconcerted and did not quite know what to do. He reasoned that this eerie experience might be somehow related to BRAND, so he felt he would make the best of it, do as he was told, so he could see where it all led to. He appealed to his captor to let him dismiss his driver so he would not have any feeling that something was amiss. They walked together with the gun still nudging unnoticeably into his side. Anyone who saw them would just think they were like father and son. He did not give anything away so his assistant drove away knowing, as he was told, Billy's new friend would bring him home. And within an hour Billy was safely delivered to his family.

"Professor Briggs I am sorry I had to use the gun to get you to follow me even if you did not want to. It might surprise you that we do indeed need your cooperation. First, let me disabuse your mind as to how someone like me with a good Master's degree was here doing what I am doing now. I do not shoot, I do not kill, I do not engage in any act of bloodshed; but I am an activist and may use some harsh persuasive measures to obtain the necessary results. I work closely with BRAND as their economic adviser. I was without a job for four years running and I could not go on depending on my mum. My dad is late. Someone in BRAND asked me to help them out with managing their finances and I agreed."

"Please, you are way over my head with all that you are

telling me. Before we know it, I might be arrested as an accessory after the fact. Please who are you?"

"That is exactly what I am doing now, sir. I told you I know you very well. I told you you taught me in the dying days of your illustrious career, and I have also told you we need your cooperation."

"Well, tell me, here you are, with a gun by my side, and you're telling me you need my cooperation, will it be cooperation at gunpoint ? Would this be a proposal I can't refuse, as in *The Godfather* movie?"

"I am very sorry, Professor Briggs. You know sir, this damn gun isn't even loaded. See, I'll fire some shots and nothing would happen." True as he said, he fired many rounds and, indeed, no bullet exited.

"Yes, sometimes it is loaded, but then I won't be alone on such escapades. Others would handle any serious eventualities. So let me continue, sir."

Billy had never seen this before, nor heard anything akin to this belligerence. He too was an activist on the side of indigenous cultures and their preservation. He took time to study the culture of his people, the Ijaw, who live close to and on water, in the creeks, and tributaries of the Niger as it flows south seeking the Atlantic, and the Ogoni, who are mainland dwellers. He took particular interest in Brass, the southernmost people of the Ijaw, at the southern tip of Nigeria. He always said Brass could be readily sawed off from the rest of Nigeria. For this reason, he was always on the side of the indigenous people whenever they had an encounter with the oil companies. At the same time, the oil companies sought his assistance whenever they thought reason was on their side. Billy was, thus, well known in Kokoma and in both Rivers and Bayelsa States.

"Sir, you see I mean no harm. My name is Jaja Fiberissima. I am from Nembe, not too far from your own family. So two of us come from the same place, sir."

"You're not serious, you're the son of Winike and Tonye. Yes, your dad is late. I knew him very well. And your dear mother has been going through a difficult time to train all her children. She is a pride to womanhood. I keep in touch with her from time to time and get to know of her progress against all odds. You have a wonderful woman for a mother. So, what happened to you?"

"Thank you, sir, Mum has seen hell on this earth. But now it is all smiles. We have all graduated and are all working, if you call what I am now doing working."

"Well, we have come a long way. We both are looking for some assistance: There's a reason you seized me, and there's a reason I was going around from hotel to hotel. Well, you're the younger man. Perhaps, you can tell me how I can be of assistance to you."

"Sir, you know what happened lately, where BRAND channelled the ransom money for the kidnapping of Mr. Emeka Akadike and Dr. Bjorn Erlander to the Faculty of Engineering in Kokoma University. It was my handiwork, yes, sir, I arranged it and got the leaders of BRAND to forgo the funds from the ransom. Sir, was this not a good thing?"

"Well, that is one of the reasons I have been going from

one place to another because I was sure I would run into someone who would help me. And here I have seen you. Let me answer your question with a simple, firm no. No, it would be disastrous for universities to be funded through blood money. It would destroy our universities. What I really had in mind was to bring BRAND to meet BOND. This is where you can obtain all the funds you need for sustenance."

"Sir, this is almost impossible. We do not want to kill and we are not killers, we are not murderers, we do not shed innocent blood. No, sir, we do not. Yes, we are militants and the cause we fight for is well known. You too, sir, are a militant."

"Yes, you call me what you may but I am not of your type. We negotiate and negotiate and negotiate some more. And still we negotiate. You yourself know this."

"Sir, as we are talking BRAND is planning another kidnapping somewhere else. But you will not believe this; I told them to hold on till I have had a talk with you. I had heard that a number of you older professors are hard against BRAND and will not stomach any more of this entry of blood money into the universities. I believe I will be able to dissuade them from this new plan. They need money. In this new enterprise, they would have split the ransom money between BRAND and the targeted university. They need money real bad, sir."

"Well, money will not be the problem. When I said we would like you to approach BOND it was only for you to get to know the workings of their minds. No, you will not confront them in battle; no, they will not kill you. We want you to use your keen Intellectual prowess to fish out the leaders of BOND, know their whereabouts, how they live, what they do when they are not killing people, how they choose their victims, where they store their arms and ammunition, and everything else that would help us to capture them in their sleep without shedding one drop of blood; that is to say, you are to smell them out."

"Well sir, this will cost you some money."

"Like how much?"

'Sir, at least fifty million naira, as wages, throw in another twenty million or so for logistics, making it seventy million; but it might creep up to, say, a hundred million."

"Well, money will not be our main difficulty. I've heard you and we'll talk some more on this. But assure me you can get the job done. You will see your people, and I, too, will see my people, then we'll meet again."

"Sir, my people move in the creeks, on boats, we are not used to movement on land. Land is an obstacle to our actions. I don't know how we will take this."

"Jaja, that is exactly why I have come to your people, to BRAND; nobody would be expecting someone from the riverine lands to come up to northeastern Nigeria where there is no water, at least nothing like the vast rivers, estuaries system of Nigeria's delta region. They don't need to be experts, and therein lies their strength. You may not believe it but there are unexpected fruits from amateurism. Amateurs often walk into serendipity and make amazing discoveries. They are not afraid, often impetuous, and they do not mind making mistakes, above all, they know they walk a thin line of safety, and so take every necessary measure to stay alive."

"What you're saying sir, would go well in one of your lectures but in the hard, real world of life and death, and, in this case, where death lurks in around every corner, amateurism is another word for death. You die without knowing it. You just find that you walk into your death, even as you're dancing to drums of war."

"Let me ask you, Jaja. Do you still have the notes from the lectures I gave you?"

"Yea, I do, sir. In fact some of your apophthegms are still with me to this day."

"That's wonderful, I wonder is there any you can just whip off the top of your head?

"The one I use all the time, which you said you picked up from a book of quotes is, 'Look at it, Noah's ark was built by amateurs, and it survived the huge deluge that drowned the whole world. By contrast, the wondrous Titanic was built by experts and it sank on its maiden voyage." I will never forget this, sir. And another one is, "A man with a gun is a man afraid."

"So what do you say now that you can understand my standpoint?"

"Sir, let me see if I understand what you would like us to do; whether or not we will do it, is another matter."

"Well, Jaja fire on."

"You want BRAND to go to the northeast, to the home of BOND, to gain as much information on them as possible; as you say, to know their thinking, how their minds work, their habits, where they sleep, what they eat, everything."

"Yes, Jaja, that's pretty much what you would be required to do. I'm happy you added the word, "everything". You know this comes from you. It tells me your mind is set on this effort and you're going to do it and do it well."

"Sir, please let's not get ahead of ourselves. We have a long way to go. Our people have not yet said yes, and I myself have not yet said yes. So, sir, can we meet in this same hotel in a week's time. You will get a yes or no from us."

"Okay, Jaja, that's fine with me. I'll be here at 9 p.m. next Wednesday. I really would like to wrap things up soon. We want to get to BOND without much delay. I have a feeling BOND right now is ready to negotiate. We must seize the moment."

CHAPTER ELEVEN

Okeosisi

February, 2013

Lately, Chioma had been on the mind of her great-grandmother, Ma Nneoma, and every other day she would dream of her. Ma Nneoma woke up, or rather, her eyes woke up at the sound of the cockcrow. She had been sleeping on her left side for some time now and must change to her right side, where she had less pain. The right hand moved more readily than the left and she can more easily scratch her head. She could do a lot more with the right side of the body, like stretch out her arms, raise her hand, touch her right and left feet, and scratch her oft-itchy back. She would glory in her right-side freedom and say she was born to do all things with her right hand. She was born right.

She changed her sleeping position to garner the last strands of distant sleep. She still slept in the brick mud house which she had shared with her dear husband, Akadike, while he lived, and firmly refused to move to the modern more comfortable bungalow her son, Ugwuoma, had built for her. She still slept in the same room that adjoined Akadike's and from time to time would walk over to his room, lie on the bed for a while, singing praises to his name.

> Hero of my dreams
> My life my knight
> I greet you
> I salute you
> Wherever you may be
> May you be happy
> Full of joy
> Watch over me your Peace
> Pray God grant us peace

She walked over to the bed, laid on it, and soon after, returned to her own bed as though a thousand needles had run all over her back. She could hardly walk, even with her strong walking stick in stubborn support, never leaving her alone, ever ready to steady her gait round the room. She was distinctly uncomfortable, even as she lay on her usual bed-friendly right side. She sneezed, then again, and the maid, Nkeiru, who slept in her room with her, quickly rose up and asked,

|"Mama, is all well with you?" There was no answer. Then she asked again, "Mama, you don't seem okay. You have sneezed twice; it is not cold and the fire is on, in fact, it is quite warm. Mama, what could be the matter?"

Mama turned to her left side and, now, distinctly troubled, pulled herself with all her might and sat up.

"Nkeiru, are you the only girl in this compound who does not know what is going on? Are you the one deaf person who cannot tell the market is on fire?"

"Mama, please forgive me, don't be angry with me." She quickly tried to search her mind for any particular events that might be in the offing, but she could not find anything that could be described as an "event"; everything for the foreseeable future seemed of the normal run of events and she could not make out which market was on fire. Perhaps, there were things she did not know, or had not been taken into confidence over. After all, she was not one of the family and, besides, she had been only seven months with Ma.

She remembered. Running across to Ma's side, she knelt down asking for her blessing before she said whatever she had in mind. She stood up and Ma invited her to her side, to her more friendly right side. She stretched out her hand, reached out to Nkeiru's right shoulder, and held her with all the love of her age-strong heart.

"Ma, I know what it is, but it did not occur to me in time. It is about Chioma, Mama, isn't it?"

"Yes, my child, it's about Chioma alright. Go on. "

"Ma, I hear she will be in the country soon, that she will come to Okeosisi, that Papa Maduka brought you the message of the visit. Mama, that is why you are sneezing. You have already seen your dear great-granddaughter in your dreams, and you agree with the gods that she should come."

"Wonderful, my child, wonderful, you are a true child of your father's who knows where he keeps his snuffbox. Yes, I cannot wait to se my baby. It is over ten years now I saw her last. It's like she was born in Sokoto and I in Uru, too far, too far."

Nkeiru stoked the fire; it was burning low but she did not add more wood for it would soon be morning and it would be warmer. With the duster, she removed the ash, fanned the flame and the dry wood came back to life. She helped Ma sit on her cosy chair and moved the bed closer to the fire. Ma laid down on her left side and, surprisingly, fell asleep straightaway. It was now six o'clock in the morning and Nkeiru herself soon slept off. She never left Ma alone and could be ever found by her side.

Ma slept in fits and starts. Her left side was not cooperating and she shifted to her right side. It was not any better. Concluding that the thought of seeing Chioma again had delightfully broken her feeble bones, she finally woke up. It was seven o'clock and she stretched out in bed to say her morning prayer. Her prayer was always brief.

"Almighty God, I thank you for this day, I thank you for my life, I thank you for the wonderful world you have given me. Forgive my sins especially now that I am old and don't remember much, not even the day the tortoise went to the market to look for his wife who had run away with his helmet. Help me more to be better and serve you well-well. Bless all the football-teams of children you have given me. Help me throughout this day."

Nkeiru was awake and added, "Amen". She went over to walk Ma to the bathroom. This was the only modification she could accept to the classical brick house of her dear husband Akadike. Maduka, her eldest son, had insisted the bathroom must be close to her bedroom so she could simply walk straight there from her bedroom. It was built in such a way that Ma could be fully supported on all sides while standing or sitting to have a bath. She would not slip and she would not fall. Nkeiru always ceremoniously gave her a bath of cold water. Surprisingly, Ma usually had a cold bath, even in the relatively cold months of the harmattan. But she would sleep warm by the fire.

Her health was failing and she took several tablets a day, in the morning, afternoon and night to keep her blood pressure, bones, bowels and appetite well controlled. But this morning she refused any of her medications. Nkeiru was surprised and ran across to tell Pa Maduka. He had planned to see his mother later that morning and felt he need not trouble her any earlier. He asked Nkeiru to return and use all her caring skills to bring Ma to take her medication. And she succeeded: without much ado, Ma asked Nkeiru to bring her medicine.

"Ma what happened, a while ago you said you would not take them."

"Well, I do not want to see Maduka this morning and I am afraid you may have reported me to him and he would come to see me. I do not want to see him this morning. Two of us will have a talk as big as the iroko tree.."

"You need not worry, Ma, he will not be here just yet."

"Good."

Mama studiously took her medication and sat down to breakfast. Nkeiru had prepared boiled plantain with some stew. Mama did not like that.

"I thought I told you last night that I would like some *agidi*, and nothing more. You have cooked yam again. Today, you can give me anything you like but not boiled yam, please."

"But, Ma, I told you last night that we do not have *agidi*. The woman who makes *agidi* has travelled to the village. She will come back next week and then we can buy some from her. But if you like, I can go out and buy *agidi* from the market."

"Nonsense. You know I do not eat any cooked food from the market."

Mama's breakfast was often boiled yam with palm oil, *akamu* with *akara*, beans and stew, or her favourite *agidi* with stew.

"Well, you can give me whatever you can prepare in a hurry. Make it quick, today is a long day."

Mama dosed off to sleep and was soon awakened by the baked aroma of boiled yam from one of the kitchens in the compound, reminiscent of the days on the farm, when she was younger and she and her dear husband, Akadike, would set out at cock crow for the farms. After ploughing about twenty rows of yam, or, in her case, about fifty heads of cocoyam, they would take a break, partnered by the accompanying sun, for a lively breakfast. She was not particularly fond of yam, but they were easy to pack to go to the farm; and since Akadike loved yam, in time, she grew accustomed to them.

Breakfast over, and supported by her faithful companion, her walking stick, Mama went out for a walk around the compound to see whichever of her grandchildren or great-grandchildren were at home. As far as she could make out, she had over forty grandchildren and fifteen great-grandchildren and she could never tell who was at home at any given time. Of her children, only Maduka was at home but since she knew he would be seeing her later in the day, she did not bother to go in and see him. It seemed some of Maduka's children and grandchildren were visiting; still she avoided his house altogether and went instead to see her grandson, Emeka, who was home from Kokoma.

There had been problems with militants who would not allow SureGas, the oil company he worked for, access to their oil fields and Emeka had been asked to take an extended leave until the insurgency was over. But this would expire in a few days and he would have to return to Kokoma. He ran out as soon as he could make out Mama's ritualistic walk, her grunts and the rough sound of the walking stick striking the ground with all the force her weak arms could muster. He helped her up the steps and she was soon in his living room.

"Grandma, good morning, you're out so early, that means you're quite strong and healthy."

"Emeka *nwam*, is that how you know good health, dear son? Thank God I'm fine. This means any day you do not see me walking around you will say I will soon die."

"No, Grandma, no. You know I see you everyday, but since I came home about two weeks ago, I have not seen you walk as you are walking today. You are strong, Ma. I shall be going back to Kokoma tomorrow but I shall be back again in a week or two. So you will be seeing me here off and on. Mama, please come in, sit down, I'll get you cold water, it's getting warm."

"I'll come in. That's what I wanted to do when I came out. But I will have ordinary potted water, nothing cold passes down my throat. You will remember you yourself took me to the doctors and they gave me all those medicines with a warning never to drink cold water."

"What is all this trouble in the Niger Delta? Who are these troublemakers? Do they not want the money we get when we sell oil, what do they want? I am now too old to know anything except love and tolerance. And, you know, as our people say, the old know better, they are nearer the gods and their voice is the voice of the spirits."

"Grandma, you are quite right that love and tolerance were the virtues you would find everywhere in the land when you were a child. There is nothing you are doing now you did not learn in your childhood, what your parents taught you. They themselves taught you and you passed the language of wisdom to your children, including my father, who has now passed it on to me. In a way, I have learnt everything your parents taught you and your language of love is also my language of love."

"Then why all this katakata? Don't the militia"—

"Militants, Grandma."

"Don't they want peace and love too, just like you and me, like your father and all my children and grandchildren and great grandchildren? Why, why?

"Grandma, it's a long story. We will never be able to finish talking why there is so much evil in the world and the only language we speak now is one of war and more war."

"But we fought a war, and we suffered; plenty, plenty. Do we want another war, or does everybody now want to fight his own war?"

"Grandma, I told you it's a long story. And we don't have an answer to this frightful question. How do we live in peace with our neighbours, how can love and tolerance reign in this world?"

Mama drank some water but refused the malt drink Emeka had offered. Emeka called out his two children who were then on holiday, Emeka Jr. and Obinna.

Mama took one look at them and was filled with joy. "Thanks be to God for you, what have I done for God to give me all these good things when this world is full of evil and mili..mili.. —

"Militants, Grandma."

"Mili..ta..nts fighting ordinary people who wake up in the morning and go to work. Oh, thank you God, thank you. God bless you my children, God bless you, Emeka, little one, God bless you, Obinna. May this world have a big, big heart of love like your own, like our own."

"Amen!" They gladly proclaimed.

Mama tried to move to a more comfortable seat. Her companion walking stick accidentally slid and missed its firm hold on the floor and Mama fell on her good right side. She yelled out loudly, *"Chineke muo o-o-o"*, and Emeka frantically ran to her help. He had left Mama to take a call in the bedroom.

"Mama, what happened? How did this happen?" He held her up and helped her to the upright chair that received her sprained back. She sat up straight, took a drink of water and dosed off to sleep.

"How am I here in this seat? What happened?" No one answered, relieved that she must be alright. She stood up to the delight of her grandson. Emeka smiled, a smile of great joy at the little things of life that can just go wrong but do not. He reasoned Ma could have broken her leg, her hip, or even her head!

"Emeka, I remember now, it is all those your mili...mili.."

'Militants, Mama."

"Yes, my child, it is all those trouble makers in your Niger Delta; they pushed me down, but they won't win. They will never win."

Emeka watched his grandma closely thinking how much longer he would have her company. In the fast-paced world in which he lived, in Kokoma today, Houston tomorrow and the United Arab Emirates the following week, and then to other countries far and wide, he found himself culturally eclectic, adjusting to varying and often perplexing ways of life. Even in his native Igboland, he was fast becoming a stranger and he often found himself on the opposite side of any argument on the towering values of human life. Honesty as far as he could make out was fast disappearing; truth no longer prevailed and hard work and diligence were habits for the stranger from another world. He really wanted to stay close to his grandma to be able to maintain a humble and sincere sense of self.

When Mama worried where Nigeria was going with militancy and insurgency on the rise, Emeka wondered whether that was a clarion call to escape from the country and live elsewhere in peace. This question tormented him over and over again and he decided he would stay close to his dear grandmother, even if all he got out of this was simply to see her God-given face each new day. Every step grandma took, her cough, her smile, her sweat, her silence filled Emeka with pearls of joy. She gave him his ancestry and his history. The recurring question that riddled his mind was, where will he take this to, the rich and honourable tapestry of his autochthonous culture? How would it serve the restlessness and bloodletting ravaging the land? He must wait until Chioma came home; they then would decide what to do with themselves in their estranged homeland.

Mama woke up with a stern look on her face. She had been dreaming and was disturbed by what she believed would come to pass soon. She called Emeka to her side and advised him not to return to his job as yet, but to wait till Chioma came on her visit to the country. Yes, she realized that though his job was one of great responsibility and the company could ill afford his absence, she did not think he would fare well in the prevailing climate of wanton and unprovoked bloodshed. The millennium she had hoped would happily see her in the dying days of her life was developing into one of restless pestilence. Emeka on his part was amazed Mama had the same idea as himself, to wait for Chioma's homecoming. Neither he nor Mama would, however, say what they thought Chioma would do and how her presence in the family would solve their aching problems let alone Nigeria's horrendous quagmire. What can one person do, and a woman at that!

CHAPTER TWELVE

July 12, 2013
Okeosisi

The kidnapping of Emeka, hit the Akadikes with the power of a Muhammad Ali upper cut. They were bruised and felt their world in tatters. It was unthinkable that such barbarous, savage act could be visited on one of their sons. Beside himself with rage, unbearable distress and mounting despair of his loving country, Maduka, Emeka's uncle, most unusually, drove himself by ten o'clock at night from Enugu to Okeosisi, a distance of about a hundred and twenty kilometers, the moment he heard of Emeka's kidnapping on the news. Just before he got to the gate to his residence in the sprawling Akadike estate, he phoned the security guards asking them to open the gate with as little noise as possible. He did not want to rouse his mother, from her fitful sleep. She would immediately draw the conclusion that something terrible must have brought her dear son home at that late hour.

Maduka drove in quietly and parked the car behind the building. He did not want to leave any sign that he was around, certainly not to Mama, who would be out religiously in the morning walking around the compound. Still to keep his presence a secret, one of his relations drove his car far away from his own house. Emeka's father, Ugwuoma, Maduka's younger brother lived in Okeosisi and from there the two of them would constantly confer on Emeka's fate. Being the elder brother, Maduka would lead the conversation always assuaging his brother's worst fears. Maduka walked over to his residence immediately his car was taken out, his phones in hand. He had called his younger brother to tell him he was at home in the Akadike compound and that he would be with him shortly.

Calling his elder brother *Nna'm,* his fond greeting for his elder brother, ever since they lost their iconic father, Akadike, Ugwuoma proceeded to pour out his distress. He swooned on Maduka's chest, his head, his arms, all of his upper frame collapsed on Maduka. Tears flowed without end, his eyes red and fluttered, Ugwuoma could hardly manage any words.

"*Nna'm*, it will all be fine. Emeka will emerge from this barbaric evil. He will come back to us smiling his engaging and infective smile, cracking all sorts of jokes of his sad experience. You know he has the uncanny ability to turn a tragedy into hilarious comedy.

"*Nna 'm*", Ugwuoma continued, still weeping freely, "yes, I believe we will get Emeka back. But, Nna'm, things won't be the same ever again. The Akadike family may have suffered a permanent, irreparable disaster."

"No, oh no, Ugwuoma. Nothing of the sort has happened, or will ever happen, to us. Never! Our great father, Akadike Okeosisi, taught us never to be afraid even if our lives were in severe danger. He taught us that death was simply a passage, not an end, a passage to another far more fulfilling life. . . . "

Ugwuoma briskly but respectfully interrupted his brother. "Nna'm, yes, Papa taught us a lot and we are ready for anything this life throws at us. But, Nna'm, there were no kidnappings in Pa's days, nor were there needless deaths from terrorism, nor even armed robbery. Pa, I imagine, spoke from the standpoint of his day, as far as he saw it."

Maduka looked as younger brother, "When Pa said we should not be afraid of anything, he meant anything, even if he did not know, or could not have known, what this thing might be. His advice was for all time. Surely, you passed this on to your own children as far as I can tell and they too have passed it on to their children. I know what your grandson can do; and you yourself sit with Chioma, and listen to all her stories of how she dares life and succeeds. Don't worry. We are well steeled to face life's challenges and uncertainties."

It was two o'clock in the morning by the end of this conversation. Maduka slept in the same room with Ugwuoma to be near him and give him every possible support, their phones lined up on the night table beside Maduka. They were expecting a call from the kidnappers and if that happened, Maduka would handle the negotiation. Not long after, by three a.m. or so, Maduka jolted his brother from sleep that they may go over to his own house and stay there throughout the ordeal. Ugwuoma lived closer to Mama and she would soon go to greet him in her ritual, 'Great Mountain'.

Ma always called him in this uncharacteristic style, in English, from the day he was named by his legendary father, Akadike. He had said, "I have climbed many hills in my life; some have led to running streams of joy, others to rocky roads of hardship and suffering. But I have come through each one, and I'm still alive. Today, the gods have given us a great mountain, high and towering, and from here we will see the world. Yes, the gods want us to climb high to the skies and go where no one else has gone. I call this son of mine Great Mountain. He will stand tall. He will go places. He will fly high the Akadike flag and plant it on palaces of joy."

Ma Nneoma went over to see her Great Mountain but was told he had gone to Onitsha to replenish his store with new arrivals of goods. His was the only shop in Okeosisi where one could make exotic purchases. Well, no one in the compound actually knew where he was. Maduka's household had been sternly instructed not to let anyone know of Ugwuoma's whereabouts. The news of the kidnapping was on the air and everyone in the compound had been instructed not to let Ma know of this. Somehow, she felt all was not well. The usual laughter and gaiety of the compound was not there; everyone seemed tense and sombre.

Mama spoke with her caregiver, Nkeiru, enquiring if there was anything untoward that would bring this unspeakable silence on the family. Nkeiru laughed this off and simply said everyone was serious with their work and there was indeed much fun amongst them all, that nothing had changed.

Mama received this explanation with her usual aplomb, sat in her rocking chair and started to sing a song of foreboding:

> "Ye gods high in the sky
> come down and see us
> bring us news of joy
> that we may live again."

She slept off after she had sung this over and over again more than ten times. Mama continued in her sleep but her brain started buzzing. "What kind of spirits are these, the one is here to help me, the other, to fight and fight till I die. How is this?"

A war had erupted among the spirits and Mama found herself in the middle of the fray. One spirit would lift another, throw him to the ground, and cut him with his sword. Blood would flow but would then be sucked back into the spirit world from where it rained on all who were fighting. Some of the blood soaked Mama's bed sheet. The wetness woke her up and she could not quite make out what was going on for her bed was dry all over, and she too was dry. What sort of dream could this be, she wondered, half asleep half awake. She looked around her and there was nothing amiss. Nkeiru was fast asleep beside her; her bible was on the table and her clothes were as she had left them, on the chair beside her bed. Mama sat for a while. She knew only too well that dreams came without any advance notice; that they may or may not be indices of future events, and that most of the time they meant nothing. But of this dream of spirits at war, after one of them had warned her she would fight and fight to the end, she would ponder more deeply when it was morning. Being old and forgetful, who would pay much attention to her if she described her experience that night? Finding no quick answers to her problem, she slept off again.

When SureGas was contacted by the kidnappers, they immediately got in touch with Emeka's father, Ugwuoma, and told him the terms of the release. Immediately he handed the phone to Maduka and he took it from there.

"Thank you for telling us Emeka and Bjorn are safe and well, that you will fulfill the demands of the kidnappers and that everything humanly possible would be done to return Emeka to us as soon as he is released. I am Professor Maduka Akadike, Ugwuoma's elder brother: I act on behalf of the Akadike family and I'm the one you will be dealing with on this difficult matter. As much as we are relieved you will handle the situation appropriately and efficiently, we want you to know the entire Akadike family will come to Emeka's rescue if need be. So, please, do not hesitate to come to us at any time for any assistance you may require should this be necessary," Maduka firmly told the SureGas representative on the line with him.

"Thank you, sir, you will be hearing from us once we are able to secure Emeka's release," SureGas assertively replied.

Ugwuoma had heard his brother's reply and was satisfied with its firmness and singular family oneness.

"Thank you, Nna'm, we shall fight together and we shall win," Ugwuoma said to conclude the conversation.

Maduka made a note of the phone number SureGas used to call them and had this checked out by some Akadike children in cyber security and they assured him it was a genuine number. All they could do now was wait, ready to act if it was clear SureGas was biding their time. However, no action was necessary: Thirteen days after Emeka was kidnapped together with Bjorn, the same SureGas representative called to say they had safely secured the release of Emeka; that he would be on a flight to Norway, to their specialist hospital in Oslo for a thorough medical checkup to make certain he was in the best condition of health before his return to Nigeria. They apologized they had not brought Emeka straight to his family but had decided Emeka must be medically certified as of good health in mind and body. They assured Maduka this was purely routine and there was no reason whatsoever for concern.

Emeka would return to the warmth of his Akadike family after a week in Oslo and almost three weeks after his abduction. On a hot, sweaty Tuesday afternoon, July 30, by two o'clock or so, a Toyota SUV with opaque windows drove into the Akadike estate with an esteemed cargo, the body and soul in living harmony of Mr. Chukwuemeka Ndubisi Akadike, B.A. (Mechanical Engineering) (Manchester); M.Sc. (Hydraulics Engineering)(Birmingham). But he would gladly trade all his degrees and expertise for a day of sunshine and romance with his dear grandmother, Ma Nneoma, and a little of good, old palm wine, set on a table of pounded yam and beefy egusi soup well garnished with dry fish and stock fish. And that was exactly what Ma Nneoma had herself prepared waiting for her bosom grandson. She had been told Emeka would be coming home again after a brief holiday in Norway with his dear friend Bjorn.

Maduka and Ugwuoma kept their emotions in check so Ma would not suspect that anything sinister had happened in the family and left Emeka to his grandma, in the usual demeanour he would exhibit on any of his visits to Okeosisi.

"My son, are you ok?"

"Yes, Ma, I'm fine. Any problems?"

"My dear son, in my old age I am beginning to see things and hear all sorts of stories."

"Ma, what kind of stories are you hearing, and who is telling you these stories?"

"My son, I cannot tell you who they are, I am not sure. I think they are spirits, yes, they are spirits."

"Spirits, Ma, did you say that spirits are now telling you stories and that you hear them quite well? Ma, did all this happen in your dream or did the spirits come to you in broad daylight?"

"Yes my son, they spoke to me in a dream. One of them said he was here to help me, another said I will fight many wars, one war after another, no end to trouble."

"Well, Ma, there's nothing to worry about since it is all a dream."

"But, son, the dreams of an old woman are not the same as the dreams of a young woman or a young man like you. You know an old woman sees the smoke before there is fire. The old are nearer the spirits, you know, and so our people show great respect for old men. So, the dreams of old people may say something about tomorrow, whether good or bad. For me, the dream is good and also bad."

"Well, Ma, let the spirits do what they like, we are all here and we are all well."

"My son, have you been well all this time? Did anything bad happen to you? Did you not go to a strange place, a place you do not want to go? Please tell me the truth, did you go to some place where you are a stranger, with no brother or sister; where nobody would give you water to drink or food to eat? I know anywhere you work, you do your work well, and the people like you. There is never any shame. So you can go back to the people you were working for and they will still love you. Your grandfather himself taught you this when you were in primary school, here in Okeosisi."

Emeka did not know what to do now or how to proceed without lying to Ma, his one and only Ma, who always held him close to her breast and made sure he lacked nothing as a child. They were now inseparable and whenever he came to Okeosisi, Ma's would be his first stop. He saw her first before going anywhere else and he had grown exceedingly fond of her; they would share jokes and she fed him well on his favourite egusi soup cooked in her delectable style. How could he then tell her an untruth: Perhaps he could tell her the truth but not the whole truth. Yes, he would answer Ma's question one after another as truly as he could.

"Yes, Ma, something bad happened to me quite alright, but it was not worse than what happened to me before. You know I have suffered some troubles in my life, and this time it was not too bad. Yes, it all happened where I would not like to return, but that was not because of what I did but because the people I worked with were bad people. I could not trust them to do anything good. This happens in life from time to time, Mama, in the oil-gas industry where I work."

"I have done it!" Emeka felt. He did not tell his Ma an untruth, and she was quite satisfied with his reply.

"Yes, my son, you are right. I believe the devil himself cannot win a war against you, son. Perhaps, this is why one spirit said he will help me and the other one said I will fight and fight. So, you have fought in the war of the devil and we have won. We won, we won, did we not win? Tell me my son, did we not win?"

"Yes, Ma, we won. And the good will always win."

Satisfied that his dear grandma would now have a quiet undisturbed rest, Emeka ran to the waiting heart of his father, bursting with effervescent joy.

"Marvellous!. Fantastic! Stupendous! Absolutely magnificent! It is time for a wild celebration of a type the Akadikes have not seen, ever. We shall celebrate with a Mass of thanksgiving to God tomorrow morning without any delay. But today, we have called our friends and relatives to join us in a sumptuous party here by the swimming pool, in the garden. Yes, we shall sing, we shall dance, we shall laugh, we shall drum our joy to the hearing of the mountains. Yes, we shall rejoice," Maduka proudly announced. Ugwuoma had run out to meet his son as he was ascending the steps to his brother Maduka's house where he had lived since the kidnapping terror.

There was a party for about a hundred people starting around six in the evening till it was past ten o'clock at night. Emeka was there to receive the toasts of the party and then was excused to go home and take a rest. His uncle, Maduka, joined him. And they went on talking and talking till it was cockcrow by five in the morning! Ma Nneoma had gone to sleep, a deep sleep of relief, once she was satisfied her grandson, Emeka, was safely home. No one really worried how she would take all the noise going on. In any case, the Akadike family was known for its fabulous parties for the community, and people would not be surprised at the party going on in full crescendo on this wonderful day.

CHAPTER THIRTEEN

August 1, 2013

Okeosisi

"Uncle, have you ever heard of this before, that terrorists were now the ones to save our education now wallowing in the depths of organized ignorance? How can this be? SureGas has come in to provide equipment and consumables for the Faculty of Engineering at UniKoko; is this the way university education would travel to obtain funds? The government has accused Union of Academic Staff of Universities - UASU - of having a hand in what they described as 'orchestrated maligning kidnapping'–Uncle what do you say?"

"My son, you are a living witness of this nightmare and have suffered indescribable agony during your kidnapping," Maduka replied to Emeka. Exasperated, he continued: "UASU has stoutly denied any complicity whatsoever on its part in the kidnapping saga. Of course, they would never condone any insurgency by whatever name, or kidnapping, or terrorism. In fact, they have condemned all such horrendous acts in the recent past and are ever in support of any government effort to bring the miscreants to book. Just forget that part and let us look at what is happening to us now as opposed to what your father and I were used to in our days at the university."

Maduka then went on to talk about the standards of education in his time at University College, Ibadan, when a degree from that institution was the equal of that from any of the finest universities in the world. After all, they were taught by some of the best from the very same universities, notably Universities of London, Oxford, and Cambridge. But all that had changed from the late sixties onward.

"Uncle, do we now support terrorism and insurgency that education may prosper, that social amenities may grow and flourish?"

"No, my son, we will not support evil that good may arise. Never! I would say knowledge has been kidnapped by our leaders. We are all held hostage and are being fed children's milk when we need solid foods for adult appetites that hunger for knowledge. What we need most has been taken from us. You know, it's like you're eating your good pounded yam and egusi soup; you roll a ball of yam and flood it well with egusi and dry fish and, as you get ready to load the whole works into your gaping mouth, the ball falls off your hand and you find yourself shutting your disappointed mouth."

Emeka saw the whole scenario as preposterous, totally beyond reason. He returned to his room, laid on his bed and let his thoughts roam where they may. He heard his late grandfather, Akadike, telling him:

"Please keep cool, we must keep praying for conversion. Needlessly, blood has been flowing everywhere. BOND is killing people in the North. In the South, in the Delta, it is BRAND. These insurgents want to undo the deeds of the oil companies or else blood will flow. Whichever way you go, it is a way down a river of blood. And don't forget, we fought in Biafra! Be watchful and pray all the time."

Emeka wondered: "What sort of boats do we need to ply

this new sea of blood that surrounds us, in our bedrooms, living rooms, kitchens, even toilets, mixing with the water in our reservoirs. We cannot be free of this deadly blood. Will the gods come out with golden oars and row this boat for us? Why do we kill, and kill, and kill innocent people who have done us no wrong, people just going about their daily business? Have the gods not given us blood that we may all breathe and live?"

"Yes blood will flow. We know a lot about fluid systems and water bodies. The body is the best example of this. From the time of birth until death, one fluid system is at work. The heart and its arteries and its veins pumping blood, receiving blood. And blood is being continually made. I want to study the peculiar engineering of the fluid dynamics of the blood system in the human body." But he quickly remembered that blood flow in the human body has been well studied over the years and there was little any new work would tell us.

Emeka continued: "Well, I am not sure that the system has been studied by engineers. Here we are at SureGas, we go deep down to over five miles beneath the earth's crust to bring up to the surface some fluids buried down there. And we must do this under enormous pressure to bring it from down under to the surface. The heart does not have this type of problem. I wonder, would the heart ever demand money to pump blood through our body? Or, what sort of money do humans spend to keep their hearts working? Would they call this blood money?" Emeka could not make sense of the horror that had befallen his beloved country, Nigeria.

July 13, 2013

University of Kokoma

Right from BRAND's kidnap of Bjorn, staff of the University of Kokoma, and their announcement that the ransom money would be used to purchase equipment for the Faculty of Engineering, the entire university campus was in a feverish mood: everyone on campus was agitated and sought avenues for some mental relief and escape from what they saw as a gathering storm. The Staff Club of Kokoma University was a restful home of quiet and elegant interaction of conversations flowing from fervid minds on various subjects that engage human attention. Here, the human person grows in imagination and creativity on fertile soils of truth and discourse. All who come there breathe the air of companionship and friendship.

"Please a Star," Dr. Dominic Lolomari requested from the steward. "Hey, Charles, how are you? I hear you've not been sleeping well."

"Come on, Dom, who's been spreading this rumour that I have not been sleeping well?"

Dom and Charles, President of UASU, Union of Academic Staff of Universities, University of Kokoma branch, met at the university staff club after the kidnappers had issued their demands commanding SureGas to direct the ransom money to the Faculty of Engineering, University of Kokoma.

Dr.Charles Finima, was greatly troubled once he learnt of the abduction and even more so when the terms for the release of the victims were announced. This was utterly unimaginable and fearing for his own life, he quickly left his residence on campus, not far from Bjorn's, and spent nights with friends in other homes outside the campus. But he made sure he was in his office during working hours even though the university was on long vacation and most students, apart form postgraduate students had left for their homes. Many lecturers had also left for travel overseas for conferences and meetings. Only a few were still on campus.

"Dom, yes, I have not been sleeping well. Have you? Has anyone? Can any of us sleep, let alone sleep well? The university is now going to be dragged into the present blowing insurrection."

"How are we a part of something entirely strange to us, which we did not arrange, and more poignantly, which we have resolutely and absolutely condemned in the strongest terms", Charles quipped.

Charlie's Star arrived and he asked his friends what they would like.

"You know me, it's a malt for me." answered Dom.

"I'll join you in a Star, Charlie, don't mind this our botany professor who runs away from beer with the speed of Usain Bolt." was Tam's response. Three others on the table with them ordered Gulder, Heineken and a malt drink.

"The police have been coming to see me every day since the kidnap. They come with their ridiculous questions varying from my relation with Bjorn to student cultism. The list is long; they even referred to my paper on the military coups and terrorism which I presented two years ago at the Prague Conference on International Terrorism. They believe BRAND used the points I raised in that paper to foment their terrible acts." Charlie painfully told his friends.

The security agents had been to Dr. Charles Finima's office searching through all his books and papers for any evidence that may help them link him to BRAND. First, they changed the lock to his office to a double lock that would require two separate keys, one with the security personnel and one with him to open the office. This way, they were sure he could not get into his office alone to remove any material and he would be secure in the knowledge that they themselves had not introduced anything foreign and untoward into his office.

Every day, they would search through a new area until they had searched the entire office within five days. They did not want to take away his books and papers again for a similar reason. They found a number of papers he had written on insurgency and questioned him extensively on their contents. In the end, they were satisfied the papers were purely for academic discourse, had no ulterior motives and simply examined insurgency for its academic interest. Besides, they had been published in reputable international journals and were well critiqued in a number of national dailies.

Dr. Finima was relieved nothing came of their investigations. He wondered: 'suppose BRAND had asked that the ransom money be used in his faculty, the faculty of the social sciences, where would he be, how would he extricate himself from being a suspect in the planning, if not in the kidnapping itself'

"You can't be serious, Charles, your paper was academic

and explored the problems as best as you could from the Magna Carta to the French Revolution to slavery to liberalism. All was academic." Tam was extremely upset and gave vent to his feelings. He continued: "This university is living through terrible times. Whichever way you looked at the equation of social order and peace, you find we are on the losing minus side. We are close to the oil companies and their gas flares disturb our daily peace. Many of the acts of insurgency take place in this state, and even our students have sometimes been suspected of being participants therein. Whenever the oil workers are taken hostage, the security agencies linger around our campus and monitor the visitors. Kokoma, once a garden city has transmogrified into a colossal empire of intrigue, rabid capitalism and violence."

The drinks arrived and the conversation became more relaxed, and many members just talked away.

"Well, folks, let's not make this whole thing overbearing. As academics, we will always be fodder for insidious political wolves."

"Yes indeed, but we are more than equal to the task. You know, the beer tastes better when we talk about the buffoonery of our gross security system."

"Buffoons indeed, they try to find invidious reasons to earn their salaries."

"How will this whole thing work out? With the success - if you can call it success - of the present kidnap scenario, are we now in an era of kidnapping for knowledge?"

"Well what's so wrong with that? Why can't these neo-imperialist oil companies fund education, clean up the environment they mess up and bring succour to the millions in the delta suffering a despoiled life?"

"You're not serious; will the oil companies now be the new government of Nigeria? Will they pay twice for oil exploration, one to NNPC, that is to the government, and then to the ordinary people of the delta? This is the fault of our government who don't care a hoot about the people. Blame it all on the government."

The conversation went this way and that with everyone in the club giving their views as they saw fit.

Then Charlie threw in a bombshell:"Let us face the facts: We do not have a government in Nigeria. The oil companies will be our saviour. Whether or not we like it, let us cultivate friendship with them. We do not have a choice."

"Are you then saying you support the kidnapping?" questioned a member of the club who had been silent all the while. "You don't seem to know what you are saying: suppose this same futile government closed down our university indefinitely for suspected acts of sabotage, what will we do?" he continued.

"You must be the only person in this country who cannot read the signs of the times we live in. Let them try closing down the university; let them try it to their utter shame. We still have the law courts, and we still have other sympathetic federal universities in this country. So, let them go ahead and they will be sorry they ever ventured into such horrid troubled waters." Charlie replied.

"Come on, before this gets out of hand, and we find ourselves screaming our heads off, let us get something to eat to quiet our rumbling stomachs and then we can continue after a hearty meal. Abdul, come and take our orders."

That was the president of the club trying to keep the conversations from degenerating into mere diatribe. The orders varied from *eba* or *iyan* and *egusi* soup, *amala* and *ewedu* or *okro* soup, to jollof rice and stew or fish and potato chips. There was a choice of beef, fresh fish, dry fish, chicken or stockfish to go with the meal. It was now evening and *suya*, goat meat, *shaki*, kidney and liver were being roasted on skewers out in the garden.

Charlie had not placed any order and Dom teased him, "Good old Charlie, you have not asked for anything. Your mother being Igbo, didn't she serve you goat-meat pepper soup? Didn't you have a goat sacrificed every now and then to entertain your father's multitudinous guests?"

"No, Dom, thanks. It will not be any pepper soup today. The frequent interrogations and visits by the security details have left my stomach ill-equipped for that highly irritable stuff. No. I'm not ready for any more pepper. But since you asked, I think I'll just have fish and chips. That, my sensitive intestines can handle." Charlie replied.

"Thank God our parents sent us to good schools." Dom steered the conversation in a different direction. "We are not part of this rot we see today."

"No kidding, did you say your parents sent you to a good school, Dom? Do you now regard Ologbolo Grammar School, out in the mangrove swamps of nowhere, as a good school?"

"You are right, Toria, Ologbolo is in the swamps, but you know only too well it has produced many good people for this Rivers State—professors, medical doctors, teachers, lawyers and artisans of various types, from tailors to masons to construction workers to carpenters. In fact, the contractor building your house now is from my school. We were classmates. And we do not go to London or Paris for our clothes, we buy them here in Kokoma. The last dress you got for your dear wife, was it not from Bibi's Boutique here on Grand Street? Yes, we may be in the swamps but we have a fine school in Ologbolo and I am proud to say I am their alumnus."

"Yes, you have all these people you mentioned. But I can count them off my fingers. Good schools like mine, Government College, Ikot Ekpene, founded in 1925, beats yours hands down, built just after independence in 1962. Where you may have one doctor, we have fifty or more, lawyers the same. Name any field, we are tops."

"Get serious, Toria, you know only too well that time is not the primary determinant of standards. After all, with all the equipment that has come into our faculty of engineering now, for example, we are well on our way to achieving excellence in engineering. And you know too there are some private universities now that would beat the older more established ones."

"Give us some examples; give us their names", Toria queried.

Dom parried the question: "Come on, Toria, it would be invidious of me to start naming names. I'm sure you know the examples I have in mind. But you might be right. Forgive me, let me not go on this way. All I want to say is that we shall never again see the good days of high educational standards in Nigeria, from the primary to the tertiary."

Charlie had been quiet all along; but now the conversation raised his anger and he roared: "Dom, you're all witnesses of what we are trying to do in UASU. It's not that we'll ever get back to the good old days of the fifties and sixties. No. All we are trying to do is to keep the slope of our sliding mediocrity from dropping too steeply into oblivion. You might remember the valedictory lecture given by one of our first professors of mathematics at the University of Ibadan where he told us that the good days of that university were during the years 1953 to about 1961, or, if stretched to 1963. It was carried by a good number of our dailies. More painfully, he hoped that there was no one in the audience that day who would look back on his departing days with the same sense of nostalgia with which he looked on those glorious years of the fifties into the sixties. And his lecture was given in 1985! Please tell me, would you not say that 1985 was a heaven compared to the hell of today, 2013? And if we go on at the present rate, this hell would look like heaven in the foreseeable future."

All was quiet. The food had arrived, with drinks all round, but no one was eating, no one was drinking either. As dry as their throats were from this wrenching talk, they were too sad to move their hands, or mouths.

* * *

Two men had come into the club premises and had taken

their seats outside the main hall of the club and sat in a corridor nearby. From there they could overhear all the goings-on but did not take part on the conversations.

A steward walked up to them. "Good afternoon, gentlemen, please are you members of the club. We do not think we've ever seen either of you here."

"No, you are right; this is our first time in these premises. We've come to see Dr. Charles Finima; we understand we can find him here, so we came to see him."

"Do you know him? Have you an appointment with him?"

"No, we don't know him and we don't have an appointment with him."

"Let me tell him he has visitors. Please hold on."

"Thank you", one of them replied.

The steward walked over to the doctor and told him two men wanted to see him and that they were sitting in the corridor outside.

"Good evening, gentlemen, I understand you want to see me. What can I do for you?"

"Sorry, we are disturbing your peace, Dr. Finima."

"No problem at all, just tell me who you are and what good fortune has brought you here."

"I am Fern and my friend with me is Mahogany. Well, I am not sure you would say our visit is one of good fortune. We've come to warn you that education will die a sudden death in the next few years. What you're seeing now is mere child's play. With BOND, we shall soon unleash a deadly war on all your schools and put all your girls in quiet seclusion away from any schools and parents and churches. Good bye, Dr. Finima."

Dr. Finima had wanted to have the visitors arrested by the Club security staff and handed over to the campus police but, with the recent happenings in Kokoma, and not wanting to exacerbate the fears of many people on the university campus, he thought the better of it and did not pursue that line of action. Instead, he simply replied: "Well, all I can say is that we'll wait and see how you will be able to succeed. Till then, good evening, gentlemen." Both Fern and Mahogany left in clear view of all who had been watching them.

* * *

Professor Williams Briggs, called Billy to his motley of friends who like him, had come to UniKoko right from the ground-breaking ceremony in the seventies, and came to the staff club from time to time after his retirement to, as he put it, meet his former students now professors, and live out the nostalgia of his earlier years. He had heard all the goings-on on this eventful day and sought a corner where he could be alone. He asked for beans and stew with dodo and a glass of wine. He sank into his book and sought for a just world in its comforting lines.

Try as hard as he could to concentrate on his reading, however, his mind kept returning to the albatross of blood that now runs a ring around the neck of education. He thought of his secondary school days in Christ's School, Bama, where it was the rule that any two students who were caught fighting would be rusticated. Under no condition was violence by whatever name tolerated. Mere use of swear words or abusive language attracted a penalty varying from cutting half a whole soccer field to running round the field ten times.

It was drummed into their heads that needless arguments should be avoided and only matters related to learning and morals were worthy of discussion. Everyone was trained to be tolerant and understanding while, at the same time, defending what was right. Bill had his secondary school education in the fifties, under the colonial government when Nigeria had a standard of education as good as in the colonial master's own country. He asked himself: "We are now in 2013, and nothing sordid, however awful, would raise eyebrows: all is accepted. But how would universities now be funded by ransom monies painted red in blood?"

Billy broke out in a sweat. His order arrived along with a friend before whom he could weep his heart out. After exchanging their usual greetings Bobo—nickname for Christopher Bongo from his childhood days to those who knew him then—joined Billy in a meal of rice with egg-stew and a drink of Guinness.

"Why are you sitting alone, Billy, when the club is full and lively?"

"It just so happens I do not want to be part of the gang. They talk deeply and fervently about the new social order in the country with pervasive bloodshed everywhere."

What bothered Billy most was that education was being

dragged along a muddy slope into the gutters aided by open-faced terrorism that wanted to return the country to illiteracy, without books. This took them immediately to BOND now they had overrun large swathes of northern Nigeria and, in the process, boldly and fiercely dictated a whole social shift from all that was humane and reasonable. Nigeria was being rowed on a sea of blood from their beleaguered bodies. Most painfully, the government was effete and powerless apparently without suitable weapons for the fight.

Billy and Bobo agreed: they would build an underground resistance. They needed a leader and would seek out their old friend, Prof. Maduka Akadike. To save Nigeria, old, adroit hands must develop forces with the young who will be at the forefront of this fight. Without coming to a definite conclusion, something told them they would need a woman as their leader: they were best in crushing brutal, excessive power with romantic designs.

CHAPTER FOURTEEN

Aprli 17, 2012

Bethesda, Maryland

After their momentous meeting in Hamilton, Canada, Baraah, Cheryl and Funeka sought out other women at Cambridge who might share their views on knowledge and the woman as members of GAP, Girls Are Precious. To their joyful surprise, a majority of those they spoke with gladly welcomed their initiative as though that was just what they had been waiting for all their life. They were, indeed, surprised for it seemed they had hit on a theme with a peculiar appeal to women.

"Baraah, how did you come up with this idea that humans were nothing if they were not knowledge; that knowledge and the person were interchangeable, and that girls were the supreme banks of this knowledge?" Sarah Simpson was all ears awaiting an answer.

"Sarah, what can I tell you? Let me first say we are overjoyed you found our motto helpful. I say "helpful" because you're already one of us, so you must have been thinking what we too were thinking. I think, though, "interchangeable" may not be the right word; it is not the right way of putting it, for it really does not convey the meaning of what a human being is. Perhaps, we could say knowledge best expresses what a person is. And this knowledge is not about books and what is learned from the printed word. No, it is more about morals, knowledge in all that is good; gained in life itself, through everyday living, in all the different circumstances of life; and women are the banks of this wealth, which they transfer to their children."

"You've got me here, Baraah, for I always tell anyone who has time to listen that women embody all that the human person represents: only a woman can give birth to a child. When I think of it—although I must say I don't fancy myself being married and having a child—that two persons, mother and child, can both live intimately together and yet separately, there is no knowledge greater than this apparently simple, yet exceedingly complex, act of nature. Nature does the whole thing and it looks simple to the eye: therein lies its mystery and supremacy. The rest of what we do is to follow nature and know her ways, and none of her ways comes close to conception and child birth that she has given us; none." Sarah spoke with excitement and conviction and asked Baraah what next GAP planned to do.

Baraah was enthused: "I agree with you entirely, Sarah. This natural process of birth, of bringing forth a child into the world, encompasses all that is good for the child to develop into a worthy person. It is the mother who introduces the child into the world, and thus gives humanity the fruits of creation. As for what we'll do next, I suggest we have a meeting and agree to champion the cause of the girl-child who suffers anywhere in the world. We have already raised a sizable fund for this purpose. In fact, our amazement is that many of our donors found our ideas and ideals readily acceptable, I would even say, formidable. When we meet, we shall decide how best to proceed."

"And when will this be?" Sarah wanted to know.

"I don't know exactly when," Baraah replied. "You might find this funny but we don't yet have a leader, or a chairperson. We are making overtures to Dr. Chioma Ijeoma, at University of Maryland at College Park in the United States. I understand she finds our ideas fascinating, worthy of pursuit, but she has not yet agreed to be our leader."

"Why don't we invite her to Cambridge to meet us?"

"You might be right, Sarah, but we don't want to give her a chance to say no. From all our efforts so far, the best we have in hand is that she is one of us, making us seventeen in number. In fact, she says our membership is sixteen and possibly one more; that she should not be counted as a regular member yet. She will, however, assist us in whatever we set out to do."

"If things are this way, why don't we all go over to the States and surprise her? Certainly, seeing our faith in her so strongly expressed, she will not turn down our invitation."

Sarah seemed to have brought up a subject that would help resolve the impasse and both she and Baraah approached the other fourteen GAP architects and in a week they were off to the States landing in Washington D.C. on early Tuesday morning, April 17, 2012, on a direct flight from London, having informed Chioma of their coming. She was at the Dulles International Airport to meet them, and got them into airport shuttle taxis to the Wellington Hotel in Bethesda. Thoroughly jet-lagged, they checked into their rooms, all on the same corridor, on the fourth floor, the rooms facing each other. They agreed they would get some sleep, or rest, shower, get into fresh clothing and be down for lunch at 2 p.m. Chioma also took a room at Wellington, which she would use during the day, that she may be close to her friends and give them all of her company for the next two days they would spend with her.

Chioma was amazed that sixteen women of cheerful merit and outstanding commitment, were out to give selflessly of themselves directly and unimpeded to others, especially the girl-child. She recalled that it was in 2009 when three of them got together and established the roots of the organisation and since then, GAP has undertaken huge tasks in Iran, Pakistan and the Philippines. They have built schools for girls in these countries and provided their teachers.

The case of their spectacular intervention in Pakistan in March, 2012 was exceedingly poignant. A group of Pakistani Taliban fighters rampaged a girl s' school, in Peshawar and killed over twenty-three students. Only a handful survived: one of them, Buthainah Jamal, barely fifteen years old, was shot in the head. She was immediately rushed to the hospital but as the facilities there were grossly inadequate for the delicate attention Buthainah needed, arrangements were quickly made and she was flown to England, to Manchester, for the necessary surgeries. The great women of GAP contributed two hundred thousand pounds sterling to cover the hospital charges with an undertaking that they would be responsible for any shortfall should the initial amount prove insufficient.

Within hours of Buthainah's arrival in Manchester, Sarah, Cheryl and Constance were by her bedside, and throughout her first week in the hospital, GAP kept a twenty four hour vigil, in eight hour rotations, to be by her side continuously and provide whatever assistance she needed, as she had no one in Manchester to give her the full warmth of love and care. At any given time, two of the women would keep watch over Buthainah. They were on the press, on TV, on social media to express their unflinching support for the girl-child's full and comprehensive education. In the case of Peshawar Girls Academy, they would help to rebuild the school to its original natural aesthetic architecture.

Buthainah, who was near death on arrival, made a miraculous recovery. After a three-month period of recuperation, she was able to continue her school work in Manchester with GAP's assistance. Two other students were flown to Manchester at GAP's behest but they died a few days after their surgery. A number of other students who did not suffer severe injuries were successfully treated locally in Peshawar.

The life of Buthainah gave GAP enormous fillip to step out and loudly proclaim unqualified support for the girl child. She had four sisters and three brothers and she was the third child in the family and the eldest daughter. The family was extremely poor, lived in a cramped two bedroom house and ate a meal of mainly rice, milk, cheese and some fruit. Buthainah had only one set of school uniform; she would wash it out when she came home from school every day, dry it in the open air and iron it in the morning with an iron heated over a charcoal flame. Usually her dress would be sufficiently dry in the morning for ironing; but if not, she would press it with the hot iron until the wetness evaporated in water vapour. Her father, Sarangei, believed that his children should have an equal educational advantage as any other child in the district and so sent all five children of school age to school, not minding that, ordinarily, girls were not sent to school where the family was poor and could ill afford the fees for a female child.

In spite of the poverty she lived in, Buthainah radiated charm, peace and joy. Ever tidy, ever studious, ever attentive, she topped her class in most subjects particularly in mathematics. One day, Buthainah came back from school to meet the pots empty and her mother not at home. She searched the house everywhere but did not find any food to cook. Would she walk across to their relatives next door and ask for some rice? This did not seem a good idea for never had she seen her mother go anywhere to obtain a food item on loan. They were poor, yes, but proudly so, and Buthainah finally sat down for a while to sort out her thoughts. She then took a cup, and went to get a drink of water. And there was no water in the reservoir. Her younger brothers and sisters were unexpectedly not at home either. Something must be awfully wrong, she concluded. And something indeed was awfully wrong: her dear mother had been rushed to the hospital, to the emergency ward, with a ruptured uterus. She was saved but poor Buthainah was now the mother of the family.

She searched through her mother's bags for money and finally found under the bed five hundred rupees folded in a letter placed in a pair of sandals. She rushed off to buy some rice, milk, and cheese, fetched water from their neighbourhood stream, Bastara, and set to work on the meal for the evening. Her father stayed with his dear wife in the hospital and spent the night with her. Buthainah fed her brothers and sisters, who had returned from the hospital, and had no time to wash her uniform. In fact, she did not think of this at all. In the morning, much to her distress, her uniform had been sullied by all the running around of the previous day. Most uncharacteristically, and gutted with trepidation, she searched through her mother's clothes and found the appropriate white shalwar and blue kameez with a matching white hijab that would pass for her usual uniform. It was in these her mother's clothes that she was shot and seriously wounded on that fateful murderous day.

The inimitable GAP members trickled in for lunch as they had agreed until Funeka sauntered in at thirty minutes past two o'clock, still in her travel clothes.

"Funeka, didn't your luggage arrive at the airport? I thought we all collected our bags", Julia curiously asked, seeing Funeka looking a little worse for the flight.

"I'm sorry, Julia, yes I collected my luggage at the airport quite alright but I don't have the energy to rustle through my suitcase and find suitable clothes to wear. Please don't mind me."

"You know Chioma might think less highly of us if we did not present ourselves in good light", Angela chided.

Chioma laughed effusively saying, "Hey, since when is sartorial elegance a barometer for courage and discipline? I thought we were on to great things and not merely worldly trivialities."

"Did I hear you say, "we", Chioma, that is, that you are one of us, one with us", Cathy wanted to know.

Chioma laughed some more, settling more comfortably in her chair.

"Yes I said "we", alright for indeed we are on to great things. As to my role in these "great things", we still have over a day to look closely at ourselves and see who is best for what. For, indeed, the tasks are enormous."

Not knowing what exactly this feisty group of women had in mind, but guessing they had descended on her to champion the cause and successfully lead them to more daring escapades, she said little else. But she was their host and she was playing this part graciously, she thought. She even wondered: 'suppose they want to see how well I handle any issues that may come up on their visit, and how well I take care of them before they inflict on me the awesome pain of their leader, I must be at my Akadike best and bring my rich Okeosisi, nay African, ancestry to bear on all I do. This must be good occasion for me to speak about African mysteries and spirits. But not yet; everyone feels sleepy'.

The group had been standing in the lobby chatting away. They now walked about two blocks to Gordon's restaurant. A waiter met them at the door and took them to their seats. Chioma had reserved seating space for seventeen people, nine on one side, and eight on the other, facing one another. It was hilarious how they were switching places like little girls, wanting to sit next to Chioma who sat last. One got the feeling that laughter was on the menu as the first course. The waiter greeted everyone, passed round the menu, and then took his leave.

More laughter: though they could easily make out the American-styled dishes, they each preferred that Chioma should guide them through the menu. Baraah was vegetarian so her choice was different and Chioma placed her order first. Lo, the rest wanted whatever it was Baraah was getting. Chioma saw this as mere banter, waited a while and full of smiles said: "I'm sorry this restaurant carries just enough vegetarian dishes to serve a few plates. They would not have enough to go round. I know that eight of you really love sea food, another six, steak rare, and only one liked her steak medium rare.."

"Yea, that would be me," Funeka delightfully said.

"Funeka, are you no more a veggie, since when is steak medium rare your delight?"

"Since I came here to be beside you and follow you wherever you go. Anyway, I do eat meat from time to time and today is one of those times."

"Baraah I know is vegetarian," Chioma concluded.

"And what about you, what would we say was your specialty?"

"Oh, I like them all, sea food, roasts, steaks, even veggies if I am stretched," Chioma replied.

"Well, for today, what would you have, since you already know what we are all having?" Andah asked.

"Andah, I know you love your steak rare, I'll have mine rare too, just like you," Chioma answered.

Everyone placed her order and it came time to choose the wine to go with the meals and they all shouted "Cheryl"; they wanted Cheryl to make the choices being a wine aficionado.

A lonely voice from Baraah protested, "Just because I am a Muslim and a veggie you think me a wine hater. Shall we talk about wines?"

"Hey, Baraah, you can talk about wines all you like but I lived with vines, I grew up with vines from my childhood till I came to Cambridge. I breathe their air, smell as they do, curl like them and bear fruits as they do", Funeka quipped.

"Bear fruits, did you say, Funeka, are you heavy with

child, fruit of the vines?" Baraah questioned innocently.

"Are we not all pregnant, pregnant with knowledge, which must express who we are? Is that not what we are? Surely, that's what we are doing." Funeka took the conversation to a different level and Cheryl had peace to order some Chardonnays and California Cabernet. Everyone waited for Chioma's toast and the eating commenced.

"What are we doing tonight? Chioma, what do you suggest? Sorry, I forget myself; of course, we are in your hands," Joanne answered her own question.

Then seemingly out of nowhere, two gentlemen approached their table. "Did I hear someone mention *Chioma*? We are here to see Dr. Chioma Ijeoma. We asked after her at the hotel and we were told she had gone out to dinner. We just took a chance and came here because it's just the type of restaurant that would be much to Chioma's liking. Thank God we are lucky to find her here with her many friends."

Chioma had been expecting such a confrontation with Fern ever since he had vowed she would be martyred. She showed no surprise whatsoever and maintained solemn calm. "Mr. Fern, thank you very much. I remember correctly that when we last met, you tried to frighten me with warnings that my life was in great danger; that knowledge would bleed. My sisters of GAP know of you and we shall take every necessary step to make absolutely certain that your plans will not succeed. We are indeed able to deal decisively with your group. In the meantime I take it that you have seen me and you've heard me. I shall further add that, if you changed your mind and decided to come to our side, we would be only too happy to receive you in our midst. But know that you will not be able to deceive us, for we can always tell what you really are."

"But you do not know what I have in mind. It may be totally unrelated to my threats and warnings. And I do not intend to participate in any of your activities."

"You have the poison of a viper on your lips but we have the right vaccine for your venom. So go ahead, do your worst: we offer nothing but excellence for the girl-child."

Chioma firmly stood her ground. She was nonplussed and said nothing more. The fiery ladies of GAP elegantly stood up, each joyously clasping her neighbour with all her strength in an outpouring of victory over evil. They had all heard Fern and Chioma quite clearly and wondered just what the conversation meant with Chioma relating some past events they knew nothing about.

"Chioma, who was that man? Why did you respond to him menacingly? And why did you say we, the GAP girls, know of him?" Waithira asked.

"I'm sorry, Thira, that was Palm Frond Fern, or Fern for short. He came once to harass me and warned me from his spirit world that he would destroy me for my stand on the girl-child. Don't worry about him, for he really cannot do much harm. I see his outbursts as mere threats."

"Well, we are all here and it's a good thing we heard him. If he is after you, he is after us too, and, as you said, he can do us no harm." Thira concluded.

"Let's all go to the concert recital tonight at College

Park; our department of antiquities is offering us a rendition of Rachmaninov's piano concertos, and some of his idyllic romantic sonatas. The bus ride will be right from our hotel straight to the university and we get down outside the concert hall. I know you all love Rachmaninov. So it would be a delightful evening. The concert starts at 8 p.m. and ends at 10.15 p.m. It's only 4 p.m. now so we should have lots of time to freshen up or even catch a nap before we leave at 7.15 p.m."

Chioma was testing out her followership, as it were, and they cheered merrily, "Great!"

"That was breathtaking, the performance by the pianist Bara Brostin. He held me spellbound with his mastery of time and space, waiting, then running at top speed, in full control of the world before him. He made me feel the whole world lived in the piano and his deft fingers simply followed the flow of the tide, the warm rays of the rising sun peering through forests, yes, forests, thick and blind, awakening to the thrills of a life of joy." Julia could not hold back her vast appreciation for Brostin's virtuoso performance and let her sisters know same. She continued: "Can we turn GAP into this flow of unlimited love for the other; can we make of ourselves the salt of knowledge that all may savour us and be fed with love?"

No one could add to this effusive expression; the general feeling being one of silence and sombre reflection. It was clear that these wonderful ladies had been transported into that world they all longed for, and worked for, where the person was truly knowledge and poured out knowledge in love and selfless service. They chatted for a while longer in the lobby and went to bed by mid-night.

The charming sisters of GAP had only one day left and would be departing Maryland on Thursday, April 19, in the afternoon. Chioma just did not know what to suggest they do. After breakfast, Waithira, like the Kenyan she was, asked Chioma if she had ever seen the Rift Valley on one of her many travels to which she replied she had not. "Well, I'll take you there any time you are free, and it's on me."

"Many thanks, "Thira, yes you will have me with you on many, many travels, some in the air, and some in the mind. Any which way, I am with you, and that's what counts."

"Did you say, 'in the mind'?" Baraah had asked. "That's the most important arena for get-togethers. And GAP in fighting for the girl-child primarily fights for her mind. What of the Himalayas of my country. Chioma; you said that Thira would have you on many travels in the air. Note, there was no mention of land. If, therefore, you take to the air, you would be keeping company with the Himalayas, and not walk through valleys. So why don't I show you the Himalayas, including the highest of it all, Everest. There, you would be on top of the highest land formation on earth. So, Thira, I think Chioma would first fly in the air there to breathe the air of knowledge. You know, knowledge does not walk in valleys but flies to the highest peaks of creation. First the Himalayas, then the Rift Valley, from the heights to the depths, not the other way round."

Constance Faber would not be left out: "Chioma, I don't have anything to show you, I'm sorry. Australia, my country, is not as scenic as Kenya or Pakistan. But we have the desert, and we could go there after you've been everywhere else so you can do penance for our failings."

"Are we now going to invite our leader to come with us to see the respective physical beauties of our countries? Is this what would make her agree to be our leader, after she has kissed Everest and swum in Lake Naivasha in the Rift Valley? We must, however, not forget she had said 'travels in the mind'. So we can invade that mind and make it our own to work for GAP, Girls Are Precious." Amanthi Amadoru from Sri Lanka who had not been heard from for a long while suddenly spoke her mind, giving them the cornerstone of GAP.

It was already past eleven and not everyone had had breakfast. The talks continued whirling from life and death, foods and cruises, tennis and soccer, to their organisation and where next their assistance was most needed.

Agnes Onyango, also from Kenya, was by now uncomfortable with this type of talk that she thought went nowhere. She was ever serious and wanted to bite into the blistering disasters of life. She suddenly queried, "What about Nigeria? These obnoxious killers under the acronym BOND, Bring On Nigeria's Development, seem to be having a field day all over parts of northeastern Nigeria. And what they call development is to make Nigeria an Islamic state where women won't go school. In the process, they have brutally, ruthlessly, and needlessly murdered thousands of Nigerians, Christians and Muslims alike. And they do not want girls in school. They burn books and do not care much for education. And they call all this development!"

Charlotte Norridge, born and brought up in Cambridge gave her opinion: "Of course, we cannot take on BOND. But we can help the girls displaced from their homes and return them to their schools."

"And problems are breeding in more places than we can attend to, at least not until we have a leader," Awarah added. Shouts of Awarah! Awarah! Awarah! Good morning. It's going to noon and you're just coming for breakfast. Do you really expect us to wait for you? Cheryl and a number of the other sisters wondered in apparent displeasure.

"I have been busy arranging our dinner tonight. Yes, we leave tomorrow. I assure you we will conclude our affairs tonight with Chioma's distinctive signature. Let's all go and visit the Maryland zoo in Baltimore and meet some of our relatives and ancestors. Who knows; these same ancestors will come out in full force to fight all our fights for us", Awarah was in her usual "human-transforming-to-spirit-back-to-human self" in her response. She had arrived with the group and was with them in her human self till the night before when she departed and was not seen until that morning. Since she left at night, nobody had missed her.

No one really wanted to leave for anywhere, even for the zoo. A lone voice from Sarah asked everyone to just hang about, lounging and singing, breathing the air of friendship. "Ah, friends cannot get any closer. There is no measure for true friendship." Sarah asserted, hugging Waithira to bone-breaking point.

"Again, I'm sorry to disappoint you. The trip to Baltimore

would be way too much for us to handle and return in time for dinner at 5 p.m. Why don't we go to my parents? I'm sure you've all been waiting for me to invite you to meet my dad and mum. Being the amiable ladies that you are, you would not broach the subject yourselves. So, let me say how pleased I am to be in the midst of such phenomenal ladies. You make me happy." Chioma gladly steered the conversation in another direction for ease.

"I am very sorry to disappoint you, my dear Awarah."

"So, it's now 'my dear" Awarah, not plain Awarah."

"Whether or not I say it, you know that's exactly what's on my mind. Anyway, as I was saying . . . "

"Before I disturbed your rhythm," Awarah completed what she thought Chioma could have added to her remarks.

"Yes, I'm very sorry to disappoint Awarah. But, then, I'm not sure she really wanted us to go to the zoo. Perhaps, it was all a bait to see if I would fall for it. I very much want you to meet my parents and have dinner in our home cooked by my mum. Besides, my grandmother is visiting, mum's mother, Mama Adiaha. I believe it would be a fine evening. And it was not my own idea, though I would have asked mum to have you over. Once she heard you were coming, she insisted that she would very much like to meet the wonderful women of GAP, for whom she has the highest regard. Well you will hear this from her herself. Awarah, what do you think?"

"Well, I just wanted to see how Chioma would react. And she has proved me right: nothing would compare to an evening with your parents and your amiable Grandma. I had wanted to regale the group with your paintings at Nathan Hale Restaurant which would be just the appropriate place to make your acceptance speech. Sure. Ahoy! To the Ijeoma's in Potomac." Awarah gladly agreed and everyone was jumping in joy. The Celine theme song of *The Titanic* was playing on the sound-system and soon they were all singing along, everyone holding everyone else, going on and on.

> "Near, far, wherever you are
> I believe that the heart does go on
> Once more you open the door
> And you're here in my heart
> And my heart will go on and on."

Then Awarah blurted out, "What about making this song GAP's anthem? We will go on and on and live a life of oneness with our fellows and make women the centerpiece of human societies that they may bring forth through continuing generations, children who would bear the mark of their being, children of selfless service to one another and to society."

Chioma was quiet and so was everyone else. It seems Awarah had hit on an idea they needed to digest more fully, in time.

CHAPTER FIFTEEN

April 18, 2012

Potomac, Maryland

"Sarah, Baraah, it was your idea that we come to College Park and meet Chioma and we were all thrilled at this marvellous thought that would end an era for GAP and start a fresh course for us at the same time. Well, it is all turning spectacularly," Funeka was beside herself with joy at the thought of getting ever closer and closer to Chioma.

Chioma's parents, Mr. Okeadinife Ijeoma and Mrs. Onyebuchi Ijeoma, both of them attorneys, lived in Potomac, Maryland, in a two storey brick building that reflected the house in Okeosisi of Pa Maduka, Onyebuchi's father. It thus gave them a grand feeling of the Akadike legendary mystique. Arriving about 6 p.m., Chioma led the group into the residence. The sun gave the ladies of GAP a brilliant welcome and stayed in full force for another hour or so.

Chioma quickly ran to embrace her mother as she welcomed her guests to the living room. Weeping happily, she held on strongly to her mum so no one could see her tears.

"Mama, I am richly blessed; look at this fine retinue of exceptional women coming all the way from the U.K. to see me. Mama, what can I do to show them how much I love them and care for them and for what they do?" Chioma spoke in joy immersed in unbridled excitement. Her mum held her close, and then greeted the party one by one as

Chioma introduced them. Then Mr. Ijeoma hugged them with the traditional Igbo welcome: "*Unu abiago, nno nu*", that is, "You have come to see us, you're welcome."

Mr. Ijeoma proceeded to pour encomiums on his guests. "You have seized the world by storm and the world will never be the same. Anyone who has a daughter is in your debt. You are now the mothers of all the girls of the world. Please be comfortable and do whatever you like while I organise the drinks."

"Here is my grandmother, my mother's mother, Mrs. Adiaha Maduka." Chioma introduced her Grandma as she came down the steps, on the last two steps or so.

"You are most welcome my children. You make us proud. You make me proud. How have you been?"

Funeka found her voice in the presence of what to her represented the nobility of the woman, "Grandma, we have been having a rollicking time, just being with one another, doing nothing else but chatting and eating and drinking."

"Well, tonight won't be an exception", Grandma assured them.

One by one, beginning with Funeka, they drew near to Grandma sitting at her feet until it grew into a semicircle.

"Tell me a little about what you've been doing."

"Grandma, we are not doing much in this rapidly changing world that we just can't understand. On the contrary, neophytes of today are dying to hear of your life in Nigeria. Families are dying today, so we wonder how it was in your days." Ingrid Ekengren from Sweden eagerly asked.

"Well, my child, yes the times have changed in some ways, and in others they have not. People fall in love, get married, have children, take care of the family, and some even live happily ever after."

"I fell in love with my husband, Maduka, the first time I saw him and, after he took me out to meet his friends, I knew I would marry him. It all happened fast and was most unAfrican. The man is the one who asks the hand of the girl in marriage. But I ended up asking Maduka if he thought we would make a happy couple."

"This is very much like what happens in Scandinavia even till today. Either one, man or woman, can ask for the hand of the other in marriage. Love is for both the woman and the man." Ingrid spoke her mind.

"So, Grandma, was there anything else unAfrican about your early love life?"

"Yes, my child; it is not a matter of our early love life. I don't think my life can be pigeonholed into one or the other genre. Love is universal and the language is one of blood and caring and suffering and laughing and suffering some more. Everywhere we find that giving of self is the language of decent societies."

There was silence as though Grandma had hit a radical note which they all shared: to say suffering was love would make her the grand patron of GAP.

"Grandma, Chioma told us you and your dear husband studied at the University of Uppsala, one of the finest universities we have in Sweden." Ingrid wanted to hear this again.

"Are you Swedish, Ingrid? Of course, you must be, Ingrid is a Swedish name. Yes, we were in Sweden and we were exposed to the liberal Swedish way of life, social, accommodating and friendly. They were some of the happiest days of our life. And women were given full respect and held in as high in esteem as any man of equal status. Girls and boys grew up loving and caring for each other."

"Chioma tells us her grandma is Efik, born in Calabar and that she owes any finesse she may have to you; that the Efik are highly refined and emancipated." Julia Newster from erstwhile colonial Great Britain observed. "Please, Grandma, tell us a little about Calabar."

"Well, my child, the story of Calabar is a most interesting one and, I must say, highly engaging. If I start now, we won't end until you are ready to board your plane. Of course, you have all heard of Mary Slessor of history, the Scottish missionary who came to Calabar in the early nineteenth century and through her courageous nature, was able to get the villagers to keep their twin children and not dispose of them in the bush. Being a woman, and wielding authority, she was able to transfer her legendary attributes to the Efik woman. They wore dresses instead of the wrappers that other Nigerian women tied to their waists and they wore hats with their dresses just like English ladies did. So the Calabar woman came to be looked upon as 'civilized' as opposed to the women from the hinterland."

"So, grandma, colonialism seemed to have done good to the woman, to the Calabar woman. What about the men?" Julia asked further.

"The same can be said of the men: they received early training as lawyers and civil engineers and as professionals in colonial Nigeria. But this was to be expected, after all, it was the man who was the head of the family, *Ete Ufok,* we would call him. Ordinarily, the woman did no more than housework. So whatever she did that took her away from home was seen as social advancement. The offshoot of this was that the Calabar woman came to be seen as one who would readily fulfill her dreams as she saw fit."

"It seems, Grandma, that when women assert their independence and want to live a life of their own choice, they unwittingly expose themselves to exploitation of one sort or another by society." Ingrid quickly added.

"Yes, Ingrid, this happens, but perhaps more so in colonialism when very few women were educated. There was a mad scramble by men for girls who went to school, at the time, no more than a secondary school. Yes, Mary Slessor also did open schools in old Calabar and her girls were greatly valued and sought after by any eligible men of the day."

"Grandma, were you a product of this Mary Slessor's culture? Did you go to school in Calabar?" Waithira asked.

"By the time I was born, of course, Mary Slessor belonged to history and her influence was felt more in the Presbyterian churches. My parents sent me to a primary school in old Duke Town, Calabar, and I attended a Catholic secondary school, Cornellia Condy Secondary School, Uyo, better known as CCC, Uyo. Well, where were we, as for sophistication, I would simply say I was well brought up by my parents, Mr. and Mrs. Eno Henshaw who made sure I had a sound education in learning as well as in morals. And I take good care of my body. The body must ever be the garden of the soul. And, please, don't forget, Chioma is an Akadike and that is quite a story."

Okeadinife arrived with the beef and chicken barbecue, salads, samosa, and drinks, white wine, including Chardonnay from Stellenbosh, another from Napa Valley, California and one from Ontario, in the region of Niagara-on-the-Lake. Cheryl recognized the label, *Angel's Gate,* as the wine they had in *Village* restaurant in Niagara-on-the-Lake when she, Baraah and Funeka first mooted the idea of forming GAP in 2009, three years ago. She quickly ran over to Mr. Ijeoma and before he could show them the whole repertoire of drinks for the evening announced:

"Grandma, Mr. Ijeoma and my dear sisters of GAP, here we have the wine that made GAP possible. Funeka, Baraah, you might recall that it was with this excellent bouquet that the thought occurred to us that we should start an organization with the sole purpose of saving the girl-child wherever she may be from the horrors of illiteracy; knowing that the whole knowledge repertoire is imbued in the human foetus in the womb of the mother, and is then slowly manifested in time through learning. We believe in knowledge that offers service and self-giving. The social development of the human person depends on the mother, the environment of the mother, especially during her pregnancy with the child. Thus, the woman is truly the one person on whom humanity depends for survival as a human species created to be good. I am sorry, Mr. Ijeoma that I'm talking this way, but when we meet your wonderful family and the superb way in which you have brought up Chioma, I just can't resist to give credit to the woman. All this outpouring from me recalls the heartfelt conversations we had in the company of *Angel's Gate* on that unforgettable evening in Niagara-on-the-Lake. In fact, as I think of it now, I think only persons who have the humility of their knowledge can pass through angel's gate. Forgive me, Mr. Ijeoma for my impetuosity but I just could not resist making these comments; and thank you for giving us Chioma."

"You're much in order, Cheryl and this family is much pleased that this fine wine has a rich history behind it. No wonder, your efforts are all crowned with success: the good angels have granted you safe passage through their gates and your dreams rush through to give solace to suffering souls. May the angels give the girl-child free passage to knowledge and fulfillment. As for giving you Chioma, I think it is my dear wife, the woman, of Akadike fame, who deserves the honour. As you well said, your organization emphasises the singular role of the mother in the evolution of society along noble, selfless lines. May your organization prosper and may the women flourish."

Everyone said Amen to Mr. Ijeoma's heart-warming remarks.

'Many thanks, sir; you did not know what role *Angel's Gate* may have played in our lives. But I'm sure you know I'm from Stellenbosh, South Africa. So let me thank you most profusely for your thoughtfulness in giving us this piece of my country." Funeka was all smiles as she cradled her Stellenbosh Chardonnay with flowing pleasure.

The conversation returned to Grandma Adiaha but not before Chioma corrected her dad to say that he must not forget that she was as much her daughter as she was her mum's; that the collaboration of the father was unmistakably crucial in the growth and maturity of the child, and that women depended on men, and men on women, but women offered the greater service to families, and thus, to society.

Andah softly asked, "Grandma, tell us a little about love. Our generation seems to have lost the real essence of love."

"And what, Andah, do you think is this essence, to turn this love coin on its head?"

"I can tell you what I think, Grandma: it is no more than what we say when we take the marital vow."

"And if you're not married, just as you aren't, Andah, is there no love in your life?"

"Of course, Grandma, there is tons and tons of love but it is not erotic love."

"Thank you, my child, for love needs not wear the erotic coat to be called love. Unfortunately, the love we speak most of is erotic love. Surely eroticism has its place in nature, and nothing really can take its place. But it needs to be completely immersed in chastity."

"Grandma, how do we get the world to understand what chastity really means and its fundamental contribution to all of life itself? We extol the body and its alluring attractions. We see a curvaceous body and we say this woman is beautiful. Is this what beauty is all about, a beautiful body, what of the soul? Of course, when we look at film stars all interest is on what we see, their bodies. And, Grandma, when we grow old and wrinkled, do we stop being beautiful?"

"Oh! My child, you take me far, far our to the reaches of the earth itself. And it seems you want us to sail the seas from shore to shore, telling stories without end about the essence of life itself only for us to come upon a new shore and discover fresh nuggets for our hungry appetites. This is your first time meeting me and, painfully, the last time we are together before you leave tomorrow."

"But, Grandma, we can spend the whole night listening to you. We have nothing else to do. We shall spend the night with you and continue with your stories at sunrise. Yes, Grandma, the sun will rise on your face tomorrow morning.

Andah kept prodding Grandma to tell them more and she was not quite sure how to begin as the stories would take all night. But when Andah said they would spend the night with her, Grandma's eyes welled with excitement. She just did not know how best to control her emotions. She would have begged off and gone to her bedroom for a discrete while. But she thought the better of it: she would stay with her guests throughout the evening as long as they wanted to be with her.

"Yes, oh yes, we shall spend the night here with Grandma; how lucky can we get." everyone echoed in effusive joy.

"My dear children, you make an old woman remember all the days of her childhood, her school days, the early years of her marriage, her husband, her children, grandchildren, and now I have a new set of grandchildren, that is Sixteen plus One, you and my Chioma."

"I protest, Grandma, it's no longer 'my Chioma", it's "our Chioma"; and it is no longer Sixteen plus One, it is now Seventeen. Yes! Grandma, if, unimaginably, Chioma would not give her whole life to our cause, then you, Grandma, would lead us through the jungles of bloodied insurgence to the green fields of freedom and love. You know what love means more than any of us, and you're the most free person we know of. So, Grandma, your legions await you and the bugle has sounded for the first battle." Angela Farmer, from Surrey, England, threw down the gauntlet ready for war. Everyone laughed and laughed and could not stop laughing till Chioma came to Grandma's rescue.

"Please leave my Grandma alone," she pleaded. "Since when did a seventy plus old grandma lead the battle? I am still here and I have not said no to you. Of course, if the competition is between my grandma and me, I yield to her totally and unreservedly."

More laughter, everyone was beside herself with the gaiety of the moment, with the irresistible feeling that they each held heaven in their hands.

"Okay, my children, Seventeen it is with Chioma completely immersed in you. I am sure we shall hear a lot from her tonight. I believe she has a lot to tell us."

Their amiable hosts, Okeadinife and Onyebuchi, with Chioma helping, had set the table and all was ready for dinner.

"This is a buffet and I will guide you through the dishes, a good number of them African." Grandma cheerfully announced.

Chioma had told her parents the ladies of GAP would arrive the United States on the morning of April 17, 2012, to spend some time with her and, she feared they had gone to all this trouble that they, GAP, might recruit her to their side as their leader. She was dumbfounded and did not quite know how to show them just how much she loved them.

"Do not worry, my dear." her mother assured her, "They will see love in your eyes, hear love in your voice, smell love near you and eat love from your hands. Yes, they will eat love when Mama and I cook up a storm, the like you have never seen. Nothing of this sort has ever happened to us, ever. It is a story for the gods. Yes. Mum and I will cook our hearts out." And they did cook their hearts out!

From Monday of the week they arrived, Grandma had gone from store to store, from Potomac to Bethesda to Chevy Chase, in search of the finest foods from different parts of the world. The fest day was here and Grandma and her dear daughter, Onyebuchi were ready. Chioma's friends and colleagues, Sutapa, an Indian, Vivian, and her Iranian student, Sahab, offered a hand. They had prepared the basic meals of rice—boiled or fried in coconut oil—and potatoes — baked, chipped, boiled whole or mashed—fish curry; fish, beef, and lamb kebabs; a variety of curries—pepper beef, beet root, and egg curry; periwinkles sautered in white wine and bay leaves. For desert she had orange and almond cake and traditional American cheesecake. She took particular care for Baraah's tastes as a veggie and served vegetables fresh and vibrant green, coconut pancakes, beet root curry and deviled potatoes, been curd and treacle. She also had plantains, boiled and fried, green unripe and ripened. This repertoire, she said to herself, would serve all foreign tastes from Sri Lanka to Iran. She topped it all with exquisite African dishes, including Kenyan *ugali* and accompanying *sukuma wiki*, but especially her favourite *edikaikong*, *afang* and *ntong* soups, specialties of her Efik people, vegetable *onugbu* soup, of Anambra State fame, incomparable *ofe* Owerri, pride of Owerri people, and cosmopolitan *ofe egusi* to complete her Nigerian cuisine. The soups could be eaten with rice, beans, plantains, mashed potatoes, maize or *poundo* yam, made from yam flour, a product of a Nigerian company out in San Francisco.

Okeadinife came in with more drinks, wines white and red, fruit drinks, punches, soft drinks and good old chilled water.

"Let us pray." He always began before each meal, "Bless us oh Lord and these your gifts which we are about to receive from your bounty and these wonderful guests you have sent to us." And they all responded, "Amen."

"Mama will guide you through the menu and you can take it from there." Okeadinife announced, feeling much like a fulfilled son.

Grandma took her time with each cuisine explaining the merits of each one. Of course, she spoke at length about her favourite Nigerian dishes and everyone ate out of the *edikaikong, ntong, afang, ofe* Owerre, *ofe onugbu,* or *ofe egusi,* with baked or deviled potatoes or plantains, boiled or fried rice, maize and ugali. And if the spices were too hot, one could opt for regular potatoes or plantains. Having consumed the first course of salad, frozen youghurt and quiche Loraine, Baraah ravenously surveyed the dishes and, with the studied alacrity of an athlete, made for the pounded yam which she doused with rich-green *edikaikong.* Okeadinife served her her favourite Chardonnay and, right from the table, she began to devour the meal. Onyebuchi hailed her appetite and all the rest, without any order whatsoever, descended on the dishes. Fortunately, they did not all go for the same dish at the same time: some went for fish kebabs, *egusi* soup and rice; others for beef kebabs, deviled potatoes and *afang* soup. By far, the favourite, however, were *edikaikong* and fresh and green *ofe* Owerre, mashed potatoes and fresh fish kebabs. Desirous to sample everything Nigerian, they also added egusi, *ntong,* or *afang* soup to whatever was their special delight. To demonstrate her deep appreciation for Grandma's effort in providing *ugali* festooned with *sukuma wiki*, Waithira took a small portion, consumed this in a flash and went for what she felt must be Grandma's special dish, *edikaikong*, pounded yam and periwinkles.

Chioma was the last and they all waited for what she would select. Knowing that she liked everything Grandma set before them, and that it would be impossible for her to try them all, she, instead, went from person to person picking a little of this and a little of that from each plate. She did not do this in one go but went a number of times so her plate was never overstuffed and she was able to eat from each of the sixteen plates. Then Grandma, Onyebuchi and Okeadinife helped themselves to the meal and joined their GAP guests.

Andah returned to her earlier questions on morality, chastity and eroticism.

"Andah, let us finish eating. This food does not go down well with words, for me. It calls for all my attention and undivided interest. You know the legs of a culture stand on the feet of their food and the way they eat it, that's what my Efik people say."

The feasting continued and, one after another, they went for seconds, off and on, until all the varieties of food were tried and there was little left. Drinks kept flowing and it was time for desert. Grandma stood from her seat and approached the table to clear the plates. Onyebuchi and Okeadinife quickly ran to the rescue but only for a few seconds for the wonderful ladies of GAP and Chioma darted out and helped them. New plates were laid out, and Chioma relieved Grandma and her dear mum of setting the desert: she would now speak to everyone casually as she set the dishes, addressing each dish as though she were addressing GAP. And she started to sing right from the top of her head:

Nature grants us warmth unending
Papaya plants knowledge in girls
Banana gives after dinner speeches
Blood learns the womb commands
Seeds find nouns grow to pronouns
Adjectives arrive unmask their adverbs
Head to foot and foot to head they run
Verbs whistle new bloods grow humans

No one paid any attention in the beginning thinking Chioma was into one of her habitual songs, and she really did not want anyone to make out the words. She continued for a while singing, 'Blood learns', with 'Nature grants us warmth' as the chorus. In a while everyone got on to the song, humming along not knowing the words themselves. It was Awarah who had the notion that Chioma was warming up to being their leader, and without any practice, joined her in singing as though she had rehearsed with her and knew the lyrics. Chioma was surprised but did not show it. She simply invited her friends to the table:

"Desert is ready and you can go from bananas topped with ice-crème, or with yoghurt; and other tropical fruits, papaya, pine apple, oranges, of course; and we have traditional American dishes—apple pie and cherry pie, cheesecake, crème caramel and frozen yoghurt."

"Please what song were you singing? Could we hear it again, with the words more clearly said so we follow them and join you?" Awarah pleaded and Chioma obliged her. She repeated the song a number of times till the lyrics were clear and could be easily followed. They sang, oh! they sang, for they now realised this must be the battle hymn of GAP: *Blood learns, the womb commands.*

Waithira could not hold her excitement: "We now have our own words, nouns and pronouns, adjectives and adverbs, and finally verbs, captains of action, command that new bloods circulate. Who are these new bloods and in whom will they circulate? Will they flow only within a particular person, or will they flow from person to person, and how? Nobody needs tell us for Chioma has spoken for us all."

Grandma got into the rhythm, stood up and started singing too. Her daughter, Onyebuchi, her dear husband, Okeadinife, and all the wonderful ladies of GAP were pleasantly moved in exulting admiration of her splendid voice that rose to a high, "blood is learning", and fell to a low, "the womb commanding". Their joy kept them rooted to their seats as all they wanted was for their unspeakable dreams, manifested in the natural simplicity and tenderness of the music to go on and on without end. Chioma ran out and with all her loving strength held on to her dear grandmother as though she would never see her again, and started dancing with Grandma. Then they all swooped on

Grandma and Chioma, Onyebuchi and Okeadinife. And Chioma sang:

> *Blood is learning*
> *the womb commanding*
> *Nouns announce pronouns*
> *Adverbs advertise adjectives*
> *Verbs vaunt babies ahoy.*

They coined all sorts of variations of the song, everyone with her own version as long as the music and the rhythm stayed the same. Whoever wished would go to the table refresh her plate, refill her glass and return to the dance. Grandma stayed on the floor and just did not want to leave. Then Chioma came with another one, while still dancing.

> *Martyrdom a love supreme*
> *suffers to free, frees to suffer*
> *Learning twirls girl in womb*
> *GAP we are on pages unborn*

"I am with you in blood, my Sixteen plus One. We are indeed GAP, Girls are Precious. We are bound in love that the woman may give all of her best to nurture and grow societies in selfless service. Knowledge will flourish and girls, nay women, will grow our children to the heights of their God-given abilities. The innocents, brutally murdered by terrorists out to destroy civil society, will ever be our abiding intercessors with God. I give you all my assistance and all my assistance you have without reserve."

"Chioma is our leader by a thousand votes of the angels and the singing snows of the Himalayas. Her blood flows in

GAP; in love, togetherness, and service. She tells us life is of sincerity and service, that liberty may blossom in all human efforts and thrive amongst the conceited thorns of rabid insurrection." Awarah stoutly exclaimed.

CHAPTER SIXTEEN

August 7, 2013
Kokoma

Maduka knew he had a daring task ahead, and in the later years of his life he was not as agile and alert as he would have liked. He knew, however, that he himself would not have much to do in direct confrontation with BOND; what was needed of him would be wise counsel and a daring determination to achieve victory over evil, no matter what. He went to work immediately: first, he got in touch with his brothers, some Akadikes in northeastern Nigeria, in Damboda, Kasikum and Mafiaya, letting them know that they would be enlisted in the war against insurgency and terrorism roaring in their part of Nigeria, the north-east. They were each the president of the Igbo Community Union in their towns.

They were on top of whatever affected the Igbo person and since BOND was ravaging northeastern Nigeria, it was of immediate interest to everyone, but more so to other Nigerian ethnic groups from the south. Maduka got their unreserved support: in fact, they had long wondered when ordinary people would get together and say 'enough is enough' to the rampages and murders perpetrated by BOND and crush them to smithereens. They would be ready to get into the fray convinced that civilians could combat and defeat BOND. They were exhilarated that something would be done with their great brother leading the fight. After the Biafran civil war, they felt any other strife would be mere child's play. But then, they were not just ordinary civilians.

Next, Maduka got in touch with his granddaughter, Chioma, to find out what she and her Cambridge Group were up to. It was a long telephone conversation with Chioma wailing as she listed the litany of all the woes her group was dealing with, from Iraq to Afghanistan, to Somalia to Syria, wherever the girl-child was threatened with ignorance and gender differential. In particular, they built schools where there were none, and provided teachers and materials in collaboration with international agencies that worked on shoestring budgets but with flowing, profound passion. They were keen to get their money into desperate but trustworthy hands that would put it to the immediate use of suffering women. Chioma went on for over an hour and her poor grandfather was speechless. When, therefore, he mentioned BOND, Chioma wailed the more as she was told that more and more girls were too petrified to go to school and were either at home, or were married off at an early age.

Maduka did not broach the subject of BRAND confronting BOND for he felt Chioma had had enough grief to last her for a while. It was clear to him, though, that GAP, Girls Are Precious, would come to the assistance of girls' education in areas suffering from the fear of BOND. He was able to extract from her a promise that she would visit Nigeria briefly next Christmas, that is, in late 2014.

Jaja met with his group that same night after he left Billy. It was already past midnight but he knew where he would find them, in a remote house on the outskirts of Kokoma. There were over a hundred active militants in BRAND but, for security reasons, only a few of them lived in Kokoma, and they would change their homes from one strange place to another. They had purchased about twenty houses each of which was far from the other, in different locations, and they were ever on the move from one place to another. The rest of them, numbering another hundred or so, lived in the creeks, on remote islands where naval, speed boats could not readily get to. And they were the ones who would destroy the pipelines in their stealth canoes whenever they were running short of cash.

"Something new has come up and I have a big job for you, I mean big, and when I say big, I mean big." Jaja stood face to face with Dagogo, the leader of BRAND, with light from a kerosine lamp.

"So tell me, what kind of work is this one?"

"You will go north and engage BOND."

"Those bastards, we will show them. They think they own this country. We will burn them and throw their ashes into Lake Chad. Great. Let me get our people to come and hear this."

Jaja repeated what he told Dagogo and they all screamed in unbelievable delight.

"Now, Nigerians will know we have power, that power pass power. We will show them." they all shouted confidently.

Jaja was surprised beyond belief. He had not said anything about what the engagement involved. To them, all was fight and fight, and win and win. But that was not what Jaja had in mind at the moment, though, in time, they might have to fight BOND. For now, he would act only on Billy's instructions: so he told them their job would be essentially intelligence gathering at the moment in preparation for a later onslaught should this be necessary.

"What kind of talk is this? Don't waste our time Jaja, will we fight or won't we fight?"

"Yes you will fight when your employers say so. I am only their go- between."

"Well, tell them we will go there and take out those people. We have our own intelligence reports and have our plans to deal with them. The Nigerian Navy has been using us to gather information for them, to keep us busy and out of mischief, they say. Now we have a rich employer, let them bring their money and give us the weapons we need. Tell them we know BOND and we are ready to deal decidedly with them."

"Dagogo, don't feel offended if I ask you this question: Do you know the workings of the mind of BOND? Do you know where they live? Do you know how they think? Do you know their daily habits, when they wake up, when and how they eat, where do they sleep, how do they manage their wives and children, do they live with their families, how many of them live together and how?"

"Please, Jaja, enough is enough. Don't you believe me when I say we have been doing some business with the Navy? What do you call intelligence, is it not all the useless questions you're asking me? How can anyone know how my mind works? Too much book that is what is killing you people. We are ready; tell your people who sent you."

"So what do I tell those who want to employ your services?"

"Tell them what I have told you. We are ready to face BOND. I and two of our people will meet with those who sent you. Tell them. I will tell you the house where you will bring them."

Jaja was full of unbelief. Surely, BRAND was invincible in the waterways of the delta. But , when it came to land, Jaja saw them as dinosaurs. He must come again on another day and hear Dagogo and let him confirm what he had just said. Two days later, Monday, August 5, Dagogo, in a furious mood, ordered Jaja to relate his readiness to fight BOND to Maduka and Billy. That same day, Jaja passed on the message to Billy reminding him of his firm arrangement to meet him on Wednesday, August 7.

Billy and Maduka met in Lagos, in the house of a mutual friend to forge their plans for BRAND's confrontation of BOND, even if this meant armed warfare. They found they had taken on more than they could chew, certainly more than they had bargained for. And now, as they saw it, they were in trouble. How could they now be prepared for the eventual battles between BRAND and BOND when all they wanted was to find a subtle way to support BRAND and get BOND to give up their arms.

"Billy, you have put us into trouble going much farther than we were prepared for. Our main task was to get BRAND to forgo their schemes for funding university education with their ransom money, and our interest in their going to the north was simply to provide us with some intelligence reports for future use, if this should arise. Now you have called out your forces to war. Is this what we agreed?"

"Is this what you call trouble, You Fool? When you see real trouble what will you do? Jaja will phone us today and tell us where it is he will take us to meet Dagogo and his people."

The following day, August 7, Maduka and Billy were off to Kokoma by air. They did not go to Billy's house, but stayed in a hotel in case BRAND had other ideas in mind to hold them to ransom. Jaja picked them up from their hotel and after driving around and around for over an hour to cover his tracks he finally delivered them to Dagogo's hideout. It was a prefabricated house near the waterfront, a good twenty kilometers or so from Kokoma, in a village called Brima. The house looked deserted and would not attract the attention of any one passing by. Jaja dropped off his passengers about a five minute walk from the house and then sped off leaving them to deal directly with Dagogo and his men who were already inside.

Neither Maduka nor Billy had ever been in this sort of situation and suddenly they found themselves gripped with fear as the room was dark, without any light. A torchlight flashed and a voice asked the visitors to sit down on the hard floor and be comfortable. How could they be comfortable on the dusty floor, they wondered. The flashlight went off and another one, bright red shone in another room, tightly adjoining where they were. The thick smell of what must be marijuana smoke filled the air, making Maduka cough and sneeze without end, and bottle after bottle of alcoholic drinks littered every corner.

"My good friends, how are you?" That must be their leader, they thought. Instead it was Jaja all over again. "Our leader has asked me to bring you to another site, that he was happy everything was working well. So let's go."

There were two other men with Jaja. The one who had asked them to be comfortable helped Maduka to stand up. Billly got up readily, wiped his backside of the dust, and they walked out to the rear of the hideout. From there, they walked for another thirty minutes or so to where they would meet Dagogo. It was another ramshackle of a dilapidated building. This time around, Billy and Maduka really feared for their life for the building was littered with firearms and shells. Neither person could talk: they did not know what might set Dagogo off and he would get rid of them especially as the whole place reeked of alcohol and drugs. Maduka could not help asking Billy in the most quiet of tones, "My dear man, have you any idea what's going on?"

"You Fool, when you deal with the devil, why be afraid of hell?"

Dagogo emerged, shook hands with Maduka and Billy and the three of them got into a waiting SUV and drove off to the same hotel where they were staying.

They had been booked into a suite and they were all seated on the outer room. But Dagogo said they should go into their bedroom. It had two beds and Dagogo decided he would spend the night with them. How would the three of them sleep on two beds?

"Oh don't worry about me. I never sleep on beds. Just throw some pillows on the floor and that's my bed. Call for some drinks. I'm sorry if I caused you some anxiety." Maduka and Billy were visibly sweating and needed a drink.

"Mine will be Coke, diet Coke. I know you drink Guilder, Maduka, and you, Billy, Guinness stout."

The drinks arrived and Maduka cordially offered his guest the Coke. He was going to serve it in a glass when Dagogo objected saying he usually took his drinks straight from the bottle.

"You don't mind, sir, I do not trust glasses."

"Anything to eat, if I may ask?"

"Nothing yet, sir, till we are done with the business at hand. So let's get to work. Jaja told me all you wanted was for us, BRAND, to provide you with some intelligence reports on BOND which you would be able to use later. I told him that given the evil atrocities which they carried out day in day out, that we should go ahead and take them out. We had already done some work for the Nigerian Navy and we know how they operate. We are ready if you are."

Dagogo spoke fluent English, without any pauses, and both Maduka and Billy could not believe their ears. Besides, he exuded the air of a cultured gentleman. Maduka could not help asking him, "Dagogo, which university did you attend?"

"Sir, you might be surprised to hear I attended Obafemi Awolowo University where you taught. I did engineering, so you can understand that I would want the faculty of engineering here at Kokoma, my home town, to be well developed. I did not know you in person but we all heard of you. So, you are not entirely a stranger to me. It is Billy, the great Professor William Briggs, that I know of from his works on the socioeconomic effects of poverty and its manifestation in militancy. We in BRAND love him. So, you see, we can do business together."

It was now up to Maduka and Briggs to say what they were there for. But, somehow, neither of them could say anything: they were too nonplussed with the situation they found themselves in. Dagogo had astonished them and they did not know how best to proceed. So they were silent.

"Gentlemen, I am here waiting for you. What do you want from me? Jaja has told me a lot already and he has passed my message to you, I am sure, or we won't be having this meeting."

Maduka responded: "Thank you, Dagogo. I think what you want to hear from us is that we will fund and support your full military confrontation of BOND. You must know that was not what we originally had in mind. But the initial work we wanted you to do, that is, gather intelligence reports on BOND, you have already done for the Nigerian Navy, we understand." Maduka was simply beating about the bush unable to come out and say specifically that BRAND should go ahead and fight BOND. Billy kept solemnly quiet leaving the final decision to his leader, knowing his Akadike charisma would see him through any possible mishap.

September 3, 2014

Kokoma

Billy, Maduka, and their supporters met several times to work out the details of providing all the assistance that BRAND would need. In the middle of their discourse, however, in September 2013, Billy took seriously ill and was hospitalised in Abuja till early March 2014. No further arrangements could be made until he got better. Fortunately, by June, he had regained his full health and was raging to proceed with the BRAND onslaught. A meeting was, therefore, arranged with Dagogo in September.

Dagogo was overjoyed to see Billy in good health: "We are very happy to see you on your feet, Professor William Briggs, our own Billy. Thank God, everything is now okay. I'm sorry I could not come in person to see you in your hospital bed and you can easily understand why. I have been restlessly waiting for you, only getting bits and pieces of information from Maduka from time to time. But we kept in touch with you throughout your illness and are so happy to see you up and about ready to fight. Terrorism is increasing by the day. We must act now. I am indeed happy to see you again, Billy."

Billy responded equally warmly. "Thank you Dagogo, many thanks. Yes I am now well and ready to do all I can in this war against terrorism. Maduka, my good friend had kept things under control but he was getting very restive and did not know exactly what to do. Surely, he could not go on alone. I am here now and we can get this job done and root out the damned terrorists."

It was now time for full scale discussion and Maduka seized the moment.

"Many thanks, Dogogo. We had feared for Billy's health, but all is now well and we are, as you say, ready to act. Well, let me say it bluntly, Dagogo: we will give you everything you need to get rid of BOND; you must make sure you rid us of this evil. So everything will be predicated on your success. We are very concerned about the problem of women's education and total well being. And you know of what my granddaughter Chioma is doing with GAP, Girls Are Precious, to put girls in school, in many poor countries of the world. This really is our main interest; but since we cannot successfully address the hazards of the girl-child unless we rid our society of the malaise of BOND, we will now go ahead and degrade BOND."

Maduka wondered how BRAND would succeed where the Nigerian army had failed. Furthermore, he wondered how a small band of fifteen people or so, however superior their arms, would be able to subdue hardened terrorists whose only purpose in life was to kill without any show of mercy, to let blood run freely where it may. Maduka was not convinced in his mind that BRAND would be equal to the task. He wanted to hear from Dagogo just how they would accomplish their dare devil counter-terrorism.

Dagogo brought out his pad and started to sketch what exactly they would do. First, they would attack with fifteen men in one night and kill their leaders, all ten men who control BOND. They knew where to locate them, though they were not all in one place and lived some five to ten kilometres apart, in groups of three and four. Their attack was poised on surprise, speed and alacrity with immediate elimination by strangling of the enemy, without struggle, without any noise.

"My dear sirs, I have just received a phone call that changes the whole dynamics of our discussion; in fact, I fear it will change the military-political culture of this country. So I'll see you tomorrow and tell you all about it. It will be in the news tomorrow morning so you'll surely hear about it. Good night."

Dagogo left summarily, the meeting at a standstill. Maduka and Billy were at their wits end what to do. Utterly confused, distraught, and destabilized, they sat there with their faces blank and distorted, eyes sunken and sallow.

CHAPTER SEVENTEEN

September 4, 2014

Kokoma

"What do you think, Billy? Is this some sort of game or is he hoodwinking us? Can he really be trusted?"

"Madu, I'm trumped. This is unbelievable. Dagogo could have told us what happened, what kind of news would this be; that BOND would do more harm than they had already done? As far as we are concerned, that would make our life all the more difficult. That is clear."

"Well, it is late and we've not had our dinner yet. It is late, I know, but let us eat, have a drink, and sleep on it."

"You Fool; you mean you have an appetite to eat after receiving such terrible news. I'm not hungry, so go ahead and eat all you like."

"Don't put it like that, please. We are not children. We are full grown adults and old enough to bear whatever this world throws at us, however horrible it may be."

"Say what you like, I don't have the stomach for any food now. Suit yourself. Do whatever you like. Just leave me out of it."

"I think this your "you Fool" is getting out of hand. You and I are in this together, all the way. Don't forget you got me into this, and so far I've not seen much of those your young activists. So what happened to them?"

"You stupid, gosh I'm sorry I won't say it again. It's just that that is what I call you and have always called you since our UCI days. Back to the point: I know your temperament and how unsociable you are . . . ."

"Is that what you now say after our days together of mirth and joy and sociability, and what have you, and shared experiences and fortunes, our lives intertwining and now you say I'm unsociable. You are now the Fool."

"You see what I mean, now I am the Fool, and what of you, what does that make you, a nincompoop?"

"Call me what you like, it does not make any difference one way or another."

"Well, I'll eat whatever you're eating and drink my usual Guinness, so we don't have to fight."

"I'm going to have a big meal of okra soup and pounded yam."

"At this time of might? It will kill me."

"That would be a nice way to finally get rid of you."

"You Fool, I'll show you. Ok I'll have pounded yam too and okra. We'll see who will wake up tomorrow with a running stomach."

Jaja came to the hotel by six in the morning to collect Maduka and Billy for their meeting with Dagogo. The route was tortuous, taking them through side streets and narrow alleyways not usually used by traffic. Maduka and Billy were not particularly troubled for their life since they were now quite relaxed with Dagogo as he seemed ready to do business with them. On the way, in an area where the narrow road firmly and desperately hugged the car, Maduka's stomach was troubled, eager to dispose its rumbling contents. Billy would only laugh reminding his embarrassed friend of his foreboding the night before. They had to leave their tracks and quickly race to the nearest petrol station where some convenience may be found. Luckily, there was one and Maduka was able to relieve himself of his vexing baggage. Jaja did not say anything about the message delivered to his boss the night before;

and if he knew, he would give nothing away. Dagogo had said the morning news would carry it, but Maduka and Billy left the hotel before the news at seven. Was this Dagogo's way to make sure he's the one to deliver the news himself, perhaps, to extract maximum remuneration for his efforts?

* * *

"My dear friends, last night, Wednesday, September 3, as we were talking, at about 10 p.m., our intelligence reported that one hundred and fifty eight students, all girls, would be abducted that night, from their school, Kagara Girl s' Government Secondary School. We later learnt the girls were roused in their sleep around 2 a.m. and taken away to an unknown destination. As we speak now, today, September 4, I can't tell you the site they were taken to. Everything has now changed. No one yet has claimed responsibility for the abduction, but you and I know it bears the insignia of evil BOND. Chioma and her group will loom large in this unfolding debacle: GAP will want the girls released at all cost. I'm certain they themselves would be prepared to come to Nigeria and see to their release by whatever means. Thus, the whole picture is getting more and more complex. Besides, the Nigerian army and police will not be sleeping on their laurels. Right now, they are panicking and are awaiting orders from above. And what they call "above" is waiting for orders from the president who is praying and praying for higher orders from above. So, we are all waiting for 'above'".

Maduka and Billy concluded that this new development had changed the entire landscape of their involvement with BRAND. Reasoning that the government would immediately fight to rescue the students, they felt they would hold fire till they saw what successes the government would have gained and how the international community would react and, possibly, send in arms or armed assistance. Dagogo also felt the same way.

"Gentlemen, everything has now changed. First, let me thank you for the ten thousand dollars you sent through Jaja. He duly gave it to me saying that you hoped it would facilitate our reaching solid agreements. Now, we wait and see. Professor Akadike, I hear your granddaughter will be in the country for Christmas. Surely, this abduction would be of unbearable trauma to her and to her friends in GAP, and I'm certain she will move mountains to gain the freedom of these girls. Don't be surprised: in fact, be at ease. We have our sources and I can confidently tell you we will secure the release of the girls, should the anticipated government efforts fail. I, for one, would like to make a Christmas present of the release of the girls to your granddaughter, Chioma, and to GAP. We shall be in touch. We watch for the signs of success or failure. We shall act in good time to free the girls. You are now able to reach me directly, but it's always best to do so through Jaja. Thanks. You're wonderful."

The meeting thus ended and Jaja took Maduka and Billy back to their hotel with all the promise of a beautiful future awaiting them.

On their way home, Maduka stopped at a petrol station to use their conveniences, once more; his torrid stomach was restless and he had to empty its contents.

CHAPTER EIGHTEEN

College Park
December 2, 2014

"I have your letter before me supported by your dean, requesting approval for a one- month leave for you to travel to Nigeria to deliver a lecture at the University of Jagowa and attend to some urgent needs of the girl-child in your country."

That was the President, University of Maryland at College Park, Dr. James Mansfield. He had asked Dr. Chioma Ijeoma, associate professor of African Spiritualism and Culture, to see him on Tuesday, December 2, 2014, whenever she was free. She found she could see Dr. James Mansfield at eleven o'clock in the morning after her lecture.

"When you told me the whole story of your deep involvement with GAP, Girls Are Precious and later as their Leader, I was quite concerned that you were getting into hot water in a world that was happy to boil water wherever it could. Peace is now a stranger in our midst and we all want to send her to the gallows."

"Mr. President, sir, you put it right, but what are we to do, sit around with arms folded, unmindful of the insidious evil that generates all the heat? Yes, peace is gone, but not too far to be unreachable. We shall lampoon it back to our homes."

"Chioma, this university owes you a lot for what you try to do to promote African culture here, and now you've gone much further to take on some tough gender and educational problems of the world."

"Sir, you know very well it was not my doing: the leadership was thrust upon me based on my affinities with girls' education. And I am happy with my work with GAP."

"This is all wonderful, Chioma, and College Park is all the happier for you. But you have my personal sympathy especially now you're going home to your native Nigeria to battle some of the problems posed by BOND. Your letter told me the whole story of what has been happening in Nigeria. Yes, you can help, but are you not afraid that you yourself might turn out to be just the kind of target that BOND wants to hit? Don't you think they would like to abduct you and Islamise you in a way you would find abhorrent and force you into a fight for your faith?"

"That, sir, would be the least of my problems if I would have to fight for my faith, for my God would not abandon me."

"I see you will be away for a month or so. It is my most sincere prayer that you come back to us cheerful and full of joy. I do not want to make any comments on the abduction of the Kagara girls, because I'm sure you're far too distraught on this to be able to talk about it. It is horrifying, it is unspeakable, and I know you will fight to your last drop of blood to get those girls back to school. GAP, I am sure, will see you through any unexpected interruptions on your normal schedule. Their reach is long, and they will be able to serve as your security shield, if necessary. We will follow your everyday activities with great interest."

"Thank you, sir, I am touched by your warm sentiments. I believe I shall come back to College Park just as I am now, or even better."

"Oh, I'm so sorry, Chioma, before you leave for Nigeria, please see me; we have raised some funds for you. I don't know if your students have told you this. They came to me and said they have formed an association they call SURF, Students United for ReFugees, they said they have been able to raise ten thousand dollars of their own money and sought the assistance of the members of our Board of Trustees in their personal capacities, to make donations to SURF. At our last meeting which was just last week, I broached the matter to them and they each gladly matched the contributions of the students: each member gave ten thousand dollars and the chairman, twenty. So you have one hundred and twenty thousand dollars for GAP. They wanted you to use the funds to help the refugees fleeing the terrorism of BOND in several cities in northern Nigeria."

"I am speechless, sir. I say a very big thank you to the Trustees and shall, on my return, give a full account of how their assistance has been put to use. This will help many refugees obtain urgently needed food, shelter and medical supplies. Thank you, sir."

December 9
College Park

Chioma went to her class on the sociology of refugee societies and concluded the lecture with a question she had asked before, "what is the worst form of refugee-ism?" One hand shot up.

"Ma'am, are you asking us this question because some of us did not contribute to SURF, or do you really want an academic answer, or one that wrings the soul of any falsehood?"

"Well, Gerald, give us any that you can think of and we'll take it from there," Chioma replied.

Another hand shot up: "Without any question, Ma'am, the worst form of refugee-ism would be to be a refugee to oneself, to run away from a worthy cause in insouciance, in total indifference to the world. That to me is the worst refugee-ism you can have."

"Thank you, Andy."

"I was going to add, Ma'am, that not having a cause worth dying for was the worst form of refugee-ism." Gerald concluded his contribution with a firm handshake with Andy who sat next to him.

Chioma congratulated the class for their germane contributions and agreed with them that, indeed, the worst form of running away from any danger would be to run away from oneself, to be indifferent, to be selfish, and not to have a cause worth dying for. She expressed her profound gratitude to them for what they had done with SURF, in particular, their bold approach to the president requesting his help that resulted in the members of the board of trustees making personal donations to SURF of one hundred and twenty thousand dollars. She now had in her hands a total of one hundred and thirty thousand dollars. She could not contain her joy filled with the hope that soon, but not soon enough, BOND would be disintegrated.

She contacted her friends in GAP, gave them the good news of SURF and told them she would be with them on December 12, on her way to Nigeria.

CHAPTER NINETEEN

December 12, 2014
London, U.K.

Chioma could not have imagined this: All sixteen members of GAP were at Heathrow airport, London, at the ungodly hour of six o'clock in the morning to receive her on arrival.

"As soon as we received your e-mail that we should meet to discuss some pressing issues for the brief period you would be with us on your way to Nigeria to give a lecture at the University of Jagowa, and that you would use the opportunity of the lecture to bring BOND to the negotiating table and provide succour to its victims, we knew we all had to come out and show our love and support from the very minute of your presence with us. You are rousing GAP to come out and pay its bills with blood of love. And here we are." Baraah, apostle of all that was good and proper, all that was worth dying for, spoke for the group, as it were, without much ado.

Taking the train, they were in Essex by eleven in the morning. Chioma had slept all the way from Washington D.C., prepared to take on a full day work on arrival.

"Please, tell us, Chioma, what is this about degradation of BOND we've been hearing in the news. If you were to succeed in bringing them to the negotiating table, who would lead the negotiations, GAP?" Sarah wanted to know as soon as they were comfortably seated in the lounging sofas in Mrs. Farmer's estate. Her daughter, Angela took Chioma's bag to her room upstairs and everyone else huddled up around Chioma to hear what she had to say. But first they must have breakfast. Their amiable host invited them to the table and they helped themselves to tea, coffee, cereals, toast, eggs, ham and fruit.

"I have a strong feeling that BOND will do everything they can to abduct me once I am in Jagowa. I'll be there for two nights and they would plan to kidnap me on the second night after my lecture. As you know, they've already abducted one hundred and fifty-eight girls from a girls' secondary school in Kagara, in northeastern Nigeria, what is now known as the 'Kagara Debacle'. Happy to report that fifty-three of the girls have successfully fled to freedom. How they did this, is still not well known, but the whereabouts of the remaining one hundred and five girls remain a mystery. I suspect BOND would use me as a major negotiating tool to obtain the release of thousands of their folk held in detention. This would be the beginning of the negotiations, for BOND would want to exchange me with the prisoners held by the Nigerian Security Services, NSS. Also, I am in touch with my grandfather and he has mobilized the entire Akadike resources and manpower to watch over me. He is not afraid. I know the University of Jagowa will provide me with adequate security but I also know that their security system is porous and penetrable by BOND.

My grandpa also tells me that something else is afoot to bring about the end of BOND. So, whatever happens, I'll be fine, praying that my visit might, somehow, be the beginning of the end of BOND. As you all know, we've already made arrangements for the full care of the Kagara girls who escaped. Surely, we have a role in this, and it won't be a simple case of providing resources for their education. Their freedom is dear to us and their whole lives are now before us."

"Then, why are you going? You say you know your life might be in danger, why are you still going? You don't really have to get entangled with the release of the girls. Let the Nigerian government see to that, for all it may be worth. You must stay out of it. We want you with us. We have far too much to do yet for us to risk losing you in your own native country. Please, Chioma, you know whatever you want to do, not only will we support you, we will be there with you. If the worst comes to the worst and you believe you have a direct role to play in the Kagara Debacle, we will be there all of us with you."

Waithira was troubled and all the group with her. She continued: "We did not think that your talk of dealing with BOND might pose any danger to you. And you tell us all the time we are not out to shed blood anywhere but to turn whatever blood that is shed into a new language of love by coming to the assistance of families suffering the pains and anguish of terrorism."

Others joined in and one by one they all tried to talk Chioma out of going up to Jagowa where she would be easy prey in BOND's hands. In particular, she should distance herself from direct entanglement with the Kagara Debacle.

Finally Cheryl felt they should all go along with Chioma and if it meant her abduction, so be it, they too would all go to Jagowa.

"Yea, indeed, why not, wherever Chioma goes, there we go too. That's why she's our Leader, with a capital L.

Chioma smiled. "You know it can never be like that. If I were to take you anywhere, I would make sure you were all ready and well prepared. Right now this is my own personal scourge, if it should turn out to be so. We all have a cause worth dying for: to save the girl-child, give her a good education, and a great start in life. . . . My travel to Jagowa is to give a lecture. I know I have other duties to perform when I get there. I would like to move across the border to Chad, to see some of the refugees in person; for, as I told you, we have some money for them from SURF. I surely would give my life for the students who have made such a bold move and have taken the initiative to get the message of the suffering refugees across to our board of trustees. My role as your leader now takes me into new uncharted territory and I must not fail you in any way. God with me, I shall be able to do my duty."

"No doubt, Chioma, God is with this group, and he gave you to us as our leader. We thank him for that. But what's this talk about the great Akadike machinery coming to your aid?" Waithira pressed for more clarifications.

"Believe me, "Thira, I do not know anything about it. It's entirely my grandpa's handiwork. He sometimes comes across as fierce and ebullient, when he steps into his great father's shoes, for example; but generally he speaks only the language of friendship and scholarship. It is all his doing. Of course, I shall go along with him and do as he says."

It was now afternoon and as GAP entourage had taken the day off, they could all relax quietly and spend the time looking far into the future of the human person on this earth, given the evil menacing pace of murderous militancy and insufferable insurgency.

"Chioma, can we suggest something?"

"Please go ahead, Funeka."

"Suppose we implanted an app on you so that we'll know wherever you are at any moment. Now that you're going to Jagowa and you say you might be held captive by BOND, why don't we fit you out so that we can keep track of you and you can be in constant communication with us. You know we have all we need to creep stealthily in situations where we might be hostages. Our work is risky and we are ready for all marauders."

"Yes, Funeka, you know I asked that we be fully equipped for our escape from any difficult situations and I think I'm getting into one such situation now. You will have to come to Nigeria and stay near me, no further than a hundred kilometers, within the farthest range of our best devices. I'm sure you have your ticket and visa for travel. As soon as I told you what I would be engaged in, in Nigeria, I knew you would go one step further and ensure my safety."

"Wow! That's my leader, our Leader." Funeka felt good in her soul that GAP would not be vanquished.

It was becoming clear to Chioma that providing assistance for the girl-child would inevitably involve dealing with the terrorists and she had made the necessary arrangements for the security of GAP should they have an encounter with the enemy. Many individuals who knew of their activities in different parts of the beleaguered world came to their assistance with large sums of money, especially when Chioma strongly indicated their possible activities in the field that might bring them face to face with the terrorists. Thus, GAP had close to five million US dollars in its kitty. Some of this, had been expended on remote sensing devices which Waithira and Cheryl had successfully used in Kenya and Syria and which would now be put to work in Nigeria.

December 14, 2014

Okeosisi

Chioma arrived in Lagos early in the morning on December 13 and after attending Mass, flew the same day to Enugu on an afternoon flight, and was met at the airport by her grandfather, Maduka. They had not seen each other for eight years now and Grandpa held his granddaughter to rib-breaking point. He released her, took a look at her, held her again, released her one more time, took a closer and longer look at her, and held her as though tomorrow would never come. Chioma was frightened, thinking she might never see her grandpa again, that something amiss may have happened to Ma Nneoma or that her presence in Jagowa might be pregnant with inconceivable danger.

"Grandpa, is everything okay, you seem apprehensive and hesitant, is anything wrong?"

"The only thing wrong, my dear, is my joy that makes my knees buckle, my lungs gasp for air and my heart eager to fly out of my chest. God bless you, my child, God bless you. How are you? You are hardly ever in one place; today you're in Kenya, from there to Somalia and tomorrow you are in far away Kosovo."

"Grandpa, you exaggerate, as is your wont. You've not seen me for eight years and so much has happened in that time. So, what happened two years ago seems like yesterday, and what happened last year seems like today to your ever contemplating mind. Your mind never rests."

"Welcome home, my child. I thank God for your life, for all you do for women and for the girl-child. Welcome." They drove from the airport and were home in thirty minutes. Ma Adiaha ran out to the front gate not waiting for them to come through.

"Oh, my Chioma, welcome, oh, I've missed you, I have longed for you so much my heart still aches from the pain of your long absence. Oh, how are you?" Ma Adiaha, her grandmother lovingly inquired.

"I'm fine Grandma; it's just that I'm very tired from the long flights. It was two years ago we saw each other in

Potomac. You were in the States for three months and I saw you frequently, almost every weekend. Sorry for my silence which may have made you feel my absence all the more."

"You're right my child; when I don't see you for a day it seems a year to me. Besides, it's one thing to be with you in the States and another thing to be home here with you."

"Ma, I've never been to Enugu, you might recall. All the while Pa Akadike was alive, it was Okeosisi and Okeosisi only. And when I came with my students eight years ago, we did not venture out of Okeosisi. We spent all our time there with Ma Nneoma. And you were with us to provide much-needed assistance to Ma—what with your irresistible Efik cuisine that the students consumed like Mother's milk. And you, too, do not spend much time in Enugu."

"You're right, my child, life in Igboland now is no longer what it used to be, so we end up spending more time here than in Okeosisi. Anyway, we'll be in Okeosisi tomorrow and you'll feel much more at home, especially when Ma Nneoma sees you."

Maduka took his granddaughter to Mass early Sunday morning, the day of their departure to Okeosisi. Chioma slept on their way and when she came out of the car, could not stop thanking God and glorifying him for the splendid architecture of the cathedral. Their two-hour journey to Okeosisi, from Enugu, took them through a rough road that was meant to be an expressway.

"Grandpa, is this the famous, now ignoble, Enugu-Port-Harcourt expressway, riddled with unending potholes? I can't believe my country can be this bad."

"That's Nigeria and her leaders for you, my child. Nothing from the oil money gets to the common man. It all ends up in the pockets of our disgraceful, greedy and ravenous government aristocrats who call themselves our leaders. You must know of all the the terrorism that has been sweeping through parts of northeastern Nigeria. It has been very visible in our capital, Abuja, and it hasn't ended yet. We've been in constant contact over the Kagara Debacle. How do you explain this? Where has all our money for development gone? BOND says they are for our development, and see what they have been doing, see what they call development, to Islamize Nigeria through terrorism. Terrorism is now the way to development! Ah! We're home."

Chioma quickly ran out of the car and made for Ma Nneoma's cottage. It was around noon and Ma would be wide awake at this time.

"Mama, Mama, it is me. It is Chioma." She knelt down at Ma's feet, rested her head on her knees and clasped her chest.

Ma shouted at the top of her voice, "Chioma, Chioma, Chioma, my child. Is it you? Am I in a dream or what is this? Chioma it is you. Hey . . . ! God Almighty come and see my Chioma-oooooh! She is here in Okeosisi. *Chukwunna ji Ike nine*, thank you for bringing my child home-ooooh! Oh God, thank you-ooooh!"

"Yes, my own Ma, God is wonderful, he has kept you for us."

"Now an old woman can go home. Akadike, my wonderful husband, your daughter has come home so that I can now come to you and join you. Remember, you told me I will not die until I see her. So, do you think I will ever see her again? I do not walk well any more and I do not see too well. But now Chioma is here, I will be well for at least one month. Chioma, I hope you can stay for more than one month. So you will be here when they bury me."

Ma Nneoma could not believe her eyes when she saw her great granddaughter who had not been home for the past eight years. She started telling stories of the visit of Chioma's students, how she gave them each an Igbo name bearing *"Chi"* either as prefix or suffix, and how they all devoured her dishes asking for more. She could not forget those days that she said made her feel young again, as though she was cooking for her husband, Akadike, and their children.

"Chioma nwam, please rest well, we shall continue in the evening. I am sure you and your grandpa have a lot to talk about."

"Ma, thank you. Grandpa and I will talk over many many things as he likes."

Ma Nneoma dropped off to sleep.

* * *

"Before we talk about your visit, please my child, tell me all you can about GAP: how you got involved in such a huge enterprise now of great benefit to the international community. It seems you're able to succeed where many countries fail. I even hear GAP is now well versed in negotiations with terrorists using all sorts of liaisons in many countries. Nations have come to develop strong affinities with you and have a global trust in you."

"Well, Grandpa, I'm sure Grandma must have told you about the visit of the sixteen members of GAP, when they came to see me in the States. I have already told you everything in my e-mail, but I know nothing would beat your hearing it from me myself."

Chioma told Grandpa the history of GAP from its formation to her acceptance to be its leader as well as the activities of the organization. She took time, however, to dwell on the problems of the girl-child in the countries where they have offered assistance and to the tremendous and unimaginable donations from a good number of notable people from different countries.

As to the negotiations they had been involved in, Grandpa already knew the details of their workings and how they evolved. It appeared he wanted to hear her little girl say, "Grandpa, we believe my great grandfather, Akadike, will ever be able to help us as an intercessor for his family." Grandpa was filled with joy basking in the memory of his great father, Akadike Okeosisi.

Grandpa now took time to drill Chioma on the pervading terrorism in northeastern Nigeria, in particular, the latest Kagara Debacle, which Chioma knew of from the news, but not once did he tell her the details of how the girls were able to escape. In particular, he made sure Chioma knew nothing about the involvement of BRAND in the whole effort to free the girls. He assured his dear granddaughter that she had nothing to fear: his brothers in northern Nigeria had been alerted of her arrival and were ready to do all they could for her safety. On her part, Chioma said nothing of what GAP was prepared to do for the girls of the Kagara Debacle.

CHAPTER TWENTY

October, 2014

Abuja

Ever since the abduction of the Kagara school girls, the whole country had been awash with tales of their imminent rescue. The following day after the abduction, that is, September 5, the president went on the air to assure Nigerians that the girls would be rescued within the following seven days and that the presidency would do all in its power to ensure that the safety of all Nigerians in school would be secured whatever may be the location of the school. He ended by telling everyone to go about their normal business without any fear whatsoever. All seemed fine at that moment and Nigerians felt confident the girls would be found and returned to their parents.

A month passed and there were no indications that the military would be able to solve the problem, now known as the Kagara Debacle. "We want our daughters back" filled the air and banners with this inscription straddled many a highway. Thirty parents, including some whose daughters were not abducted, drove to Abuja in a ramshackle bus chanting,

> "We want our daughters
> They went to school
> A gov'ment school
> They came for them
> In middle of night
> We want our daughters
> Bring them back home"

They drove round the city for about an hour before they were stopped by the police and asked to go home. At this point, they all came down and marched toward Aso Rock, the president's office and abode, wailing and chanting. On their way, one of them fell down and swooned. He was rushed to a hospital where he gallantly stood up after treatment. Fearing that they would likely be hindered from seeing the president, they changed their route and returned to the bus and went by Ahmadu Bello Way to Shehu Shagari Way from where they walked to the National Assembly, tired and exhausted. By this time, the crowd had swollen to close to a thousand men and women and children. Everybody on foot on the road joined them and the chanting grew threateningly vexatious. The police drove ahead of them providing some security from any miscreants who might seize the opportunity provided by the angry crowd to cause commotion. Quite unexpectedly, the police was understanding and shepherded the crowd to forestall any mishaps. One got the impression the police were supportive and would really like the parents to have the opportunity to lay their grievances at the feet of the legislators. Only later was the news relayed that the Inspector General of Police had directed that the parents be accorded every possible assistance they might need and that they should be afforded every necessary protection.

At about four in the afternoon, the Speaker of the House of Representatives, Alhaji Babatunde Ojesimi, came out to receive the aggrieved parents. Their leader, one Chief Jerome Okunade, approached him with a petition which he did not read: he could not for he was now weeping uncontrollably. The chanting resumed, "We want our girls! We want our girls!" In a deep show of sympathy, Alhaji Ojesimi embraced the chief, held him close and started chanting himself,

> *"We will find your girls*
> *They are our girls too*
> *We will find your children*
> *They are our children*
> *Give us some time*
> *And they will come home."*

A number of legislators followed the Speaker and huddled with the parents. One of them, Chief Mazda, could not restrain his agony and told the story of how his family had been faring since the abduction.

"Oga, sir, please don't be annoyed. I am suffering. My suffering is too much. We are all suffering. We have no money, so our friend gave us his bus to come to Abuja from Konduga. We have been in the bus for three days now. It broke down on the way two times and we slept in Lokoja last night. I have two daughters at Kagara, twins, Alice and Agnes. We are Christians. I have five children, three boys and my beautiful twins. I am a shoemaker, most of the time, I repair old shoes. People don't make new shoes nowadays in Konduga. My twins and two of the boys are in school, the last child is at home eating mama's food. All my money I use to pay school fees. They tell me, girl education is waste of money. I tell them, my boys, my girls, they are from the same God and the same mother. So, what I do for the boys, I do for the girls. I even do more for my twins. You can see I am not a young man; our children were born when I was already fifty years old. Oga, sir, my twins, Alice and Agnes, I hear perhaps they are married now, that Alice is even pregnant. I am dying. I can't eat, I can't sleep, all I do is wait for news about my twins. In the morning, I bring out my chair, I sit outside facing the road in case there is news. What we hear is the girls may be married, they are in Cameroon, they are in Chad, or Niger. Oh God, will I not see my twins again? Oh God, please free my girls, let them come home. I want to see my twins, I want to see Alice I want to see Agnes."

Mr. Speaker, Alhaji Ojesimi, was completely drained of any energy. He perspired profusely and kept wiping his face over and over again.

"Chief Mazda, Mr. Okunade, my good people from Konduga, we hear you. Believe me, we suffer with you: your daughters are our daughters. I am a father: I have two sons and a daughter, the youngest in the family. If I should miss her, I think I would just die. I would not know what to do. God will help us. We shall find the girls and you will see them again. We shall take care of you on this trip and make sure you get back home safely. Please be patient for a little while longer, not too long, I assure you, all will be well. Thank you."

He then instructed his personal assistant to book them into a decent hotel, take care of their meals until the following day, and take their vehicle to a good mechanic for repair. Each parent was to be given twenty thousand naira as allowance for their travel.

CHAPTER TWENTY-ONE

November, 2014

Okeosisi

It was November and there was no word anywhere of the imminent release of the girls. Dagogo felt the uncontrollable urge to move his troops into action. As he had said to himself, he would get the girls home before Christmas. It was now time to obtain some firearms which, if necessary, would be used in self defence. He reasoned that the arms and all equipment must be in the country before the end of November. But things took a different turn all of a sudden. He had to see Maduka and Billy without any delay. This time, Dagogo himself came to Okeosisi with Billy and his twelve staunch fighter-activists, and twenty men and four women of BRAND. The women were themselves cutthroat warriors, helped to instruct the activists on the ways of women and, whenever necessary, would dress the men as women as decoys. They all were in one bus, a fifty-seater bus, with Dagogo, dressed as a woman, sitting in the rear.

Billy asked everyone to wait in the outer-reception hut where they would be more comfortable and more easily catered for. He and Dagogo now went into Maduka's living room; Maduka was already seated awaiting their entrance, after giving directions for the rest of the party to be given lunch. It was about two in the afternoon.

"Welcome Billy, who is this your woman friend, and where is Dagogo, if I may ask?

"Yes, you may ask, you Fool. Take a closer look at this woman and tell us what you see."

Maduka would guess that the "woman" would be none other than Dagogo and, before his very eyes, 'she" took off her wig, her earrings, her long kaftan, her shoes, wiped the make-up off her face to reveal the good same Dagogo in beige pants, a long, white shirt with a blue handkerchief in the pocket to match his blue cap, which he had just donned on. Laughter galore!

"Dagogo, it's you. Welcome to our home. I'm beyond words to express my profound respects to you for coming to the Akadike sprawling estate. I can only say, God bless you."

"You Fool, it is not for you to say, "God bless you"; rather, bring us kola and the gods will bless us. Kola, fast."

"I'm sorry, Dagogo, I'm very sorry. Don't mind my good friend, he is too deep into social settings that he rushes into unnecessary protocol."

Dagogo responded to Maduka's welcome with a "thank you, my good professor."

Maduka sent for kola and gave them to Billy, who received them with thanks, passed them on to Dagogo who returned them to the principal, Maduka.

'let us pray", Maduka began, "God of Okeosisi, we thank you, we praise you; Almighty God, creator of the universe and all that is seen and unseen, we praise you, we adore you, we worship you. Pa Akadike, we thank God we are your children now left to carry on the good work you left behind. May all that is good and wonderful come to us, to Billy, a dear friend you gave me, to our hero Dagogo, whom you will use to heal the wounds of many suffering innocent people. Land of Okeosisi, that brings forth good fruits in season and out of season, watch over us your children, bless us your children."

Maduka gave eight kolas to Billy to be presented to his guests in the welcome hut, two to Dagogo, one to Billy himself, and then broke one to be shared between the three of them. Drinks and light refreshments of fried chicken and fresh fish were served: Dagogo asked for water, then Coke, Billy had his usual Guinness and Maduka Gulder. Adiaha came out, greeted the party and made to hurriedly leave to have lunch ready. But her dear husband interrupted her departure.

"My dear, you don't know the third person amongst us, Chief Dagogo Fubara of Nembe fame. Don't mind how he looks."

"You're most welcome, my chief." Adiaha responded and quickly took her excuse.

Billy did not know what Dagogo had in mind when he asked him and his activists to join him to Okeosisi; so he left him to say what the meeting was about. Maduka did not take kindly to this, insisting that discussions went better on well fed stomachs.

"My dear professor," Dagogo responded, "what I've come for is agitating my mind far too furiously for me to be relaxed. It must be disgorged straightaway and then we can eat all we want. So, please, allow me to tell you what is happening right now.

"I got word from my people in the field that the Kagara girls may have been all married off or sold into slavery, making it extremely difficult to trace them and find them. Whatever the case, there must be a way to know where the girls are, and find this way, I must. We have been able to locate the major sites where BOND lives, in tents spread over a wide area; and though in the beginning the girls were all pooled into no more than five tents, at a site close by, not far from the major BOND homes, those same tents were now all deserted. I knew I must get the news to you and Billy without delay.

"I asked Billy to invite to this meeting his young activists who have been working with us in parts of Nigeria where BRAND has interests. Twelve of them are here and will play a crucial role in the plan to release the girls. I know in the beginning, when we thought we might confront BOND head on, you wondered what they would be doing if they did not have much experience with armed insurrection. Well, they do, and now you have seen them. What this means is that all those who will now operate to rescue the girls are represented here, and there are more too in the back-up group: BRAND, with twenty armed men and Billy's twelve men and your good selves, sir, our employers, as you told us. We have more numbers, do not fear, up to a hundred in all; but we shall proceed with this initial thirty three in all."

"Where we would have needed a variety of modern ammunition, now the numbers are less for the plan I have in mind involves little shooting. I cannot tell you the details right now; all I can say is that we know where twelve or so of the girls now live, with their new-found husbands or slave masters. Using them as our sample, I have designed how they, as principals, would lead us to other girls near them, and from then on, we will use the same plan or adapt it to any new situation we may find. I can assure you that this battle for the girls' release is one we will surely win. Absolutely, nothing has been left to chance, believe me.

"To end this briefing all we need now is extra funds for the whole exercise which would surely last into December, even into Christmas, when I promised Chioma would have the released girls as a Christmas present. Thank you for the massive support we have received so far. We have used it well, and no one can beat us. As it is now, we may not be able to trace the girls who may have been married off to husbands or sold to men in our neighboring countries, Chad, Cameroon, or Niger. We do hit and run escapades across the border but we certainly don't want to antagonize our neighbours whose assistance we would need. Money will solve a lot of our problems: let me give you a hint, suppose we become second tier slave merchants, that is, we stealthily and secretly buy the girls back from their original owners, or become new husbands paying a higher dowry, how about that?

Maduka concurred with Billy that Dagogo should go ahead with his plan and made arrangements to provide him with the finance for the present operation. Dagogo made it clear what they needed most were pistols, notably XD-S 4.0 Single Stack 9 mm to be used at close range, where concealment would be of the essence, and some dozen or so UZI SMG sub-machine guns that may be required should the unexpected happen and their life was in grave danger. Dagogo apologised for going into the particulars of the ammunition saying he did so just so that Maduka and Billy might have a clearer idea of BRAND's requirements. Maduka had asked his brothers in the north-east, who would collaborate with Dagogo in all details, to provide logistical support in well veiled circumstances, given their experiences during the Biafran civil war. Dagogo did not say more and left for Kokoma by five in the evening. He and his men went to work and by early December the first fruits of their success were announced just as Chioma was on her way to Nigeria.

December 5, 2014
Bomdu, Bokoro State

BRAND had sprayed the sign of the cross on one hundred and fifty eight houses in Bomdu, a village of about one thousand people. Their intelligence reports had informed them that a number of the girls had been sold to some of the house owners who were all Moslems. On the morning of December 5, certain of the house owners were heard screaming and chasing after some girls who were fleeing, accusing them of trying to turn them into Christians. The girls all ran toward another town, Mudu, aided by the entire population who did not go along with their slavery or forced marriage. BOND had taken their hands off their case once they received their money; it was up to the new husbands or masters to do whatever they pleased with the girls, now their wives, or slaves, while they pursued new terrorist acts elsewhere. Twenty seven of the fifty girls from such houses escaped. Other girls also sold into slavery or married off, but not living in any of the sprayed houses soon followed suit and the whole town was in sudden and unexpected fury. On this day, a total of fifty three of the girls escaped and were quickly herded into waiting vehicles and taken to Kasikum, home to one of the Akadike brothers, Chidozie. It had been arranged that the girls would be taken from there to an undisclosed location where they would be housed and fed, and from where their parents may retrieve them. Much to the relief of all, in particular the parents, BOND showed no interest whatsoever in the plight of the girls once they had been disposed of. The news was carried on national TV and Maduka could breathe a sigh of relief. What about the remaining one hundred and five girls?

December 12, 2014

Waza, Bokoro State

Dagogo wondered whether he should use the same plan in the succeeding efforts to get the girls freed or try out something else, since the masters or husbands in other places would have learnt a lesson from his first success. He tried a different plan: just five days from the escape of some of the Kagara girls in Bomdu, well disguised as Alhaji Dankoko of Bomdu, he met with the Chief Imam of Waza mosque, a town about twenty kilometers from Bomdu. He gave the Imam six rams for his household, and a large amount of cash in addition. He said he was there on a peace mission and wanted Bomdu and Waza to cooperate more fully in the welfare of the people. To this purpose he was making a donation to the people of Waza and would do more in future once the two towns worked together. Dagogo, now Alhaji Dankoko, got the Imam to announce at the end of Friday prayers, that he would give a ram to each family in his village, and each head of household should come to his house the following day, Saturday, to collect his own. And they all did, about one hundred of them, and then took the rams home and tied them securely. In the dead of night, on Sunday, December 14, Dagogo's men stealthily went round to the homes, slaughtered the rams, left the carcass on the front door, and poured the blood on the floor. When they woke up on Sunday, the men who bought the Kagara girls, were surprised by the sight they beheld on the front entrances of their houses, and feared for their lives. For a good number of them, their first suspects were their wives or slaves whom they charged with the abominable crime of sacrificing the rams, a sacred job meant for men, accusing them to be Christians. One after another, the girls immediately took to their heels, crying and shouting loudly as they escaped. Some of the men whose wives were Muslims like themselves believed that some enemy had done it and would return to kill them. The Imam went to the village head and narrated what had happened, from Alhaji Dankoko, to the gift of the rams, and the escape of some of the girls. The village head, who already knew of the escape of the girls, and suspecting that Alhaji Dankoko must have a hand in the whole escapade, asked the Imam to quietly go home and not bother his head since he could not have gone round and sacrificed all hundred rams in one night. They saw this as a plot by Alhaji Dankoko to free the Kagara girls who had been bought or married off to new husbands. And they were satisfied the girls had found their freedom.

By this scheme, sixty five girls of the Kagara Debacle escaped to their freedom, from Waza, first to Wazabiu and were then transported to Mafiaya to one of the Akadike brothers, Nnamdi, who quickly sent them off to another secret location where their parents could come for them. This information was carried underground through trusted secure routes from person to person. All one hundred and fifty five parents were contacted from the beginning of the release effort to be ready to collect their children at locations to be identified. Although some leaks occurred, still BOND did not raise an eyelid to combat anyone they suspected of being the whistleblower.

CHAPTER TWENTY-TWO

December 16, 2014

Okeosisi

Chioma wrapped herself around her great grandmother, every chance she could get. She sat on her bed as they looked into the heroic past of her great grandfather, Akadike, their vast farms, the rows and rows of yams in the barn from where Chioma would roast one for breakfast on any given morning well soaked in fresh palm oil. Mama would ask after the students who had come to Okeosisi some eight years earlier, the last time she saw her dear child. Though she had forgotten their names, she remembered Chigozie, otherwise called Rosemary before the name change. In typical Igbo style, she started praying for her all over again that she may be ever more blessed by God, that she may see her children's children, that no evil may befall her, that she may be the one and only lover of her husband who will find in her the most beautiful and precious qualities of a woman. Mama would go on and on about Chigozie and would end with, "How is she now?"

'Mama, Chigozie is fine; she got married three years ago and has had a son and daughter in quick succession. Mama, you won't believe this: Chigozie married a Nigerian teacher she had met when she was here in Okeosisi. She fell so much in love with Okeosisi that she asked after decent young men who would be suitable partners. I introduced her to one, he came over to the United States just after their visit, and they were married after Chogozie graduated. I am very happy for them and visit them in New York whenever I can. And they come to see me too, in fact more often than I do. Chigozie is ever after me to teach her Igbo language, Igbo foods, Igbo names and the general customs of the Igbo. She is happy with her family and from all I can tell she has taken much after the Igbo."

"Oh, this is good, this is wonderful. Thanks be to God." On what would be her last visit to Mama before she left for Jagowa, Mama strictly instructed her dear child that she must return to Okeosisi again before leaving for Lagos, then to the States, telling her that it was forbidden for a child to travel to far away places without receiving the blessings of the elders on the morning of the child's departure. This was an abomination, she stressed, if the child's parents were alive, as they were in Chioma's case.

"Mama, how can you forget, I shall spend Christmas here in Okeosisi, so you will surely see me again and give me your heavenly blessings. "

"Is that so, forgive me my child. An old woman forgets everything."

It was December 16. Nothing more had been heard from Dagogo and the liberation of the last set of forty Kagara girls. Maduka, however, knew that whatever could be done was being done for their release. He said his morning prayers together with his dear Chioma and took her to Enugu from where she flew to Abuja.

Two days earlier, that is on December 14, sixteen ladies of GAP flew from London to Abuja and from there to an undisclosed location where they would rendevous with Dagogo and his BRAND fighters. Unknown to Chioma and to Maduka, they had been in constant communication with Billy and Dagogo ever since the news got out of the escape of the first set of Kagara girls. Now that he faced the far more difficult task of securing the release of the remaining forty girls, whose whereabouts could not be traced after months of searching with a fine tooth comb, Dagogo felt he needed the direct and immediate intervention of Chioma and of GAP. Awarah had taken charge of the proceedings in Cambridge, secured visas for their travel, and shepherded them all to Abuja from where Dagogo took them by night to an isolated village just fifty kilometres from Jagowa.

CHAPTER TWENTY-THREE

December 16, 2014

Abuja

Chioma drove with her grandfather to Enugu from where she took a flight to Abuja. She had scheduled to meet in Abuja with the representative of the United Nations High Commission for Refugees, UNHCR, as she had been advised not to venture outside Nigeria to meet some of the refugees in Chad and Cameroon in person. Transport snafus could not be overcome as the only mode of reliable movement would be in military and security vehicles. And the last thing Chioma would accept was any military assistance. Since they had woefully failed to secure the release of the Kagara girls, the military were anathema to her. She met with Mr. Charles Chalabesa from Namibia, at the Skylight Hotel for dinner, feeling utterly disturbed and distressed. She hoped she would be composed sufficiently to engage Mr. Chalabesa in difficult, intractable problems of Nigerian refugees fleeing from BOND.

"Good evening, Chioma, welcome to Abuja, your national capital and my home of choice in all of Africa. You have a formidable and fantastic country. How is College Park?"

"Thank you ambassador...."

"Hey, don't spoil a nice evening; please call me Charles. Yes, Charles I am to you."

'sir,...."

"That's even worse. Perhaps you're trying to tell me that your old African habits require that you show your respect to elders by not calling them by their first name."

"Exactly, Mr. Chalabesa, you took the words right out of my mouth."

"Ok, it seems that's the only way we can proceed. Tell me, how did you become what you are today, what we all see, what the world sees?"

The waiter arrived and asked what drinks they would have.

"Chioma, what will you have, let me tell you, I'll have a Chardonnay and then we'll pick Marguax for dinner, what do you say?

"Many thanks, Mr. Chalabesa, but I think I'll skip both and have just plain water."

"Please, help me celebrate this moment, this great moment when it seems all the Kagara girls just might find their freedom. The air is thick here in Abuja, and everyone is asking, "when will the rest of the girls escape? And now you're in Nigeria, and going to the lion's den where you just might be consumed; the rumours are you're here to secure the release of the girls. You may not know it, Chioma, but this is the only hotel in Abuja, perhaps in all of Nigeria, that serves Chateau Margaux, one of the finest wines in the world. Please let us share one."

"Again, Mr. Chalabesa, many thanks. Yes, I know that Chateaux Margaux is a very fine wine, and I have tried it on some occasions, but not today, I am sorry. If indeed I'm here to secure the release of the girls, as you say, then I need my entire thinking prowess for whatever it is worth. Wine would not help in this enterprise."

Mr. Chalabesa went ahead and asked for Chardonnay and some water and repeated his question that Chioma should please tell him how she was able to do the things she did. In front of an ambassador, who would be able to offer assistance to GAP, she decided to be fully candid with her host and tell him everything he cared to know. And so she started with her birth in the Akadike dynasty, to the heirloom, *Uzo,* of unsurpassed powers she inherited from her great grandfather, Akadike himself, to the immigration of her parents to the United States. The Chardonnay and water arrived and Mr. Chalabesa was served. He opened the bottle of water and served Chioma.

"Cheers, Chioma, cheers to Africa, cheers to the Victoria Falls." Mr. Chalabesa enthusiastically lifted his glass and wished his guest an entertaining evening.

The drinks came with side plates of starters, avocado pear laced with prawns marionetted in wine vinegar, herbs and spices, cheese nuggets, and almond nuts.

"Please continue, Chioma, we were at the stage where you found yourself in the United States."

"I studied at Georgetown University, Washington, D.C., for though I had admission into more prestigious institutions, my parents wanted me near them and so Georgetown it was. In the end, it was a happy choice for Georgetown took me in her arms and turned an ordinary student into a first class scholar. The school is known for this: "just bring yourself to us and see what we will make you", they tell anyone who wants to make something of themselves. Thanks be to God for Georgetown. It made me whatever I am and whatever I may be. The rest, I believe, you know, sir, that is my life at College Park."

The steward came to take their orders for dinner and again, Mr. Chalabesa asked what she would like and quickly let her know what he would have, steak with onion and mushroom sauce and baked potatoes. Chioma scanned through the menu and settled for boiled potatoes and steamed fish sautered in mushrooms and onions. Mr. Chalabesa asked for a Margaux and tried to persuade Chioma to share the wine with him though she was having fish.

"You've provided the reason, Mr. Chalabesa, I'm having fish, but you might remember I had opted out of any wines for the evening."

"If I might return to my earlier insinuation of rumours, perhaps they are right, you're here for something more than just deliver a lecture."

"Yes, Mr. Chalabesa, our meeting this evening confirms that; I'm here for something more than just deliver a lecture. I'm here to give you a cheque from the wonderful people of SURF, my students, with the superior support of the Board of Trustees of my university. I had hoped I would be able to gain entry into Cameroon to see, and interact with, some of the Nigerian refugees there." The ambassador was not expecting this generous, huge donation; instead, he thought Chioma wanted to know of the sore state of Nigerian refugees. He thanked her profusely stating that the funds would all be used for local purchases to give the refugees real Nigerian foods and native clothing they were used to.

"All hope is not lost, Chioma, hope is still alive. You're here, are you not, the refugees are all passing before you whether or not you get to see them."

'mr. Chalabesa, you've hit the nail on its head: the refugees are all passing before me; refugees all over the world from Syria to Cambodia, Somalia to myanmar. Yes, Mr. Chalabesa they walk past me, shreds of their former selves, deserted and forsaken, even forgotten by their fellow humans, indifferent, feelingless, otherworldly."

Their meals arrived and again Mr. Chalabesa asked Chioma if she could say a little bit more about GAP.

"Where does your energy come from, Chioma, please how do you find this enormous energy? You work with your whole life on the line, you give all of yourself to whatever you're doing, and those who work with you love you so much they are prepared to die for you. How do you inspire such loyalty? I can't believe it."

"This is a question for the wonderful women of GAP who love me immensely. I certainly do not deserve their love. I can only say, Mr. Chalabesa, that GAP offers me a unique opportunity to live each day fully, cheerfully and happily serving the girl-child, any girl in distress, any girl who seeks education and is denied the freedom to pursue her dreams in a simple world, a world of love and caring and giving. That's my world, that's the world of every girl who suffers ignominy, rape even murder, because she stands up and wants to make something of herself."

It was getting late and Chioma wanted to get to bed early so she could catch her morning flight to Maiduguri from where she would be picked up and taken to the University of Jagowa.

'mr. Chalabesa, this has been a joyous occasion for me and the dinner was excellent. Thank you most kindly and here is the cheque I have for you for the refugees fleeing from BOND massacres. I'm sorely disappointed I won't be able to go across to Cameroon to see some of them."

"Well, well, Chioma, I'm just doing my duty. You make my load all the lighter and more bearable. It's not the money, it's your heart, your will, your passion. Yes, you will surely see the refugees in Cameroon tomorrow. Our light aircraft will take us in the morning into our refugee camps there and you will see them as they are."

He then opened the envelope with the cheque and right before his startled, unbelieving eyes was the sum of one hundred and thirty thousand US dollars staring him in the face.

"Chioma, this is enormous. I'm speechless. You know individuals do not give us any money, even private organizations like SURF, an activity of your students. The whole world will hear this; I'll make sure about that. Thank you, thank you immensely. The refugees will know they are cared for, that they are loved, and that their sorry state would only get better and better. I will tell them what you're doing and how SURF has been able to come in with this huge assistance."

"You're the one doing all the work, Mr. Chalabesa. We are most thankful."

"Well, Chioma, Leader of GAP."

"Please spare me this Leader talk, Mr. Chalabesa."

"I'm sorry, I mean no harm. The flight had been already set to leave Abuja at 8 a.m., so let's be in the lobby at 7 a.m. for the drive to the airport. Ok?"

"Good night, sir."

"Good night, Chioma, and have a good night's rest. Oh, we shall be able to take you to Jagowa; there's a runway there we can use. So you'll be in Jagowa by 5 p.m. I'll tell the Vice-chancellor of these recent changes. And sorry, how are you getting back, can my car take you back?"

"It's okay, Mr. Chalabesa, I came with a car from Nagode Women's Centre, and it is waiting for me downstairs. Thank you very much and good night, sir."

CHAPTER TWENTY-FOUR

December 17, 2014

Pakomba, Cameroon

Chioma had wanted to see the refugees just as they rose from their sleep to get the true and deep feeling of their desperate existence. And, indeed, their morning faces bore the story of dejection and utter abandonment; even as they received some assistance, they felt unloved, and a sense of decay and death pervaded the camp. With the aid of an interpreter, she was able to speak with Shasia, a young girl about twelve years old who had managed daringly to escape from invading BOND terrorists, now in a refugee camp in Pakomba in Cameroon. Chioma carefully studied her countenance: what must have been a flowing head of hair was now rusty, twisted beyond loosening, sandy, despoiled and wet from sweat, even in the morning.

Chioma tried to comb the hair with her fingers, to loosen the coils and let fresh air blow through them and give them a new life, but the coils, as it were, resisted any attempt to tease out their one-on-one bonds. They held on tenaciously to each other oblivious of any sense of comeliness or sightliness. Her eyes were as vacant as they were foreboding, boring relentlessly into an uncaring world, hopelessly searching for minds that would hold them to heart. They were no longer eyes for seeing, but nails that pierced into your soul in wonder that the beautiful world she once loved could be so overrun by heedless and needless terrorism. Chioma would no longer be the same from looking at her. She gently pulled her jaws apart and poor Shasia screamed in pain: the teeth were pasted with strands of the last meal of soaked garri, the spaces in between filled with the decayed rot of past gone meals. The gums had lost their erstwhile blood-red glow, and were now dark and broken.

Where there were once fleshy cheeks, Chioma would only feel the firmness of bones as she stroked Shasia's face with the tender love of a mother. Her face was now all jaws. And her neck rose in defiance to uphold her freedom and her dreams. She had received a green t-shirt with the inscription, "Gift of Sweden" that sheltered her from the ferocious bites of mosquitoes and other bugs. They were whistling in her ears, in Chioma's ears too, causing them to keep turning their heads from right to left, and left to right, to fend off the unrelenting nuisance.

Shasia's legs were mere broomsticks that could barely support her frame: she would stand and sit, sit and stand, and could not stand up erect for no more than five minutes or so. Her toes were covered with wounds and the nails long and forsaken.

She would tell Chioma the story of her escape. Some people who must be BOND people had furiously rushed into their house, a little house with three little rooms, one for her parents, one for her brothers and one for herself and her sister. Her parents were shot dead in the middle of the night. The moon was out and she could make out the profile of the window in her room. She saw one of the men outside walk across the window and she waited until he passed and went to the house adjoining theirs. Her two brothers were not touched but they quickly ran into her room and seeing they were girls they started shooting. She squeezed herself through the window as one of the bullets fell on one leg, another on her back and a third just missed her head.

There was no time for Shasia to take her sister with her and with all the bullets raining on both of them she feared she must have been killed and simply sought a way out of this horrendous and macabre murder. For reasons short of a miracle, the terrorists did not see her escape through the window. She ran as far as her bleeding body could carry her, not knowing where she was running to. Some other homes in their neighbourhood came under BOND's gunfire and poor Shasia did not know in which direction to run. But run she did until she fell into the stream that supplied water to the village.

For safety she swam to the deeper end and rested there while listening for any raging gunshots. And the gunshots rained on unabated. Soon, Shasia was joined by another girl, then another girl, and now there were three of them all buried on the deep end of the system where they would lie low undiscovered. Two of the murderers walked into the stream and soon walked out again when they neither saw anyone nor heard any tell-tale sounds. Shasia was relieved and so were her fellow escapees who had maintained absolute silence for the five minutes or so they were at risk of being discovered.

It was still night and after what seemed like an eternal interregnum, Shasia and the girls came out of the river and resumed their escape through woods that shielded them while suffering the pestilence of biting insects. Bedraggled and wasted, without food and sorely in pain, and sorely in need of medical attention, Shasia and her new found friends continued relentlessly until it was morning; and fearing they might be seen and apprehended, they hid safely in the thick wood.

She wondered, 'would they be there until it was night, that is, for another twelve hours or so without food, without water, and without any source of succour'? Needing all the help she could get, she convinced her friends that she must continue to a road where she might be rescued. Her friends, wondering why they themselves would not be the assistance that Shasia needed, tore their clothes and used the strips as bandage for her bullet wounds. Fortunately the bleeding had stopped and it seemed the bullets were harmless where they were lodged, for Shasia's pain suddenly subsided.

After five days of untold misery without food or water, they fortuitously found themselves in a totally strange environment, one whose language they did not understand without any words like theirs. They were met by five young men who must have been on their way home after a day at the farm for they had cutlasses and hoes and some head pans.

Realizing their newly discovered strangers did not understand a word they were saying, they immediately came to the conclusion that these must be refugees fleeing the horror of BOND in Nigeria. Everyone in their village of Chomba, who had heard of BOND, was ever ready to help anyone fleeing from their catastrophic killings. They walked Shasia and her company to the refugee camp of UNHCR at Pakomba who received them and were told of their heroic escape.

Chioma spent over thirty minutes sitting with Shasia and as she told her story, others joined her to listen, to cry, all of them holding Chioma by her hands, her feet, the helm of her dress, or whatever part of her body they could access. The camp was heavily populated by girls, mothers, and their children, who had luckily escaped. Chioma wondered how she would be able to return to Jagowa for her lecture: all she wanted to do was to sit with the children, listen to them, to be part of their grief and give them whatever psychological and mental assistance she could. Words were not enough, she had to live with them and care for them, but how could she do this?

"Chioma there are two other camps I would like you to see. Of course, there is not much you can physically do here. We of UNHCR are on top of the quagmire and, as you can see for yourself, the refugees are receiving humane treatment and their mood can be described as hopeful. But we are overwhelmed by the suffering, the continuous influx of refugees; as many as a hundred flee to us every day. And we have not yet turned anyone back; how could we?"

Chioma was devastated since she could not give the refugees the personal attention they all desired. It was not just providing them with food, though this was the most immediate need to keep body and soul alive. These were human beings without love and caring, who had lost every sense of dignity, of being human. Many had no idea where their parents might be, and many women had no idea either where their children might be. Of course, their husbands had been murdered by the bloodthirsty BOND. She nevertheless must give them hope and sustain their belief in the human bond of love and friendship.

What could GAP do in this regard? The only true answer lay in annihilating BOND. She must pull herself together and offer herself as best she could right there and then.

Chioma started singing inviting the whole camp to join her. Unfortunately, for five minutes or so, there were no subscribers; no one felt strong enough to sing. Then Shasia stood up and started clapping and dancing, and soon the rest joined her, with some new-found energy and enthusiasm clapping where they were too feeble to dance. Chioma went on from one song to another, making up the words in pidgin English as she went on. This continued for thirty minutes or so and soon Mr. Chalabesa came up with food rations of bread and rice and slivers of dry fish from Lake Chad. Chioma was greatly troubled and asked Mr. Chalabesa if he could arrange to have the children taught saying GAP would pick up the cost.

"I'm sorry, Chioma, it's not just a matter of costs, it is more a matter of getting the necessary hands for such an enterprise. Where would we get the teachers? The nearest school here is about two to three kilometres away and we are here at the mercy of the kind villagers who come in from time to time to offer some assistance of one kind or another, from religion to fashion."

"What do you mean by fashion?" Chioma asked.

"Were you not the one trying to tease out Shasia's twisted hair? Were you not overly depressed by her sour look? Yes, the women come here and give the girls a bath and bring them some clean clothes, cut their nails when they can and clean their teeth. They work hard to make the girls feel loved and wanted. And all these they do on their own, in their own time. Of course, they don't come as often as we would like."

December 17, 2014

Tagore, Cameroon

To save time, they quickly flew to two other camps also in Cameroon, as it was now late in the afternoon and they must return to Jagowa before nightfall as the airstrip there was in a poor state. The Tagore camp had more of young men and mothers with few babies and children. The men were of great help in fetching water from a nearby stream, even hunting for wild animals with makeshift bows and arrows for food. Their mood was uplifting as they moved around in song and laughter oblivious of their sad fate: they had decided to make the best of their sad lot.

"Well, Chioma, you can see the difference here. Even without our doing much, these kids and the women have developed life-sustaining skills and they are filled with enormous joy that they have been able to escape from death. So everything else is a mere trifle and they go on with their lives with a large dose of hope. Besides, the local community is ever at hand with food and medicine even without any medical supervision. It seems the local native doctors know how to treat the commonest disease of the camp, namely dysentery and we let them go on with their cures."

There was no time for Chioma to get on to one-on-one chat with anyone as she was ever involved with their stories and this took time. But she could not help asking a young boy his name, his village, his parents, whether he was in school, and his class, and what he wanted to be when he grew up. Wogobio gave a good account of himself saying his parents had both been killed by BOND, that he was in his final year in school, and that he wanted to be a medical doctor when he grew up. He was certain he would be able to return to school as soon as BOND was defeated and that nothing would stop him from achieving his dream. His poor English was understandable and the boys around him all cheered and hailed him as their hero. Chioma took a good look at him and swore to herself GAP would train this boy to be a doctor.

A thought kept gnawing at her: what about the rest, who will take care of them? What sort of promises would she make to herself? Yes, she felt, GAP would have to work with local authorities in their chosen places of interest to provide schools up to the secondary level.

December 17, 2014

Mubi, Cameroon

The visit to Mubi was fast and brief. Once the plane landed, Mr. Chalabesa was besieged with loud greetings and screams. Some children, who could manage it, ran after the plane as it was taxiing to a halt. In all, there was a feeling of togetherness and sharing. It turned out Mubi was the oldest camp, then over three years old and there were some arrangements for schooling and better distribution of foods. Chioma felt Mubi must be a showcase for UNHCR which they use when dealing with donors and so asked Mr. Chalabesa: "this must be your pride which you display to the world for all to see and applaud your efforts. Why, you could have brought me here to impress me and gain immediate respect."

"Yes, I could have brought you here, Chioma, if I indeed wanted to impress you with our efforts. But I have read a lot about you and GAP, and my brief encounter with you last night left me without any iota of doubt that you are a deeply caring person, and that I should, therefore, take you where the pain was greatest and the suffering unbearable. And you have not let me down. It is so much easier for us to discharge our duty to GAP and use all your funds wisely down to the last penny. You have seen where the money would immediately go, and where it certainly won't go, for now. I am happy I now know you."

Chioma was flustered and could barely mutter, "thank you, Mr. Chalabesa."

As they were walking to the aircraft, a little girl, no more than eight years old, ran after them, got close to Chioma, and gave her a handful of wild flowers with the words, "for you."

Chioma would have asked her her name but she didn't. She turned to Mr. Chalabesa and said, "her name, 'my Unknown Friend.'"

December 16, 2014

On the night of December 16, Dagogo could not quite find a way to free the rest of the forty girls still in BOND's hands. His intelligence had reported that the girls were all lodged in tents occupied by BOND's leaders and had been turned into sullied sex slaves, their only duty being to satisfy the aberrant sexual desires of their masters. They were, thus, under tight security for they were BOND's prized property that assuaged whatever may be their pains or disappointments. They lived under perilous fear of death at any time.

December 17, 2014

Kasikum, Bokoro State

Dagogo realized that to liberate the girls he must engage in a deadly shootout with BOND. His intelligence had also revealed that they were under the armed guard of no less than fifteen raging terrorists. To free them was possible but Dagogo feared he would lose some of his men in the bitter bloodshed that would ensue. This was a risk he was prepared to take.

Unknown to anyone, Fern came in to the rescue. He had fallen out with the rest of the spirits and now was on GAP's side. He wanted a new heaven. Thus, BOND had lost its spiritual moorings and could now be had for a kobo. With a handful of thirty well-armed men and three women. Dagogo entered the Gusu enclave where the girls were held. Surreptitiously, with small illumination from their torch lights, they engaged the terrorists and were ready to start shooting them one by one. It all looked incredibly easy. But no one fired a shot: in fact, BOND's militants dropped their guns and ran in one and the same direction. The girls in fear, fled in the exact opposite direction right into Dagogo's army's waiting arms. Totally in a daze, his men immediately huddled together and ran with the girls to a sandy road, to a site they had prepared to shield them.

Ahead of his onslaught on BOND, Dagogo had brought two buses with him to take the girls and his men to safety in Kasikum, to Chidozie Akadike's residence, a distance of about one hundred and seventy kilometres that they covered in the dark, through the night, arriving by sunrise. The news of their release was on the local radio and on national TV, to wild celebrations all over the country. The girls were in all sorts of pain and sorrow: some were pregnant, many bore the marks of shackles on their legs, and they all suffered from the trauma of rape and wanton and incessant sexual assaults. They were a sorry lot and were taken first to Kasikum hospital, then to Kagara hospital without delay. As soon as the girls were safely delivered to Akadike, Dagogo and his men quickly left the scene to rendezvous with the ladies of GAP housed with Onyema Akadike in Damboba from where they would easily travel to Jagowa. The girls' parents later made their way to the hospital to see their children and ascertain that the story of their successful release was indeed true. They were told by the hospital staff that Dagogo would like the girls kept in hospital till he returned for them in a few days time, before Christmas Day.

December 18, 2014

University of Jagowa, Jagowa State

Chioma went into her lecture, *Of Language and Culture,* in the opulent and ornate Ahmadu Bello's Hall confidently beaming with smiles and aplomb that immediately pervaded the lecture theatre as the students were clapping and cheering with shouts of "Girls are precious. Girls are precious". The chairman, with gusto and charm acknowledged their cheers over and over again. Finally the lecture commenced and Dr. Ijeoma strode into her subject with authority. From the history of the Sokoto Caliphate, to the Benin and Oyo kingdoms, to Igbo oracles, Chioma painted a picture of unity even in conquest, a culture of great pride in achievement and togetherness in the formation of the country known as Nigeria. She stressed without ceasing that language was not about words but about the outpouring of the goodness of the heart. In this respect, she saw language as a culture that defined all that was noble about the people of Nigeria. She ended with a poem:

> Language speaks that we may live
>
> Hear what is said, live what we hear
>
> From Jagowa to Kokoma
>
> Bokum to Okeosisi
>
> All Nigeria one blood
>
> One language supreme.

The chairman invited the audience for comments and questions which Chioma superbly handled. The lecture over, he stood up gallantly to the full benefit of his compelling stature and stoutly announced:

"Ladies and gentlemen, it gives me boundless joy to invite into the theatre the charming, wonderful ladies of GAP, Girls Are Precious."

Chioma was wild with joy at this astonishing turn of events; she could not believe her eyes as nothing had prepared her for this overwhelming spectacle. How could this have happened? Awarah stood up, and spoke for the group: "Mr. Chairman, sir, we are here to accompany our great leader home, back to Okeosisi. Whatever our leader does, and wherever she goes, there are we with her. And, as our leader has said, the good people of Bokaro State have our support for the girl-child. Thank you, sir."

The chief officer of Nigerian Security Services who led the party to the meeting walked up to the chair and obtained his permission to escort Chioma and the ladies of GAP with him to security vehicles waiting outside. All seventeen ladies including Chioma were safely taken to the vice-chancellor's chalets.

Chioma was rhapsodic, mumbling: "May God my maker bless you and watch over you." They all responded "Amen." She was short of words and did not know what next to say. But the ladies were all watching her, astounded at all she could do, directly and indirectly, for Awarah had given them the details of the rescue of the Kagara girls, and the end of the Kagara Debacle owed to the conversion of the evil spirit, Fern. They were gathered in the living room of the vice-chancellor's lodge and light refreshments and drinks were served. Professor Idris Tahir, the vice-chancellor, raised his glass in the spirit of this sensational jollity and said, "Cheers! . . . There is so much on my mind this evening we could have Chioma give us the lecture all over again to capture much of what I'd like to say. Let me doff my hat to you: you show the world what loyalty in leadership is all about. You have all left your jobs and duties to be here in Jagowa, a place totally unknown to you, to be with your Leader, Dr. Chioma Ijeoma. This is a tale for the story books; where in the world do you hear of such friendship and love for a leader, for one another, in an organisation? No, you don't hear of it, not even as a rumour. You truly live up to your name, "Girls Are Precious". We are in your debt. Nigeria is in your debt. The world is in your debt and the girl-child, wherever she may be on the face of this earth, shall prosper, thanks to you. Please enjoy yourselves, be happy."

"Chioma, I imagine the implants are still on you for I'm still able to follow you; we're all able to follow you."

"I'm sorry to disappoint you, Funeka. I have no implant on me! I let you go ahead and do what you did because it was a good idea at the time and I wanted you to feel better composed to let me go into Nigeria at these troubled times. No, I do not have the implants. They were all discarded before I came here."

"I see," Funeka responded, "then how was I able to track your movements successfully?"

"Funeka, truly I don't know. Let us thank God for his kind assistance." They all concurred. They spent the night in endless talk running from the Akadike's to Maryland to Cambridge and back to Akadike.

"Well, tomorrow, we all go to Okeosisi by road shepherded by Dagogo and BRAND. Your grandfather, Maduka, and his dear friend, Billy, will be waiting for us. So, Chioma, brace yourself for our Christmas party. There will be two buses here, one for us, one for Dagogo and BRAND, all the way to Okeosisi. We should be there before sunset if we set out by 6 a.m." Baraah took over the arrangements and gave the directions.

CHAPTER TWENTY-FIVE

December 19, 2014

Okeosisi

As she had said, they were all at Okeosisi by 6 p.m. following instructive guides from Dagogo, who left with his BRAND comrades for Kokoma without saying hello to Maduka or Billy. Christmas was getting nearer and nearer each passing day and Dagogo still had a lot of work on hand.

Maduka and Billy eagerly awaited their arrival with every car that passed their gates. Finally the bus drove into the colossal Akadike compound which wore all the garlands and joy of the Christmas season.

"You Fool, won't you go out and welcome your guests. You sit here in your living room and wait like a king ready to receive his subjects."

"Am I not a king? Have you not made me a king?"

"So what are you king of?"

"I'm king of all I survey, and that includes you, Billy."

"Is that all the poetry you know, You Fool, "all you survey", when you can't see beyond your nose."

"Ok, ok, enough is enough. Let's go out to meet them."

"You go alone, and when you bring them in then you introduce me to them, that's how it's done."

Chioma ran into the arms of her grandfather, Maduka, and knelt down for his blessings.

"God bless you, my child, God bless you with all the blessings in the heavenly places and from Zion may he watch over you."

Chioma rose with thanks and while they were still standing in the outer courtyard, all the wonderful ladies of GAP bowed in respect and asked for Maduka's blessings too.

"God bless you my wonderful children. May he grant you your heart's desires and make good all your plans."

"Amen", they all responded. It was late but Pa Akadike's grave stood out in all its solemn magnificence. Chioma took her guests to see her great grandfather and say hello to him, which they all did, each in her own way. Baraah just stood there beside Maduka, holding him by the hand.

"This is a great family, sir. See all you've been able to do. We are all astounded. We can't believe we are now part of the Akadike dynasty. May Allah be praised."

"Amen, and may Allah help us to do more according to his will."

They returned to the living room and Billy stood up to his commanding two metre height much to the delight of Chioma who took over the introduction from her grandfather.

"My dear GAP comrades, here is Profesor William Briggs, whom we fondly call Uncle Billy. He's been Grandpa's close friend ever since their days at University College, Ibadan. He and Grandpa were the brains that brought the end of the Kagara Debacle. He is a father to me and now to you. I can now tell you that SureGas, the company where the kidnappees Emeka and Bjorn worked, and which in the beginning wanted to provide BRAND with some maintenance funds, later withdrew their offer. Instead, to shield them from any direct contact with BRAND, they gave the funds to GAP at the instance of Uncle Billy, that is, Professor Briggs. Grandpa organized the necessary logistics for the safe delivery of the Kagara girls to the homes of his brothers in northeastern Nigeria, once Dagogo and his army were able to obtain their freedom."

In his usual humility, Billy would respond, "Thank you, my child. All is well."

Adiaha came out to meet Chioma and her GAP women. "Welcome, welcome to Okeosisi, welcome to the Akadike home."

"That's Grandma, who keeps my head from running off my head."

They all greeted Grandma and one after another wanted to sit with her on the large sofa but it could only take five of them squeezed like slaves on a slave boat. Laughter and gaiety reigned supreme and though she could hardly breathe, Grandma was overwhelmed with the joy of this sumptuous moment which she had never experienced in all of her long life so far. When she tried to extricate herself to arrange for drinks and food and their lodgings, they resolutely refused her exit, their thoughts drifting from the girl-child to emergent womanhood. To look at them, you would think they had all lived with Grandma all their life, so dearly did they hold on to her and falling over each other to congratulate her for her rich and exotic life.

After what looked like eternity, Grandma freed herself from their effervescent hold to see to everyone's welfare.

Chioma quickly ran to Ma Nneoma to tell her she had come back as she promised she would. She was asleep at the time but when Nkeiru saw it was Chioma knocking at the door, she quickly got up and helped Ma into her living room.

"Hey! Chioma *Nwam*, Chioma my dear child, how are you? Oh, I have missed you like life itself. Oh, an old woman thanks her God she is alive to see her child doing all the work you are doing. Your grandfather always tells me you are in that katakata (troubled) area of Nigeria, that you brought many women to Nigeria to help us. Oh God, I thank you. I thank you plenty plenty."

"Ma, the women are here in Okeosisi all of them big-big women in the university. Ma, they are wonderful and they have come with me to Okeosisi, to breathe the Akadike air, and be with us for Christmas. Ma, I am very, very happy."

"Well, tomorrow will be tomorrow when I see them. Tomorrow you will see what an old woman can do. Oh God, thank you oooo!"

Though they had been on the road for over twelve hours and were tired and scraggy from the dust, they were not at all interested in cleaning themselves up and, instead, rolled around on the floor like little children celebrating their birthday.

Drinks and food arrived and they ate and drank with fervid gusto devouring pounded yam and *edikaikong* at lightning speed. Grandma had to prepare some more and delightfully watched her GAP guests do justice to her kitchen with mouthfuls of joy.

They slept off on the sofa, some on their chairs and some on the floor. Chioma pressed and pressed for them to go to their rooms but they did not want to leave the warmth and immediacy of the Akadike romance. Totally immersed in this bohemian extravaganza, all sixteen women spread out over the place, Chioma found a pillow for head and slept off on the floor till the morn.

"Did you see all those girls hawking all sorts of goods on the highways on our way here? Cheryl asked Chioma the following morning after breakfast. "There were so many of them, about ten to one boy. Not only were they not in school but they may become easy sex preys to depraved and capricious travellers along the way. This is most horrible, what are we going to do? We can't see this happening and not do anything. Chioma, please come up with a saving scheme for these unfortunate souls before they are turned into a social nuisance. We have seen this in many other parts of the world, some are even worse. But this is Nigeria, supposedly, Africa's great hope. What will we do?" Cheryl was sorely grieved and wanted her leader's input.

"Let us take it one step at a time, Cheryl. We've just come through a most gruelling exercise in combatting BOND. As you know, their insurgencies and terrorist catastrophes all aim to destroy the power of knowledge and drive the society back to the doldrums of ignorance, the girl-child being the worst sufferer of their exploits. Yes, we will act and act decisively in concert with the government and all willing partners to whom knowledge is supremely the blood that runs through civil societies. Yes, Cheryl, we surely will act."

Chioma took her guests to see Ma Nneoma. She had got up much earlier than usual and asked Nkeiru to get her finest 'George' wrapper with a matching blouse. Her son Maduka had given her a present of golden lace wrapper and a sparkling white lace to go with it. Nkeiru brought these and got Ma superbly dressed. Her head-tie was a problem and Nkeiru ran quickly to Grandma Adiaha who swiftly tied the damask piece into an elegant crown for Ma's queenly head. She wore flat shoes and was all set to receive her great granddaughter Chioma and her retinue.

There was not much room to accommodate all of GAP's women in Ma's petit living room but the wonderful ladies made an old woman happy sitting one on the other, some at her feet and some hugging tightly to Chioma.

After the introductions, all went silent for an interminable period of three minutes or so. Ma did not say a word. She got up and started singing welcoming her children and thanking them for all they have done.

"Umum ndewo nu

Chukwu gozie unu

Unu emeka

Ndewo nu."

Ma moved to singing some noble Okeosisi songs and now broke into a solo dance, more like a shuffle, as she could barely stand let alone move her legs. There was little room for her movements so they all stood up by the walls immersed in Ma's exultations and immeasurable joy. Nobody had seen Ma dance, since her dear husband passed away and now Chioma wondered if Ma would be following her loving partner in a flight from earth. But no, her songs changed and she was now calling Mother Earth to witness all the wonders of her adorable life. Finally she leapt up in amazing delight and her great granddaughter grasped her and held her firmly by her chest squeezing out all the air in her weary lungs. Chioma was beside herself with heavenly rejoicing and all of GAP with her. They surrounded her and formed a circle around Ma. Holding each other's hands, they joined Chioma in her grand Okeosisi dance to her ancestors paying tribute to all that was noble and wholesome in the land. Ma sat down out of exhaustion breathing heavily but happily. Chioma rushed a glass of water to her. She continued the dance with the rest of GAP lifting this Igbo dance into a rousing crescendo.

'*Ma ndewo, Ma imene.* Ma thank you. Ma, you have done us proud," they sang and sat down for Ma's blessing but not before she had given them new Igbo names. She had wanted to cal them by names with Chi either as prefix or suffix, as she did when Chioma came to Okeosisi with her students some seven years ago. But try as hard as she could, no names came out of her memory. And Chioma did not want to get into any of this: Ma must do it any-which way she pleased. Finally she pleaded:

"You are all big women like my Chioma. You are all to be called Chioma, no difference from my own child. You are all mine. You belong to me."

They cheered and screamed their mountainous pleasure dancing each according to her music. Ma laughed and laughed and since she knew they would be seeing her before leaving Okeosisi she got up to take her leave.

"Ma, not yet; please take a picture with us." Waithira requested. Chioma wanted to be in the picture so she stepped out to call one of the Akadike grandchildren in the compound to help out. They even went as far as requesting that Ma should please take a separate picture with each of them. Ma was far too filled with joy to say no, basking in the glow of love and friendship that lit the air.

The GAP ladies went to their sports, some to tennis, some to swimming, some to table tennis and some to basketball while Chioma walked over to Uncle Ugwuoma's house where Grandpa and his friend Billy were staying.

December 23, 2014

Okeosisi

Dagogo had gone back to Kagara hospital on December 23, five days after the released girls had been admitted to the hospital. Having obtained the consent of their parents to take them to Okeosisi and the assurance of the hospital that they were fit to travel the following day, Dagogo and his team drove all forty girls in their two thirty-seater buses to Okeosisi on less frequently used roads to avoid public attention as much as possible. The tortuous journey took more time than usual and they finally arrived Okeosisi by 6 a.m. on Christmas Day, before anyone was awake.

Chioma had invited her guests to join her at midnight mass on Christmas Eve and they all gladly agreed, including Baraah and the rest of the non-Catholics. They were deep in slumber when the buses lumbered into the courtyard. The girls started chanting at the top of their voices, Merry Christmas, Pa Akadike, Merry Christmas Dr. Ijeoma, Merry Christmas GAP. Maduka and Billy both came out in their pyjamas wondering what the commotion was all about. Seeing Dagogo in full regalia of the Nembe prince he was, they quickly returned to the house and put on some street clothes.

"What do you think is going on?"

"What do you think is going on? Don't you see the girls? Don't you think they are some of the girls Dagogo promised Chioma he would free before Christmas Day? Look at them, see how happy they are. Yes, sir, this indeed is a Merry, Merry Christmas."

Dagogo greeted Chioma whom he was meeting in the flesh for the first time.

"Merry Christmas, Chioma! Here is my Christmas present to you: I promised I would liberate all 158 girls by Christmas which I did. Here are the last forty; BOND has been decimated they have scattered into the bush. Again, my sweet child, Merry Christmas." Then, he quickly excused himself, and made straight to Maduka's house and slumped into bed in one of the bedrooms.

Chioma had sensed what might be happening and ran out to the courtyard even ahead of her grandpa and his friend, Billy. Her first words: "Gaudium cum pace: Joy and Peace" followed by a basketful of prayers all ending in "Thanks be to God."

The girls were sweetly led to the outdoor reception hall that comfortably holds over a hundred people where mattresses were thrown on the floor for them to sleep if they wished while arrangements were being made for their baths and breakfast. Of course, they were all comfortably seated. Nothing had prepared the Akadike family for this mountainous encounter, their all proven and faithful prowess at catering notwithstanding. They were simply overwhelmed by the immediacy of this unexpected and spectacular occasion. Surely, all would be taken care of. Fortunately everyone had attended midnight mass and were now available for any duties. Dagogo sluggishly walked with Billy and Maduka into the house and quickly retired to a room to sleep.

Many Akadike children, grandchildren, and great-grandchildren were home for the Christmas celebrations and quickly set about cooking and making sure the generators were all functioning, water supply from the boreholes running smoothly and toilets and showers all ready for use. Being Christmas Day, Maduka and his brothers were well prepared to receive large numbers of visitors and were well stocked with drinks and food. However, taking care of the Kagara girls for whom this was their first Christmas after their release, with all the expected fun and joy and merrymaking, posed a challenge that would stretch their renowned charity. Within an hour of their arrival, however, the girls were served a breakfast of boiled yam and stew with beef. Anyone who wanted to clean up was directed to a convenient washroom and little by little the girls were taken care of.

Ever since the release of the first set of fifty-three Kagara girls, Billy and Maduka had spent all their waking hours together planning and scheming along with Dagogo how best to secure the release of the girls, although they were nowhere near the scene of action nor did they know exactly what Dagogo and his team would do, for even after they may have agreed on a particular mode of action, Dagogo would have freely pursued his own plans. And with his first success, he worked more and more on his own. But Maduka was constantly in contact with his brothers up in the field of battle with BOND in northeastern Nigeria. On one occasion, Billy himself had to travel to Mafiaya to confer with the brothers and give them every possible support.

On this auspicious Christmas morning, Maduka exulted: "Well, old boy it's all over. Can you believe it, that Dagogo would be able to pull this whole thing off?"

"Isn't it Chioma and her GAP ladies who gave us the funds, and the spirit to fight and fight hard, that led the way to the rescue of the girls by means you and I don't yet understand? I'm sure Chioma will tell us how it all happened. All that Dagogo did at this time was to go in and collect the girls as BOND fled."

Not long after he arrived in Okeosisi, Dagogo dragged himself out of bed unable to get the kind of deep sleep he needed. He was far too happy to close his eyes to the unfolding events of the day.

"Good afternoon, gentlemen, or is it still morning? The harmattan breeze won't let me sleep."

"Sorry to disappoint you, Dagogo, great hunter of joy and peace, it is still morning and we still have a long way to go."

"Billy, I am not going anywhere, so we don't have a long way to go. Everything will happen here, with Chioma and her grandfather. You know, when you're with these two people, the whole world comes out to greet you, as if they have been waiting for you all their lives. Yes, it is morning, according to you. But here I am and here I will stay."

"Oh, yes, master of evil who demolishes forests of the spirits that roam at night, great warrior of Nembe, hero of the creeks that water may flow to mouths that speak the truth, the eye that sees demons before they turn to masquerades, champion of champions who has wrestled BOND to the ground, we salute you. My ancestors, going back to the first Okeosisi who gave this town its name, all salute you and say, Merry Christmas. The gods have used you to conquer crass inhumanity and needless, horrible, and catastrophic bloodletting. No more will we die for nothing. No more will we be bludgeoned to death in our homes, in our schools, in our mosques, in our churches . . . ."

"Come on, You Fool, that's enough. You can see Dagogo is not even listening to you. His eyes, whenever they can manage to open up for a few seconds, are on the girls in the outdoor welcome house. Let us go there. That's all Dagogo wants to do, I'm sure."

Chioma had made herself presentable and called out her GAP team to meet the visiting Kagara girls.

"What, are they here? How come?" Baraah enquired.

"It is our Christmas present. It is simply incredible, Baraah, incredible," Chioma chirped.

All seventeen GAP members joined the girls who ran out in their doubles to embrace them.

"I don't want to go back to Kagara. I don't want to go back to Kagara," one of the girls kept repeating and the rest joined her: "We don't want to go back to Kagara. We want to live with you. We want to live in Okeosisi. Yes we want to live and go to school in Okeosisi"

"Tell me, are you twins?" Chioma asked two of the girls who looked identical to each other, even wearing the same clothes.

"Yes we are," answered one of them. I am Alice Mazda and my sister is Agnes. Two of us were abducted together and we have suffered too much in the forest. We will not go back to Kagara. We want to start a new life here."

"Yes, I want to be a doctor. My dream is to save people who are suffering too much. I want to be a doctor. Kagara can't help me," Agnes added.

"Me, I will be a university doctor of books, just like you. I want to teach and write books," another girl burst into the conversation.

They all said what they would like to be in the future until the baton was handed to Longa. She took off at breakneck speed: "I don't want to waste time at all. I want to start helping people now as a nurse. I don't want to be married. I want to be free to go anywhere in the world I am needed. I will go anywhere just to help people I don't even know. Even if all I do is wash sick people, help feed them, wash their clothes, or throw away their wastes, yes, I will feel happy. My life must help other lives."

"And what's your name, miss?" Amanthi asked of this fascinating child.

"My name is Joy. I want to give everybody joy."

"Well our Leader is here, Dr. Chioma Ijeoma. We are sure she can give you an answer today, and this will be your Christmas present.

Chioma undoubtedly was filled with joy and like Miss Joy, she wanted to give the Kagara girls all the joy they can contain in their bubbling, growing hearts.

"We shall talk to your parents and get their consent to do what we want to do for you."

"Go ahead, Dr. Ijeoma, do whatever you want to do for our children. Five of us have travelled to Okeosisi on our own to see this place that has rescued our girls. And we represent the parents of the children. I am Chief Mazda, the father of the twins, Alice and Agnes. We are sure the parents of the other one hundred and eighteen rescued children feel the way we feel. We are the happiest parents on this earth to see our children alive again. GAP will live forever. God will do more wonders for you. Ah! here's Chief Dagogo himself. We knew he was coming here. Wonderful, good morning my Chief."

"We have heard you, my girls," Chief Dagogo responded, "This compound you are looking at now, where I myself brought you, will forever be a Christmas jollity for all girls in school. You will remember this day all your life."

Chioma stood as tall as the iroko tree in the forest behind their compound. She could speak for the Akadike family for she had been bestowed with this singular honour by her great grandfather, Pa Akadike Okeosisi himself. She poured profuse encomiums on Chief Dagogo Fubara, Professor William

Briggs, the indefatigable warriors of BRAND and, of course, GAP: that this would indeed be a special Christmas Day in the annals of Okeosisi, nay Nigeria. Rising even higher to her incandescent joy, she proclaimed the Akadike dictum for the children.

"Thank you, Mr. Mazda. Yes, we shall take care of all the Kagara children and bring the Kagara Debacle to a close. Any child who wants to live in Okeosisi will live here, with us, in the Akadike compound. My uncles' houses—four of them—will be converted to dormitories and classrooms to enable you complete your secondary education here. And we shall quickly build a school also here for girls running from primary one up to sixth form secondary education. And we shall rebuild the school in Kagara for you and for all the girls of Kagara. GAP is behind you and we will always be with you offering you our best services, and all that is good and wholesome."

Epilogue

"Chioma, I think I need to tell you the whole story." Fern met Chioma at the end of her speech welcoming the Kagara girls.

"Dagogo and his men could not understand how they were able to save the forty girls without a fight, without firing a bullet. It was all mysterious to their eyes. You see, ever since I saw you with the Cambridge group, I took a greater interest in you and wanted to know you fully. Spirits do not know the past and I wanted to know every bit of your history. So, I had to read up about you from your thesis, your publications, and from being at your lectures, though no one would see me. Then I read about your father, your grandfather and your awesome great-grandfather, Akadike. I love that man! After gathering all this information, I approached my other brother spirits and tried to get them to forget any notion of hurting you, let alone kill you. But they would not relent. I still carried on the duties they entrusted to me: I threatened the president of the Senior Staff Club, University of Kokoma, Dr. Charles Finima and, as you know, we threatened GAP. There was a war and, with a handful of three loyal spirits, we defeated all the others, including my great boss, Bronze Mahogany.

And so, I made up my mind I would save you and help you to save the Kagara girls.

On the night Dagogo attacked, I had freed the girls from their chains and had seized the weapons from the guards. So, when Dagogo came in, the terrorists had no arms to fight with, quickly realized the game was over and ran away. The rest you know; but that's exactly what happened. You might remember I had once packed boxes of chocolates for you; and you were very delighted. That's how it all happened. That was the hour of my conversion — when I packed those chocolates for you."

Printed in the United States
By Bookmasters